Lord Iverbrook's Heir

Carola Dunn

Walker and Company
New York

Also by Carola Dunn

The Miser's Sister
Angel
Lavender Lady

First published in the United States of America
in 1986 by the Walker Publishing Company, Inc.

Published simultaneously in Canada by John Wiley & Sons
Canada, Limited, Rexdale, Ontario.

Library of Congress Cataloging-in-Publication Data

Dunn, Carola.
  Lord Iverbrook's heir.

  I. Title.
PR6054.U537L6   1986   823'.914   85-26598
ISBN 0-8027-0877-3

Printed in the United States of America

10 9 8 7 6 5 4 3 2 1

— 1 —

"WHITTON? WHO THE devil is Miss Whitton?" cried Lord Iverbrook in exasperation. He ran one hand through already dishevelled brown hair.

The lawyer looked at him in mild surprise, peering through gold-rimmed pince-nez that seemed as dusty as everything else in the gloomy office.

"Your late brother's sister-in-law, my lord," he explained.

"Gil's sister-in-law? Of course. I'd forgot he married a Whitton."

"Indeed, my lord. If I may continue, it is to Miss Whitton that the guardianship of your nephew has been entrusted."

"Not merely my nephew, dammit, Hubble. The child's my heir and ought to be under my protection. That's why I came to see you as soon as I reached England. Not to be raked down for freeing my slaves. Of all the cork-brained, ramshackle notions, to make my heir the ward of a female! Who put that into Gil's head, I'd like to know?"

"He is your heir presumptive only," reminded Mr. Hubble, "and your lordship was absent at the time. Mr. Carrick had the will drawn up several months after your departure for the West Indies. There was no knowing when you intended to return, quite apart from the risks inherent in a lengthy ocean voyage and a protracted sojourn in foreign climes."

"Gil might have guessed I should return as soon as the news of his death reached me. I suppose the will can be contested?"

Behind the opaque lenses, the lawyer's eyes gleamed. How many of his brethren had made their fortunes from contested wills! With luck and good management the case might be drawn out for years, decades even, and Hugh Carrick, Viscount Iverbrook, was a plump pigeon for the plucking.

1

"Certainly, my lord," he said quickly. "I shall enter a suit in Chancery at once."

"Not so fast, man! I'll call on this Whitton woman and I daresay she will see reason. After all, it cannot be pleasant for a hubble-bubble female to be saddled with such a burden."

"I understand the lady to be of a serious turn of mind, my lord."

"Bluestocking, is she?"

"No, my lord . . . "

"No matter. All women are the same. They're all out to get what they want, one way or another, and I've never met one yet who wanted responsibility!"

Mr. Hubble held his peace. It was not his place to point out that his lordship's career up until this, his twenty-ninth, year had been singularly lacking in evidence of any desire on his own part to accept responsibility. "Miss Whitton resides near Abingdon, in Berkshire, my lord," he said, his bland voice offering no hint of his thoughts. "My clerk will give you her precise direction."

Lord Iverbrook stood up, his tall, loose-limbed form filling the cluttered room. His movement disturbed motes of dust dancing golden in an errant sunbeam which, having mistakenly entered at the grimy window, was unable to find a way out. His lordship had no such difficulty. Retrieving his hat from a pile of mildewed documents, he flung a casual "You'll hear from me" at his lawyer and was gone before that worthy could rise to bow humbly and declare his everlasting servitude.

In the copying room, into which no sunbeam ever strayed, three depressed-looking clerks perched on high stools at a long desk. They all glanced up from their work as the viscount emerged from the inner office. He addressed the youngest, a pallid youth whose rusty black coat failed to conceal his patched shirt.

"Miss Whitton's direction, if you please."

"At once, my lord."

The clerk slipped down from his stool and trotted into a dark corner to consult a huge, leather-bound tome. Lord Iverbrook noticed that his boots, though well polished, were cracking at the ankles; he dropped a half-crown back into his pocket and fished for a sovereign.

"Milford Manor, my lord," announced the young man. "Kings Milford, near Abingdon, Berkshire." He flushed with pleasure as he caught the gold coin. "Thank you, my lord. Is there anything else I can do for your lordship?"

The viscount smiled and shook his head. The elderly clerk nearest the door hurried to open it for him, and crossing the dingy lobby, Iverbrook stepped into the street with a feeling of relief, to stand blinking in the brilliant July sunshine.

"Lawyers!" he muttered. "Damn the whole tribe!"

A high-perch phaeton rattling over the cobbles drew his attention. Its occupant was peering at him, hand raised to shade against the glare. It pulled up with a jerk beside him.

"Hugh! It *is* you then. Thought I couldn't mistake that gangling figure. My dear fellow, when did you return?"

Lord Iverbrook looked up into the plump, welcoming face of Mr. Lennox Hastings.

"Hullo, Hasty. That's a neatish bay you have there. What are you doing in town at this time of year?"

"Pockets to let," admitted Mr. Hastings sheepishly. "Can't afford Brighton. This nag's the only thing I've won these six weeks and more. The devil's in the bones."

"Been playing hazard, have you? You ought to stick to faro and picquet. You always were unlucky at dice."

"Promised old Crowe I'd stay away from the tables till my next quarter's allowance is due. He's a Friday-faced old proser but he's kept me from drowning in the River Tick so far. I say, my dear fellow, can I give you a lift? Going to see Schultz to order a new coat. Always cheers me up after seeing my man of business." He cast a critical glance over his lordship's apparel as his friend climbed into the carriage. "Looks as if you could do with one yourself, Hugh. Daresay there ain't such a thing as a first-rate snyder in Jamaica, eh?"

Mr. Hastings was, as always, immaculately dressed after the discreet style of Beau Brummell, from the snowy Mathematical perfection of his cravat to the high gloss of his top boots. Hugh regarded him with the tolerant amusement of one to whom clothes are a means of keeping warm and appearing decent in public.

"You're the very man I need," he decided as the phaeton moved on. "Dimbury still with you?"

"Yes, and you can't have him."

"I don't want him. Wouldn't suit me at all. The thing is, I brought a fellow back from Jamaica with me. You don't have anything against blacks, do you?"

"Against mourning? Lord no, not in its proper place!"

"No, not mourning. Blacks, negroes, Africans, whatever you like to call 'em."

"My dear fellow, you mean you've brought one of your slaves home with you?"

"Joshua's no slave, and I don't own any. Freed the lot a month after I reached Kingston. Hasty, you wouldn't believe . . . "

"Daresay I wouldn't, and I don't care to hear it," interrupted Mr. Hastings firmly. "I'll have Dimbury help this man of yours tog himself out decently, if that's what you want, but I can see you've got a bee in your bonnet about slavery, Hugh, and you're not dragging me out to Clapham with you!"

"Clapham? Why the devil should I want to go to Clapham?"

"I suppose you will want to join forces with Wilberforce? Fellow who abolished the slave trade? Well, from all I hear he's not so bad himself, but the rest of the Clapham Sect are a bunch of canting evangelicals. Steer clear of 'em, my dear boy, steer clear."

For the next few minutes, Mr. Hastings was himself occupied in steering clear. A brewer's dray, overloaded with empty hogsheads, rattled out of an alley and a flock of sheep on their way to Smithfield Market scattered across the street in bleating confusion. Narrowly missing a black and tan sheepdog, Hasty swung his carriage around the dray just as the first barrel crashed to the ground, and emerged unscathed, looking pleased with himself. He rather expected congratulations from his friend, but Lord Iverbrook was lost in thought and seemed not to have noticed how brilliantly his friend had handled the ribbons.

His memory nudged by the recent mention of mourning, Mr. Hastings recalled the sad event that had brought the viscount home. "I say, my dear fellow," he said with quick sympathy, "I'm most frightfully sorry about Gil and his wife. Went to the funeral you know. Shouldn't have mentioned Clapham."

"Don't tell me Gil and Phoebe had joined the Clapham Sect!" exclaimed Hugh.

"No, no, no. Shouldn't think so for a minute. But prison visiting, you

4

know, same line of business. Pretty little thing, too, your sister-in-law, Mrs. Carrick. Nothing of the puritan about her. Pity!"

"What do you mean?"

"Stands to reason. If she hadn't been to Bridewell, she wouldn't have taken the gaol fever."

"Gaol fever! Good God! Hubble made no mention of such a thing."

"Just a rumour," Hasty disclaimed. "Beg pardon, my dear fellow. You know what a rattle-tongued clothhead I am. Always was and I daresay always will be. Don't suppose for a moment there's any truth in it."

"No, I can believe it. Phoebe was used to spend much of her time in charity work and Gil approved, helped her even. Puritan or no, he was always a trifle straitlaced. Both of them frowned on the way I lived."

"What's wrong with the way you live?" demanded Mr. Hastings defensively. "Way I live, way lots of people live!"

"Oh, gambling and drinking and opera-dancers and . . . Devil take it! I'll wager that's why they left the boy away from me!"

"Huh?"

"Hubble said it was because of my absence." Hugh noticed his friend's bemused look. "Gil left his son to Miss Whitton's guardianship. My heir! I'll get the child back if it's the last thing I do!"

"Got another bee in your bonnet," mourned Hasty. "You always was one to get bees in your bonnet. Only it used to be about harmless things like curricle races to Newmarket or riding your nag up the steps of St. Paul's. Who the devil is Miss Whitton?"

"Phoebe's sister. Gil's sister-in-law. What does it matter who she is? My nephew's my responsibility."

"Ah, yes. Met her at the funeral. Two of 'em, come to think of it, both towheads like Mrs. Carrick. Which one is it, the pretty one?"

"I've no idea. I suppose I must have met them, at Gil's wedding if nowhere else, but I've no recollection of it."

"Can't be the pretty one; too young. All the same, my dear fellow, you'd better marry her." Beaming with delight at his brilliant solution to the problem, Hasty turned up Bond Street.

"Marry her? Zounds, man, why should I marry her?" Hugh demanded, astonished, then added suspiciously, "Hasty, you're not disguised, are you?"

"Nothing but a mug of porter for breakfast. If you married her—not the pretty one, t'other one—the child would be your ward too. Easy!"

"But I don't wish to get married!"

"Daresay you soon will, with a child on your hands."

Mr. Hastings obviously had more to say upon the matter, but a crush of carriages forced him to rein in his bay and for a few minutes he was busy shouting imprecations at the homespun-clad driver of a whisky which threatened to lock wheels with his phaeton.

Lord Iverbrook listened admiringly to Hasty's disquisition on the morals of the other driver's family, while looking around at the bustling crowds. The West Indies had been beautiful and fascinating, but it was good to be home. Several of Bond Street's expensive and exclusive shops had put up their shutters: the season was past and the *Haut Ton* had dispersed to country estates and watering places. Yet the pavement still was crowded with shoppers. Cits aping the gentry, perhaps. The men in their high, stiff collars and top hats were red-faced and sweating. Their wives and daughters, bearing parasols of a hundred different hues, made lavish use of their fans as they stood gossiping with acquaintances or passed in and out of those modish establishments which had chosen to remain open.

A figure caught his lordship's eye. And what a figure! He would have recognised it anywhere. Standing near the door of a fashionable milliner's, as if uncertain whether to enter, Mrs. Parcott was undoubtedly eye-catching in a rose pink promenade dress cut to flatter her voluptuous shape. A matching parasol framed luxuriant dark hair and cast its blushing shade on an exquisite profile, turned now towards the gentleman at her side.

"Amabel!" exclaimed Lord Iverbrook. "Hasty, is Mrs. P. still free?"

"The Merry Widow? Lord, yes, free and easy as ever, and still casting out lures at every likely prospect, especially those with titles. You had a narrow escape there, my dear fellow. Wouldn't get mixed up again, if I were you."

"Bel and I are good friends. She knows I'm not hanging out for a wife. Not that I'd marry her if I were. It don't do to marry your mistress, Hasty. Bad *ton.*"

"If that don't beat all!" said Hasty indignantly. "Anyone'd think I'd advised you to tie the knot, not warned you to stay out of the harpy's clutches! Fact is, Mrs. P. was quite put out of countenance when you left without a word. I'm not the only one who thought she'd snare you in the end."

"She won't," promised his lordship, "but all the same, I must make my bow. Pull up here, Hasty, and let me down. Tell you what, why don't you come and dine with me in Dover Street this evening?"

"Happy to, my dear fellow." Mr. Hastings drew up his phaeton and Lord Iverbrook sprang down with a farewell wave.

Seeing his quarry step towards the open door of the shop, his lordship called out, imperatively, "Bel!"

Mrs. Parcott, a frown marring her smooth brow, turned to see who dared thus rudely accost her in the street. Annoyance changed to delight. "Iverbrook!" she cried, letting go the arm of her companion and greeting the viscount with both hands.

"Beautiful as ever, Bel," approved Lord Iverbrook, taking her hands, looking her up and down for a moment, then kissing her cheek.

The stout, middle-aged gentleman on whose arm she had been leaning coughed disapprovingly. Reminded of his presence, Mrs. Parcott presented him.

"Iverbrook, allow me to make known to you Sir Alfred Bagley. Sir Alfred, Lord Iverbrook is a very old friend . . . " her sultry voice paused, " . . . of my late husband's."

His lordship, whose acquaintance with the deceased was limited to the occasional reminiscences of his widow, absorbed this without a blink and returned Sir Alfred's bow. He noted with amusement the suspicious look in the gentleman's eye.

"Your servant, sir," he said, politely if untruthfully.

"And yours, my lord," growled the other. "Amabel, we were about to . . . "

"La, Sir Alfred, if I have not quite forgot what it was I wished to purchase! And you were saying, not five minutes since, I vow, that you have an appointment at the Cocoa Tree. Upon my word, sir, you need not scruple to leave me in Lord Iverbrook's care. I daresay he will be so good as to procure me a hackney carriage, for poor Mr. Parcott's sake."

"Certainly, ma'am. For poor Mr. Parcott's sake, I will even engage to accompany you to your door. Good day, Sir Alfred."

Leaving her bewildered escort fuming, the lady permitted Iverbrook to hand her into an expertly summoned hackney and take his seat beside her.

"So easily consoled!" he said provocatively.

"Hugh, he is nothing to me! But when you left without a word and were gone so long!"

"Is he rich?"

"You know perfectly well that Mr. Parcott left me in very easy circumstances. I wish you will not tease. Only I cannot live without a man to take care of me. Why did you go so suddenly?"

"There was the duel . . . "

"Fustian! You did not even kill your man. Indeed, it was commonly said that you both deloped."

"True, it was a friendly match. But then, my agent in Jamaica dying at just that moment . . . "

"As though you could not have hired another without going there in person. Tell me truly, Hugh, why did you leave?"

"I was bored."

"You are complimentary!"

"Oh, not with you, Bel."

"With what, then?"

"With everything. With my life," he said lightly.

"You were the envy of all your friends. Wealth enough to gratify every whim, and your stepfather running your estate so that you need never concern yourself with where it came from."

"That was not by my choice." His voice was tinged with unwonted bitterness, but seeing her puzzled frown he smiled. "Never mind, Bel, I don't expect you to understand. That is long past now; I feel sure I should find farming a dead bore and am grateful to Mr. Ffinch-Smythe for his efforts on my behalf. So, I had plenty of the ready, a beautiful mistress, and not a care in the world, and was not satisfied. Unnatural, ain't it? Come, give me a kiss for old times' sake."

In the course of the afternoon, Mrs. Parcott was persuaded to give my lord a great deal more than a kiss for old times' sake. When at last he tore himself from her embrace, church bells were striking six all over the city.

"Let's go to Brighton," he proposed, "or Tunbridge, if you prefer. I have to fetch my nephew from his aunt first, and take him to Iver Place, but that shouldn't take more than a few days."

"Your nephew? The poor little orphan! A mother's care is what he needs, I vow."

"He'll manage very well without." Lord Iverbrook had issued his warning: if the Merry Widow chose to disregard it, that was her own affair.

2

"THIS MAN OF yours," said Mr. Hastings, sipping his smuggled brandy appreciatively, "the one you brought from Jamaica: what exactly is it you want Dimbury to do for him?"

"Only to help him purchase appropriate clothing. You cannot suppose that I would know what apparel is suitable for an articled clerk." Lord Iverbrook lounged back in his chair, looking somewhat piratical with a red Belcher handkerchief knotted loosely at his sun-bronzed throat.

Impeccable in a tight-fitting coat of blue superfine, a sapphire nestling in the exquisite folds of his neckcloth, Mr. Hastings snorted. "To all appearances, my dear fellow, you do not know what apparel is suitable for a peer of the realm! Dimbury would leave me on the instant if he so much as caught sight of such an object among my cravats. So he's to be a lawyer, is he?"

"Joshua? Yes. Apropos, what sort of man is this Crowe of yours?"

"Old Crowe? Starchy as a dowager duchess, but he ain't let me land in the Marshalsea yet. His clerks are well fed, I'd say."

"Good. You shall introduce us. I'd not willingly subject anyone to Hubble. Stap me, the fellow had the gall to haul me over the coals because I freed my slaves! And this business with the Whitton woman . . . Wait a bit, I knew I'd heard the name before!"

"I should rather think so, since your brother married one!"

"No, no. Sir Aubrey Whitton, that's it. A counter-coxcomb living on the fringes of society in Kingston. A remittance man, I believe, who came into the title quite recently."

"Black sheep of the family, eh?"

"Could be. Or possibly no connexion at all. Now, will you go with me to see Mr. Crowe tomorrow, while Dimbury takes Joshua to a snyder?"

After the magnificent meal he had just consumed, Mr. Hastings felt it would be discourteous in the extreme to refuse.

"By all means," he murmured agreeably.

Dimbury was not so easily persuaded. At the outset of his career, Dimbury had decided that forty was the correct age for a gentleman's gentleman. For twenty-five years now his appearance had matched that belief. He held equally strong views on all other matters pertaining to his chosen profession, the duties of which, he felt, included neither consorting with ex-slaves nor procuring raiment for articled clerks.

Mr. Hastings prevailed. Mr. Hastings usually prevailed, for he was the sort of master of whom an ambitious valet dreamed. Exquisite taste, sunny temper, never a hair out of place, and entrée to all the haunts of the ton where his servant's handiwork might best be appreciated.

The next day Dimbury took Joshua shopping.

"An eloquent young man, sir," he reported that evening, easing off his master's boots with gloved hands. "I believe Mr. Joshua will be an excellent attorney. He told me some very shocking tales of his life as a slave."

"Don't want to hear 'em! And if you turn political on me I'll . . . I'll wear the pink and green muffler Aunt Mabel knitted me! I've heard nothing else from Hugh all day."

"Lord Iverbrook has always been subject to sudden enthusiasms, sir," soothed Dimbury, paling at the thought of the muffler.

"Yes, but he always does what he says he's going to do, and I daresay he'll abolish slavery if it takes him twenty years, you mark my words!"

Two days later, his business in London completed, Lord Iverbrook set out for Iver Place. His curricle had been hurriedly refurbished since his return to England, but the matched pair of greys had been out at grass for nearly two years. They trotted out of the mews with ponderous dignity.

"Sluggards!" commented the manservant perched behind his lordship. "Take 'em easy now, m'lord. When I fetched 'em up to town after I carried that letter to her la'ship, they was puffing like a grampus afore we'd gone ten mile."

"Regular exercise will soon bring them into condition. They were once sweet goers! I look to you to take them out every day, Tom."

"Yes, m'lord. We'll soon have 'em in prime twig again."

Thomas Arbuckle, a stocky man with grizzled hair, was not precisely a groom. Nor would Dimbury have recognised his claim to be a valet, far less a gentleman's gentleman. He made no such claim, describing himself as "his lordship's man." He kept the viscount's clothes in order, drove his horses, ran errands, and had willingly followed him to the Indies in spite of turning green at the sight of the sea.

"Jamaica's pretty enough, but there ain't nowt to beat a bit of old England," he said as they left the city behind them.

The road was in good condition after a week of sunshine and they had scarce twenty miles to go. In spite of letting the horses make their own pace, it was not yet noon when the carriage turned in between the brick gateposts of Iver Place.

To either side of the well-kept gravel drive purple heather bloomed, scattered with clumps of oak and silver birch. This land would grow no grain, nor even pasture for cattle, though there were short stretches of wiry grass where a few sheep grazed, raising their heads to watch the curricle go by. The only hint of the source of Lord Iverbrook's wealth was a faint, nose-wrinkling aroma, borne by the breeze.

The trees grew closer and soon they were in a wood of mixed oak and beech. The dappled air was full now of grunts and squeals, and the odour was growing stronger.

"Devil take those pigs," muttered his lordship, nostrils twitching.

A small boy with a stick urged a large sow off the drive as they approached. He stood watching them pass, openmouthed, then whistled shrilly and shouted: " 'Tis my lord come home!"

Half a dozen barefooted boys appeared, accompanied by twice as many equally curious swine. Finding the fuss was unrelated to food, the pigs trotted back to their foraging among the acorns and beechmast, while the viscount dug in his pocket for a few sixpences.

The boys raced to open the gate at the end of the wood, and grinned shyly as he distributed the silver coins. "Thank 'ee, sir," said one, bolder than the rest, and breaking into giggles they scattered among the trees.

Lord Iverbrook gazed down the hillside at the home of his ancestors. Iver Place was a long, low house built in the local brick and flint style. A singularly ugly example, his lordship thought, not for the first time. Succeeding generations had added wings here, courtyards there, until strangers needed a map to find their way from bedchamber to parlour, and food invariably arrived cold after travelling the endless corridors from kitchen to dining room. Hugh and Gil, as small boys, had had their games of hide-and-seek frustrated by too many hiding places. The seeker generally gave up in despair.

The small park was neatly mowed, and the house had an air of peace and prosperity. As his lethargic team drew the curricle up to the front entrance, the viscount noted a pair of topiary pigs among the lions and peacocks carved by careful hands from the yews in the shrubbery. He sniffed the air. Nothing but the green smell of new-cut grass reached his nose. At least his stepfather had had the sense to build his breeding yards downwind of the house and out of sight.

Tom jumped down from his perch. He ran up the brick steps and tugged on the huge brass bellpull, then went to the horses' heads.

The butler who swung open the door had aged visibly during Iverbrook's long absence, but his gaze was as steely as ever. His "Welcome home, my lord," held no hint of warmth.

"Hello, Prynn," said the viscount, then found himself explaining his arrival on his own estate. "My mother's expecting me, I believe."

"Her ladyship has been awaiting your arrival for some hours, my lord. Her ladyship is not, at present, as robust as one might wish."

Lord Iverbrook at once felt guilty for being late, though his letter had not specified any particular hour, and for not having yet enquired after Lady Lavinia's health. "Is she in her boudoir?" he asked. "I'll go to her right away."

"Yes, my lord. Surely your lordship does not intend to appear in her ladyship's presence in your driving apparel?"

"Certainly not. Have I not already given you my gloves and my hat?"

Before the servant could respond with more than a shocked look, the angry viscount strode across the cavernous hall and took the stairs two at a time.

Several hundred feet of draughty passages and stairs, hung with insignificant portraits of insignificant forebears, cooled his temper. By the time he tapped on his mother's door, he was once again calm and resolved upon his course of action.

The door opened immediately and into the lifeless air of the corridor wafted a potpourri of heavy scents. A gaunt, grey-haired female, at least as tall as he, confronted him with an accusing glare.

"You needn't knock loud enough to wake the dead! Poor Lady Lavinia, not a wink of sleep all night, aching head all morning, and now her own son has no more compassion than to come battering down the door!"

He had forgotten his mother's companion.

"Hugh?" came a weak voice from the dimly lit room behind the gorgon. "Is it indeed you, my darling boy? My head is quite better, Agnes. Pray draw the curtains back so that I can see my darling boy."

Hugh crossed the room, fell to one knee beside his mother's couch, and kissed her hand and powder-perfumed cheek. As daylight entered, he saw that she was dressed in a flowing, mist grey robe, with a tiny wisp of a lace cap adding to her appearance of fragility.

"Still pretty as a picture, Mama," he said. "How are you?"

She clung to his hand. "You have been gone so long, Hugh. And I am never well when you are gone, I fear. I have been quite worried about you. It was very naughty in you not to write more often."

The old, familiar impatience rose in Hugh but he swallowed his retort. "I beg your pardon. I was very busy but I should have found the time. Now I'm home, though, I have a great deal to talk about with you."

"Oh, Hugh, I do hope you are not going to be dreary. If you tell me again that I must live in the Dower House, you know it will bring on a Spasm. Agnes, my vinaigrette!"

"Yes, I know," said the viscount grimly, moving aside as Miss Sneed bore down upon him waving a cut-glass vial. The pungent aroma made him cough.

"Just to drive past that place gives me the vapours," announced Lady Lavinia, revivified. "Your poor Aunt Fanny died there of a consumption and your sainted Papa vowed I should never have to live there. The house is damp. And say what you will, I *cannot* think of Ffinch House as home."

"I have not asked you to remove to either the Dower House or my stepfather's residence, Mama. I wish to discuss your grandson."

"My grandson? Oh yes, dear little Peter. Such a sweet baby."

"I am glad you are fond of him, because as he is my heir, I intend to bring him to live at Iver Hall."

"What! A horrid, noisy little boy at Iver Hall? Agnes, I feel a Palpitation! Pray bring me a little hartshorn. You cannot be so heartless, Hugh. Consider my poor nerves!"

"Lady Lavinia, calm yourself, I beg of you. Lord Iverbrook is certainly speaking in jest. No one in your delicate state of health can be expected to take responsibility for a small child. Why, I daresay it would be the death of you!"

Hugh tried to ignore the interruption. "I shall hire nannies and nursemaids and governesses and whatever else you consider necessary, and I shall come down often from London to see him, of course. But the child is my heir and will be brought up at Iver Place whether you are present or not, Mama."

Lady Lavinia produced a feeble shriek and fell back against her pillows, eyes closed.

"'How sharper than a serpent's tooth...'" intoned Miss Sneed, casting a glance of condemnation at her mistress's "thankless child" as she seized the vinaigrette.

Lord Iverbrook beat a hasty retreat. He had been on the receiving end of that particular quotation more times than he could number, and had once even read through the whole of *King Lear* to find out just how he compared with that monarch's ungrateful daughters. Since he had so far resisted the temptation to turn his mother out of doors, he felt that to class him with Goneril and Regan was unjust.

He went in search of his stepfather.

Mr. Ffinch-Smythe was leaning on the gate of his favourite sow's pen.

"What-ho, Iverbrook!" he shouted, sighting the viscount. "Come and look at Primrose!"

His lordship picked his way through the mud and looked over the fence. A huge black pig with white feet and a white star on her forehead stared back at him, then turned around to present her curly tail.

"She looks very healthy, sir," he commented cautiously.

"Aye, she's a beauty." Mr. Ffinch-Smythe was a short, spare gentleman. The tie-wig he wore in defiance of modern fashion lent him the air of a courtier, an impression completely at odds with his boundless enthusiasm for pigs. "See the piglets? I bred her to a Tamworth boar this time. Tamworths have lots of lean on them, fatten slowly, while Berkshires like Primrose mature early. It'll be interesting to see what the offspring are like, what?"

"Very interesting, sir. Speaking of offspring, I'm going to be bringing my brother's child to Iver in a few days. He's my heir, after all, and ought to be living here."

"Right you are. Last time I crossed her with a White Yorkshire." One of the piglets started squealing and the others quickly joined in. Mr. Ffinch-Smythe raised his voice a trifle. "Great success it was. Eighteen of 'em and all doing well. If they breed true, I'm thinking of calling them Windsors, in compliment to the King."

George III might be known affectionately to his subjects as Farmer George, but it seemed a strange compliment to the crazy old man. He was presently confined at Windsor Castle, not six miles distant, while his son celebrated his recent appointment as Regent. The viscount opened his mouth to argue, caught himself in time, and returned to his own current obsession.

"M'mother won't hear of it."

"She won't? Can't think why she should object. Not as if I was going to call them after her, though it does have a ring to it: Lady Lavinia's Own Breed, what?"

"Not the pigs, my nephew."

"You want to call them after your nevvie? 'Pon my soul, can't even remember the lad's name!"

"My mother objects to my plans for bringing my nephew here," said his lordship loudly and clearly. "She kicked up the devil of a dust when I mentioned it."

"We can't have that," his stepfather frowned. "I'll tell you what, Iverbrook, you went about it the wrong way. It never does to go mentioning plans to Lady Lavinia. Upsets her. Gives her Spasms and such."

"It did."

"What you have to do is present her with a Fate Accumplee. That's French for no use crying over spilt milk. I went on the Grand Tour in my youth, you know, before this upstart Napoleon made it impossible, and I must say the French have some excellent pigs. Italians too. Neapolitans and such. I wonder . . . "

"So you think I should just bring the boy here, without saying any more about it?"

"Let her think you've forgotten about it. And be sure to wear knee breeches to dinner! Wish it was as easy to bring hogs from Naples, but with Boney's brother-in-law on the throne I daresay it ain't to be thought of."

"I'm afraid not, sir. Thank you, I'll take your advice."

"Knee breeches always put her in a good mood, you mark my words. Primrose don't set any such store by fashion, do you, old girl?"

Primrose honked a reply, and Lord Iverbrook left them to commune with each other in peace.

He had been wondering how to announce to Miss Whitton that he was about to remove her charge from her care. Best, he now decided, to swoop down and carry the boy off before she had time to be cast into high fidgets. He would request the honour of an interview with her on Monday afternoon, take the child to an inn in Abingdon for the night, and be back at Iver on Tuesday. Then, duty fulfilled, off to Brighton with the luscious Amabel.

A spring in his step, Lord Iverbrook strode back to the house and called for pen and paper.

3

"I CAN READ a new word," announced Peter at breakfast. The morning sun, pouring through wide open windows, gilded his hair; he looked positively cherubic.

"Clever boy! What word is that?" asked his aunt Selena with a smile.

"Anise. I know what the rest of the label says too. It says 'For Flatulence'. That means it stops you belching, doesn't it, Grandmama?"

Lady Whitton looked up guiltily from the finger of toast she was dipping in her comfrey tea. "Yes, Peterkin, but not to be mentioned at table, pray!"

"Mama, can you not teach him to read from his primer, or the catechism?" Selena demanded, frowning.

"I spend a good deal of time in the stillroom at this season, dearest," said her mother apologetically. "And Peter does so like to help me. But I agree, he must bring his book with him in future."

"I do not like my primer," the child declared. "It has dull words. When I grow up I'm going to write all Grandmama's labels for her."

"You are excessively peevish today, Selena," observed the fourth member of the family, slathering a muffin with butter.

Selena sighed. "You're right, Dee." For the hundredth time she wondered how her younger sister managed to look so delicately romantic even while munching a muffin. Delia's long, straight, ash blond hair was smooth as silk, and her dark brows and lashes over blue eyes added piquancy to her dreamy face. Selena's equally flaxen hair was a mop of curls, and while her lashes were dark enough to be visible, her eyebrows were so fair she might as well have had none. Add a figure like a beanpole and the freckles inevitable to her outdoor life, she thought, and it was just as well she had no romantic inclinations.

Sighing again, she pushed her chair back and stood up, tall and slender in her faded blue riding habit.

"I'm sorry I was snappish, Mama. Of course it will not harm Peterkin to learn the names of your herbs, though you must admit he does come out with the most disconcerting prescriptions! I am a little worried about the weather. The wind is in the west, and clouds are building up in that direction though you cannot see them from here. I had hoped to start cutting the barley today."

"Can I come with you, Aunt Sena?" clamoured Peter. "I'm ever so good at barley. You said so when I was four, 'member?"

Selena smiled, and her hazel eyes twinkled. "You should be even better now you are five. Let us make a bargain, then. You will study your book with Nurse this morning, and this afternoon I'll take you harvesting."

"We have to shake hands to make a bargain," said the child solemnly. "Timmy Russell says so. Please, Grandmama, may I get down? I have to shake hands with Aunt Sena."

"Finish your milk first, dear. Selena, cannot John Peabody manage the harvest? You know how ill it makes you."

"Old John may know the land like the back of his hand, but he has no real authority with the men. If I am not there, they will spend hours arguing about which field to cut first and which end to start and whether the scythes are sharp enough." Looking harassed, she ran her hand through her curls.

It was Lady Whitton's turn to sigh. "Well, I shall make you some clover tea," she said practically. "It is one of the best things for hayfever."

Selena dropped a kiss on her mother's rose-petal cheek. Peter had finished his milk and climbed down from his chair. White-mustached, he shook her hand and submitted with dignity to being picked up and hugged.

"I'm going to read my book to Finny," he said, and ran out of the room, narrowly missing the butler in the doorway.

"The post is come, my lady," announced Bannister, presenting a silver tray with a heap of letters.

"Thank you, Bannister. Pray give them to Miss Selena," said Lady Whitton, as usual.

Selena sat down again and sorted through the pile. "For you, Mama, from your Learned Society, and here's a couple of household bills.

Bannister, these are all farm business. Put them on my desk, if you please."

"Is my *Lady's Magazine* not come?" asked Delia.

"No. Now what is this? A letter franked by Lord Iverbrook! I did not know he was in England. It is addressed to me, but it must be meant for you, Mama."

Lady Whitton, already deep in the report from the Learned Society of Herbalists, waved it away. Selena broke the seal and unfolded a brief note.

"He's coming to see me this afternoon! How extraordinary! I must suppose that he wishes to present his condolences on Phoebe's death, though we are now out of black gloves even, and perhaps to see Peter; but it is you he should speak to, Mama."

Her oblivious parent stood up, report in hand. "Here is a decoction of mullein leaves which will be the very thing for your sneezing, Selena. I will go and pick some at once, for it must be carefully strained to remove the bristles. It will be ready for you by the time you come in for luncheon." She wandered out, still reading.

"I'm sure we have not seen hide nor hair of Iverbrook since Gil and Phoebe were wed," said Selena. "I daresay I shall not recognise him."

"I remember him well," said Delia dreamily. "He is excessively handsome and romantic. Clive says he is a rake."

"You exaggerate, Dee, and so does Clive, I feel sure. All I remember of him is that though I was Phoebe's maid of honour and he was Gil's best man, he did not see fit to dance with me after the wedding. Dear Papa was quite incensed, and I have no patience with such ramshackle manners, I vow. And now here is another example. Does he think I have nothing better to do than to sit at home this afternoon awaiting his condescending arrival?"

"I daresay he does not know about your barley harvest. It is not at all the sort of thing in which ladies of quality are generally interested."

"I own I had as lief not go out there in the fields today. When John Peabody retires I shall look about for a bailiff who can supervise the men. But I prefer to manage my own farm, and I could never be satisfied with a life of novels and gossip and embroidery, like Clive's mama."

"There is nothing wrong with novels," said Delia defensively.

"Well, before you begin the one I saw Jane passing to you in church yesterday, give these bills to Mrs. Tooting, if you please, since Mama has forgotten them. And you had best warn her of Lord Iverbrook's visit. I suppose it is but common courtesy to invite him to dine, though if he has but common courtesy he will decline."

Leaving her sister gazing out of the window, apparently engaged in a daydream about the coming noble guest, Selena set out for the Forty-Acre Field.

It was still early when she and her groom rode down the lane. The breeze was cool on her face, but the threatening clouds had blown over and the bright sun made dewdrops twinkle on spiderwebs in the hedgerow.

"It's going to be hot later," she said.

"Yes'm. Good harvest weather." Young Jem, the groom, had but recently advanced to that exalted position. He now took care of the ladies' riding and carriage horses, leaving to mere stableboys the great, patient Shire horses that did the farm work. "Take care, Miss Selena, Orion's a bit resty this morning."

Selena curbed her black gelding as he danced skittishly sideways, and stroked his neck soothingly. As they drew level with a five-barred gate, she brought him to a halt and looked across a field towards the river. The Thames glinted through a tangle of willows; the pasture was overgrown with meadowsweet, its scent hanging heavy in the air. Selena sneezed.

"One day!" she muttered in frustration, and urged Orion onward.

A couple of hours earlier, at first light, she had sent a message to John Peabody, and he had gathered some two score harvesters who now awaited her at the Forty-Acre Field. Most were local villagers, glad of a chance to supplement their meagre incomes. A dozen or so were gypsies, swarthy folk whose encampment south of the village had been making the inhabitants of Kings Milford uneasy for days. Jem grunted disapprovingly and urged his cob protectively closer to his mistress's side.

After a brief consultation, the harvesters were stationed along one side of the field. Selena took a scythe, tested it against her thumb, and with a graceful swing cut the first swathe of corn. It fell neatly, ready to be sheafed. A cheer went up and she flushed with pride. There was a trick to it, and she had been practising for a week on the long grass in the paddock.

The reapers started across the field. Pale golden barley, scarlet poppies, skyblue cornflowers, all fell before them, and behind them stooped the binders, boys and women, tying the sheaves with wisps of straw.

Gradually the line of figures spread out. Old John and Selena marked where slow scythers kept their followers waiting, and where stragglers laboured far behind. At the noon break the teams must be rearranged, and fast workers given the longer or more awkward rows. John knew what must be done, but without Selena's authority behind him there would be argument, bad feelings, and time wasted.

Selena sneezed again, as the breeze brought a swirl of dust and pollen. It was going to be a long day.

Under the blazing midday sun, a curricle drove slowly down the deserted village street. Lord Iverbrook reined his sweating team to a halt before the inn. Though a faded sign over the door proclaimed the Cross and Gaiters, it was scarcely more than a hedge-tavern. No eager ostler ran out to enquire as to how he might serve the travellers; even mine host seemed uninterested in his aristocratic guest.

Iverbrook removed his hat and wiped his forehead with a damp and crumpled handkerchief.

"Go ask the way to Milford Manor, Tom," he ordered, "and bring some ale back with you, if this godforsaken place can produce such a thing."

While his servant trudged into the silent inn, he looked around. The dusty street came to an abrupt end here on the riverbank. Near a small jetty, a solitary coot bobbed in the water; its bright, cynical eyes seemed to regard him with amusement.

The opposite side of the river was lined with a tangle of willows upstream; downstream he could see well-tended watermeadows, dotted with black and white cattle. Beyond these, the bank rose higher above the water, and there terraced gardens led up to an attractive brick and stone house.

The viscount turned and looked back down the street. Thatched, whitewashed cottages, with candytuft and gilliflowers wilting in the gardens; a pleasant enough place, no doubt, were it not for this infernal heat. He wiped his face again.

Tom emerged from the dim recesses of the inn, bearing an earthenware mug. He watched his master drain the ale at a draught before he spoke.

"It's the wrong Milford, m'lord," he said expressionlessly.

"What the devil do you mean, the wrong Milford? We're in Berkshire, aren't we? Near Abingdon?"

"Yes, m'lord. Seems as how this is Milford Abbot, and what we wants is Kings Milford. In Oxfordshire."

"Devil fly away with that lawyer! Berkshire, he told me."

"Yes, m'lord. The landlord explained as the local Receiving Office is in Abingdon, which is in Berkshire, so the direction for the mails . . . "

"To the devil with the mails! Where is this other Milford then?"

Tom hooked a philosophical thumb over his shoulder.

"That's Milford Manor over there, m'lord. On t'other side of the Thames."

Lord Iverbrook held his breath for a long moment, then let it out in a sigh and grinned wryly.

"He did tell me Kings Milford. I ought to have given you more precise instructions when you enquired in Wallingford. I suppose all these 'fords' are merely a manner of speaking?"

"I wouldn't advise trying to drive across, m'lord. There's usually a boat, a skiff the landlord said, but all the men are gone to harvesting over there. There's a bridge about four miles on, seemingly, in Abingdon."

"Abingdon it is then. I trust the place also has a decent posting-house. I'll leave you there with the horses and hire a pair. We'll rack up there tonight."

"But Grandmama, Aunt Sena *promised* I can go harvesting if I be good!"

"Your aunt is still waiting for Lord Iverbrook, Peter, and besides, she has the headache. Be a love and fetch me the jar marked 'hyssop'. An infusion with a little honey and oil of almonds will do her a world of good."

Peter obediently fetched the herb, but repeated sadly, "She *promised.*"

"Of course I did!" Selena entered the odiferous stillroom at that moment, attired in a most becoming morning dress of amber crepe. "Mama, I am quite out of patience with Iverbrook and will not await his pleasure any longer."

"How is your head, dearest? I was just preparing a draught of hyssop for you."

"I am vastly better, thanks to your mullein tea. I will try the hyssop next time. It smells delicious. Peterkin, do you go and ask Finny to dress you for the fields. You will need stout shoes for walking across the stubble. I will change too, and meet you at the stables."

"I want to ride with Jem. Can I ride with Jem, Aunt Sena? 'Cos Jem says 'Rion is a lady's horse and I'm not a lady. So can I?"

"Jem's cob is so very large," said Lady Whitton anxiously. "I think Peter will be safer with you, Selena."

"Jem is very trustworthy, and Pippin is a docile beast, not to say phlegmatic. Peter will come to no harm if he behaves himself."

"I'll be good, Grandmama. You can come and see me riding Pippin, will you?"

"Off you go to Nurse, young man, or you'll not be riding at all!"

Not long after Pippin and Orion trotted out of the stable yard, Lord Iverbrook's curricle drew up at the front door of the Manor. He sat for a moment looking at the house, before tossing the reins to the postboy.

Close up, it seemed even more attractive. It was built mostly of a fawn-coloured stone, embellished with decorative red brick, though parts of the façade were Tudor style black and white. A curious mixture, but somehow the whole was harmonious. The mullioned windows gleamed and the open door offered a welcome.

The butler who answered Iverbrook's ring invited him into the cool hallway, redolent of lemon oil and beeswax.

"Miss Whitton is out, my lord," he said apologetically. "I fear she is not expected to return for some time. If your lordship would wish to see Lady Whitton, I shall enquire as to whether her ladyship is at home."

"My business is with Miss Whitton . . . but I daresay I ought to pay my respects to Lady Whitton," responded the viscount with annoyance. As the butler bowed and withdrew, he wondered a shade anxiously whether he would recognise Gil's mother-in-law. He had no more recollection of her than of her daughters, except for Phoebe, though they must certainly have been introduced at the wedding.

The butler returned.

"It seems her ladyship is also out, my lord. I had thought her to be in the stillroom but Mrs. Tooting says she walked down to the village, and Miss Delia with her. Will your lordship wait?"

"Dash it, I've no alternative! Is is customary in this household for everyone to leave when a visitor is expected? I suppose my letter was received?"

"I cannot take it upon myself to say, my lord," reproved Bannister.

"What about my nephew? Mr. Carrick's son. At least I can go up to the nursery and see him!"

"I understand, my lord, that Master Peter rode out with Miss Selena. Miss Whitton, that is. Perhaps your lordship would care to take some refreshment in the drawing room? Or, the gardens are particularly fine at this season."

The irate viscount had no desire to see the gardens, but the thought of being shut up in a stuffy drawing room to cool his heels was still less bearable. "Bring me some ale in the garden, dammit," he growled, then smiled his sweet, rueful smile. "I beg your pardon! I should not come to cuffs with you only because your mistresses' notions of courtesy do not suit mine. Refreshments in the garden, if you please, and if possible, a newspaper. And notify me the instant Miss Whitton returns!"

The gardens were peaceful, full of humming bees and the fragrance of roses and spicy marigolds. Brick steps led down from terrace to terrace to the river bank, where Lord Iverbrook found a comfortable bench in the shade of an oak. The Thames slid by, green-brown, smooth, hypnotic.

A pretty maidservant in white cap and apron appeared, bearing a tray.

"Here's your ale, my lord," she said, bobbing a curtsey, "and a bit of lardycake. Cook baked it just this morning and it's right good. Oh, and the paper. Mr. Bannister said to tell you it's just *Jackson's Oxford Journal* and is there anything else I can get you, my lord?"

"Not unless you can produce your mistress."

"Oh no, sir. Miss Selena's at the harvest and my lady's took a salve to Miss Pauley's cookmaid as burned her hand. My lady's better nor any 'pothercary. Excuse me, my lord. Mrs. Tooting said to come straight back."

So Miss Selena had gone to watch the reapers, had she? She had not even the excuse of a prior social engagement to plead for her absence. My lord sank his teeth into the sticky lardycake, full of plump raisins, as if he were a mastiff and the sweetmeat Miss Whitton's ankle.

=4=

BY THE TIME Selena returned from the fields, her headache was back in full force. The dust raised by the reapers had, as usual, made her sneeze till her nose and eyes were red; Peter had fallen over and scratched his hands; and a gypsy had come to blows with one of the locals, leading to the premature departure of all the itinerants.

"Good riddance," Jem had snorted, but John Peabody had cocked a weather eye at the sky and muttered forebodingly, "Hope it holds fair."

Selena entered the house through the side door from the stables. As she and Peter passed the butler's pantry, Bannister popped out.

"His lordship's here, Miss Selena."

"Iverbrook? I'd forgot him! I'll go and change and be with him shortly."

"He's been waiting near two hours already, miss. He's in the garden, pacing up and down like a tiger in a cage."

"Oh dear! Perhaps I had best go straight out. Thank you Bannister. Peter, you run up to Nurse and have her put some of Grandmama's ointment on your hands."

Selena glanced in the gilt-framed mirror in the hall and poked ineffectually at her hair. It would take more than a couple of minutes to set the flaxen curls to rights, without considering her shabby riding dress. It was six years since Phoebe's wedding, when the viscount had displayed an arrogant disregard for her person. If she had been beneath his notice then, the intervening time could hardly have raised her in his esteem. Her chin tilted defiantly, Selena went out into the garden.

His lordship was indeed pacing up and down, but his tall, lean form brought to mind a picture she had once seen of a giraffe, not the motheaten tiger that had come with the fair to Abingdon last year. She stood at the top of the steps for a moment, watching him. Certainly not romantically handsome—Delia's memory had been looking through rose-coloured spectacles. How he might look without the wrathful expression that presently distorted his regular features, she could not guess.

"My lord!" she called.

He came towards her eagerly, relief at the ending of his long wait overcoming his resentment. As he reached the terrace below her, he took in her unkempt appearance and hesitated.

"Miss Whitton?"

"We have met before, sir." Selena's voice was cold. "I must apologise for having kept you waiting."

"I should dashed well hope so!" exploded the viscount. "I've been here forever. I informed you that I was coming, did I not?"

"You did not specify the hour. *I* waited for *you* for two hours, but I had pressing business elsewhere and could not spend the entire afternoon attending your convenience. Enough said. We must not quarrel when we are scarcely out of mourning. I most sincerely condole with you on the loss of your brother, my lord."

"And I with you on Phoebe's death."

"Gil was a gentleman of superior understanding and morals, and he made my sister very happy. I expect you will wish to see their child?"

"Such was my purpose in coming here today. I intend to relieve you of the responsibility of caring for my nephew, Miss Whitton. He will reside at Iver, as befits my heir."

Selena thought she must have misheard. Then she wondered if he could possibly be jesting on such a subject. She descended a few steps, trying to read his face.

"Surely you cannot be serious?" she said uncertainly.

"Never more so. You cannot expect me to allow him to be bred up among the petty squirearchy, and in a household of females besides. It was generous of you to give him a home during my absence, but now that I am returned he should be under my protection."

"I suppose you will concern yourself intimately with his upbringing? You are going to make your home at Iver, I collect?"

"I shall set up his nursery there, and visit him frequently. My mother is in residence, of course."

"A household of females, in fact, and indifferent females at that! Lady Lavinia has not once sought to see her grandson since Gil died. Peter is an orphan, Iverbrook. He needs affection and stability, not to be left with servants!"

"I have no intention of abandoning him. Properly chosen servants are perfectly capable of bringing up a child. That is how Gil and I were brought up, and you expressed your admiration for Gilbert not five minutes past."

"But none for you! Believe me, my lord, I have heard tales of your rakish life, and if only the half of them are true you are no fit person to have charge of a small boy!"

"So now we come to the meat of the matter! On the basis of scandalmongers' gossip you would deny me the right to be guardian of my heir!"

"You have no such right. Peter is legally my ward, and I shall never betray the trust your brother and my sister reposed in me."

"I shall contest the will. The law cannot but consider a Peer of the Realm a more fitting guardian than a totty-headed female."

"This is Peter's home. There is no more to be said. As his uncle you may visit him as often as you wish, I assure you. I shall take care to be absent when you call! Good-bye, my lord."

Selena's head was pounding, blinding her. As she turned to leave, she tripped on the step. The viscount's hand was instantly on her arm, steadying her.

"Let me go," she said icily, and stumbled into the house.

Iverbrook watched her go, torn between fury and admiration. The last thing he wanted was to go to law over the boy, for he was as aware as his lawyer that the case might drag on for years. Damn the wench for forcing him to it! All the same, she was a well-plucked 'un! Amabel would have coaxed, his mother would have collapsed in hysterics, but Miss Whitton rattled in, game as a pebble, and gave as good as she got. He followed her into the house.

After the sunshine, the room seemed dark. He stood blinking, letting his eyes adjust.

"Borage!" said a voice suddenly. "You must be Gilbert's brother Hugh. You look hot, and I certainly am. There's nothing more refreshing than a glass of lemonade with a sprig of borage. Do sit down, Hugh, while I ring the bell."

A small, plump lady, her face very pink under a bonnet cap of Honiton lace, tugged on the bellpull and came towards him with her hand held out. He bowed over it.

"Lady Whitton, how delightful to see you again."

"Flummery!" she said, a twinkle in her brown eyes. "I believe you had quite forgot my existence. As though a good-looking young man had not better things to think about!"

"I plead guilty, ma'am," said Lord Iverbrook, laughing, "to the forgetfulness if not the looks! But I see now that I was mistaken not to further our acquaintance. It must be from you that your daughter got her talent for plain speaking."

"You have seen Selena already then? Oh dear, I hope she behaved unexceptionably. It would be quite useless to try to teach her a maidenly reserve, for she has no idea of hiding her feelings, and I expect she was not quite well. In fact, haymaking and harvest always make her ill, but she will insist that she must be there to oversee the men."

"Miss Whitton was supervising the harvest? I had thought her gone out merely for pleasure, as a spectator."

"Oh no, Selena has been running the farm since she was eighteen. Sir William bred her up to it, not having any sons. I must make her a tisane for her headache, Hugh, so pray excuse me. Bannister shall bring you some lemonade and if you should like it, I will have Nurse send Peter down to see you. You will stay the night of course."

"Thank you, Lady Whitton, but I left my luggage and my man at the Crown and Thistle in Abingdon. And besides, I rather doubt that your daughter would welcome my presence."

"Nonsense! The farm may belong to Selena but I am still mistress in my own house, I hope! Bannister shall send to Abingdon for your things, so do you make yourself comfortable and Peter will be with you at once." Not waiting for an answer, Lady Whitton bustled out.

Lord Iverbrook sat down in a comfortable chintz-covered chair. The whole room looked comfortable, not shabby but lived in. Here was no fashionable bamboo furniture in imitation of the Chinese, just solid, well-polished English oak. The French doors through which he had entered provided a wide view of the sunny garden, the river, and the brilliant green of the watermeadows on the far side.

Bannister brought in a tray with a pitcher and three glasses. He was followed by a small boy, tawny-haired and neatly dressed in nankeens and a frilled shirt, who came to stand before his lordship and bowed gravely.

"How do you do, sir," he said. "Are you my Uncle Hugh?"

"That's right, Peter. Don't you remember me?"

"Not much. I was only a baby when I sawed you, Finny says."

"Who is Finny?"

"My nurse. Her real name is Mrs. Finnygone but she's not gone so I call her Finny. Do you want some lemonade?"

"Yes, thank you. Shall I pour you some too? Here you are."

"Grandmama put some blue flowers in it. That means it's good for you. My grandmama is Lady Whitton."

"What about your other grandmama, Lady Lavinia?"

Peter sat down on a footstool and considered this carefully, sipping his lemonade. "Does she live in a great big house with pigs? My papa taked me to see her once, when I was little."

"How should you like to go and live with me and Lady Lavinia in the great big house?"

"I liked the pigs," said Peter, "but it's better if you come to live with me and Grandmama and Aunt Sena in this house. And Auntie Dee and Finny. I scratched my hands today. I was helping Aunt Sena cut the barley. Do you want to see them?" He carefully set his glass on a small table and displayed his palms. "I only cried a little bit and Aunt Sena said I was a big, brave boy. Finny put wych hazel on."

The viscount could think of no suitable response to this revelation. Fortunately, they were interrupted at that moment by the arrival of an excessively pretty girl. She was charmingly arrayed in pale green muslin, looked to be eighteen or nineteen years of age, and knew just what to say.

"Did it sting, Peter? I'll wager you squealed."

"I did not! Timmy says only girls squeal."

Iverbrook rose to his feet and bowed.

"I'm Delia Whitton, sir. How do you do." Her face took on a soulful look as she curtseyed. "How romantic that you rushed home from half a world away to rescue your orphaned heir, my lord!"

"I hardly think Peter is in need of rescue, Miss Delia!" His lordship revised his favourable impression. He had no opinion of sentimental young ladies who looked on life as an extension of the fantastical novels to which they were invariably addicted. The merry tease who had entered the room was more to his taste.

Delia was also revising her idea of the viscount. No gentleman of a truly heroical nature would have said anything but "It was my duty!" in thrilling tones. Lord Iverbrook's tone was indisputably commonplace, not to say damping. On closer inspection his face, though good-humoured, held neither the ethereal spirituality nor the fiery passion to be expected of a genuine hero.

"You sound just like Clive," she said bitterly.

"Clive?"

"Clive Russell. His family lives at Bracketts and his sister Jane is my dearest friend. He looks amazingly romantic but he is only interested in farming."

Iverbrook's lips twitched. "How very distressing. What an odious wretch the man must be."

She looked at him with suspicion. "You are hoaxing me," she sighed.

"I like Mr. Russell," said Peter. "He's Timmy's brother. He taked me on his horse. It's a gentleman's horse, not like Pippin and 'Rion and Lyra. Have you got a proper gentleman's horse, Uncle Hugh?"

"Lots," said his lordship promptly. "When you come to live at Iver Place, you can ride them all."

Mrs. Finnegan soon came to bear Peter away to supper and bed, despite his loud protests that it was still daytime and boys do not sleep in the daytime. Iverbrook pulled out his watch.

"I suppose you keep country hours," he said to Delia. "Your mama pressed me to stay the night but I shall be unable to change for dinner."

"We don't dine till eight in the summer, sir, because Selena is often late home. Your servant will be here with your bags long before that."

"He will?"

"Yes. Mama thought it best to send the postboy back with the hired horses and have your man return."

"Lady Whitton has a managing disposition, I see!" Lord Iverbrook, unused to having his affairs arranged for him, hovered between annoyance and amusement.

"Well, Papa was never in the least use at managing, so Mama has always ordered everything in the house and Selena on the farm. Clive's papa says Selena is one of the finest farmers in the county. She knows all about drainage and rotating crops and things."

"I shudder to think of two such females in one household!"

"Selena generally has the last word, but if Mama puts her foot down everyone does as she says. You see, Selena is a good farmer but Mama is a good *person.* Besides being our mother and honour thy father and thy mother and all that. Only sometimes she gets a bit absentminded because of her herbs."

Though admitting to himself a certain curiosity as to whether Miss Delia was about to reveal any interesting skeletons in the Whitton closets, Lord Iverbrook steered the conversation into safer channels.

Tom Arbuckle arrived with horses and baggage. When Iverbrook descended to the drawing room in his evening attire, he found the family already assembled. He nearly failed to recognise Selena, transformed from a dusty drab into a slim, elegant young woman in a lavender silk gown. Her pale curls shone in the candlelight, but her face was almost as pale and she was silent and subdued. He would have liked to think that she was regretting her quarrel with him, but it seemed more likely that she was simply not in very plump current. She nodded listlessly in response to his polite greeting, and ate scarce a mouthful when they went in to dinner.

In the absence of other gentlemen, his lordship elected to forgo the port and leave the table with the ladies. At his hostess's request, he regaled them with tales of the West Indies until the arrival of the tea tray, prompt at half past nine. He was surprised to be offered a choice of peppermint tea or the more usual China tea. In a mood of daring, and remembering the cool flavour of the borage in his lemonade, he chose the former and was rewarded with a glance of approval from Lady Whitton.

"Excellent for the digestion," she informed him.

Had she known the difficulty he would find in falling asleep, she would have prescribed chamomile instead. Unused to retiring at ten, he tossed and turned until he was sure dawn was about to break. As a result, he awoke long after everyone else had breakfasted and gone about their business.

A maid served him ham and eggs in the dining room. Well fortified, he decided to make another attempt to persuade Miss Whitton to see reason before he went to the horrid lengths of calling in the legal profession. He stepped into the hallway just as she emerged from the passage leading to the side door.

Once again dressed in her worn, outmoded riding habit, she was holding her forehead with one hand while the other struggled with the ribbons of her hat. Her face was white, eyes red-rimmed and swollen with curious brown blotches around them.

"Miss Whitton, are you all right?" Lord Iverbrook asked in alarm. "Let me call your mother to you."

"Don't be nice to me," she snapped, "or I shall cry and then my head will explode." She gave up the fight with the bonnet strings, pressed both hands to her temples, and closed her eyes.

"As you wish." He saw a hand bell on a marble-topped table and rang it, then untied the recalcitrant ribbons and removed her hat. "You are a birdwitted nodcock to insist on going out in the fields when it makes you so ill."

"I have to. The men will work for me, not for John Peabody. If I leave them they start brangling and brawling and nothing gets done. I must go back."

"I trust this Peabody knows what needs doing, and that your groom can take me to him. You will go and lie down, or whatever will best aid your recovery, and I shall see that your barley is cut."

"Why, you high-handed fribble!" Selena wanted to demand just what he thought he knew about harvesting, but the effort of shouting after his retreating back hurt too much. Besides, Mrs. Tooting had appeared and one did not squabble in front of the servants.

"Did you ring, Miss Selena?" she asked, an expression of concern on her rosy-cheeked face. "Oh, you do look ill, dearie! Polly! Polly, go and fetch my lady to Miss Selena's chamber. Now you come on upstairs, dearie, and we'll soon have you feeling better." Murmuring soothingly, she led Selena upstairs.

Her mother found her pacing up and down the room, with the housekeeper clucking at her.

"Thank you, Mrs. Tooting," she said, "but you know it never answers to lie down when Miss Selena is like this. I have given Cook some herbs.

Pray go and see that they are properly infused, and send Polly up with the tea. Dearest, whatever has happened to your face?"

Selena stopped and looked in her mirror. "I don't know. Oh, I suppose it is the sage dye you gave me for my eyebrows. It has smeared all over. I look a perfect fright!"

"At least no one has seen you, my love, and now we know it is not to be used in an overheated ballroom. I wonder if walnut juice might be more permanent?"

"But someone did see me: that arrogant court-card Iverbrook. I shall never be able to face him again."

"Nonsense! And I do not think he can be described as a court-card, for I distinctly recall dear Gilbert saying how fortunate it was that Hugh was too young to be a member of Prinny's set."

"At all events, he is arrogant. He said in that odious, toplofty way that I was a fool, and if he dares to go to law to take Peter I shall fight him every step of the way, even if we all go home by beggar's bush!"

"Of course you will, my love, but I am sure dear Hugh would never do anything so ungentlemanly. Now here is Polly with your tea. Sit down and drink it and you will soon feel more the thing."

Lord Iverbrook, mounted on Orion, followed Jem down the lane in no charitable frame of mind, in spite of his errand of mercy.

"Fribble!" he muttered to himself. "I'll show her if I'm a fribble!"

Jem looked back. "Did you say something, my lord?"

"This horse is much too high-spirited for a female."

"Miss Selena can manage him," said Jem pugnaciously. "Miss Selena's different nor other ladies."

"With that sentiment," said his lordship, "I am in most wholehearted agreement!"

— 5 —

LORD IVERBROOK THOROUGHLY enjoyed his morning in the fields. The reapers responded to his natural air of authority, not to mention the fact that a "real lord" was taking an interest in their labours. John Peabody was inclined to take offense at first, but was won over by the viscount's deference to his expertise.

When the work stopped at midday and the men gathered in the shade of the hedge to eat their bread and cheese, Iverbrook rode back to the Manor. He found a hired chaise in the stable yard and an acquaintance ensconced in the drawing room.

"Whitton!" he exclaimed. "So you *are* the black . . . a connexion of the family."

The exquisite who rose to greet him with a flourishing bow was startlingly handsome, with guinea gold hair and a Roman profile. Also startling were his vermilion coat, its shoulders peaked with buckram wadding, and his peach waistcoat embroidered with hummingbirds.

"My lord Iverbrook! What a charming surprise," he lisped.

"Sir Aubrey is Sir William's nephew, Hugh," explained Lady Whitton, "or not precisely a nephew but a third or fourth cousin. Somewhat removed, I collect. Since you are acquainted, you will excuse me while I go to see whether Selena is well enough to join us at luncheon."

Sir Aubrey's shirt-points made it impossible for him to turn his head; he twisted at the waist instead to address her ladyship.

"Of course, dear Aunt. My lord and I met in Jamaica. Your lordship was about to say 'black sheep,' I believe." He tittered. "'Pon my soul, the black sheep was not I but my father, who was exiled to the Indies."

"And what brings you to England now?"

"La, I have long wished to return to the home of my ancestors, and I

35

recently inherited the baronetcy so the omens seemed favourable. Snuff, my lord?"

"No, thank you." The viscount watched with scorn as Sir Aubrey produced a snuff box set with what might conceivably be rubies but he rather suspected was coloured glass. With a mincing gesture, the baronet sniffed up a pinch of its contents. "I thought Sir William died several years ago," Iverbrook went on, "not long after my brother married his daughter."

"Ah, so you too are a close connexion of dear Lady Whitton. How delightful! Indeed, the late baronet passed on some while since, but the news travelled slowly to Jamaica—I am sure you understand the delay—and then the lawyers proceeded with extreme sloth in verifying my claim to the title. It was scarcely worth the long voyage if I was to find at the end that some closer male relative existed."

"Indeed. So your title is proved and you are come to claim your inheritance?"

"So I believed, my lord, but I find myself in the most damnable situation! It seems the property is not entailed upon the heir and Sir William was so ill-advised as to leave it to his daughter! What, I ask you, can a flighty female want with a substantial farm like Milford? It can only be a burden to her."

"You have not met Miss Whitton?"

"Not yet. She is unwell, I collect. However, I trust I have hit upon a scheme which must be acceptable, nay, welcome to all parties. If Miss Whitton will do me the inestimable honour of granting me her hand in marriage, I shall lift the burden from her shoulders while enjoying what is rightfully mine."

"I must warn you that Miss Whitton has broad shoulders, Sir Aubrey."

"You mean she is an antidote?" asked the baronet in alarm. "I confess I had hoped to find a fashionable female with looks to equal my . . . ahem, of tolerable appearance. However, I daresay I shall soon come to overlook any minor defects of person in a young lady of amiable disposition."

"I feel sure you will, in view of the rewards to be gained thereby. I was riding about the estate this morning and it looks to be a very pretty property, and in excellent heart. It is a great pity that Miss Whitton's disposition is managing and quarrelsome."

"'Pon rep, my lord, I believe you are gammoning me. Can it be that you have an interest there yourself?"

"No, no, not I!" disclaimed the viscount hurriedly. "Pray excuse me. I must remove some of the dust of the fields from my person before luncheon." He closed the door behind him before he said aloud, "Mercenary man-milliner!"

"I beg your pardon, my lord?" said Bannister, startled. "Luncheon will be served in the dining room in fifteen minutes, my lord."

"Will Miss Whitton be down?"

"I believe not, my lord, though I understand the headache is much improved. If I might make so bold, my lord . . . "

"Yes, Bannister, what is it?"

"Young Jem says your lordship brought the labourers up to the mark in prime style this morning, and we was hoping you might think to stay, my lord, till the harvest's over. For we don't like to see Miss Selena in such queer stirrups and that's the truth."

"Stay? Good heavens, I had not intended to stay so long as I have already!"

"I suppose your lordship has engagements elsewhere," said the old butler sadly.

"Not exactly. No one knows I am back in England, you see. I have to admit I enjoyed this morning, but I don't believe Miss Selena would appreciate my staying."

"Miss Selena's got plenty of sense in her cockloft, my lord, for all she's a trifle hot to hand. It's not a bit of use coming down heavy but if you was to explain as how it's a rare treat to you to go a-harvesting and you wish she'd tell you what needs doing, well, then she'd have no reason to nab the rust. Begging your lordship's pardon."

"I'll think about it," promised Iverbrook, and went upstairs wondering why he should feel disposed to assist the cross-grained Miss Whitton.

At luncheon, the viscount was dismayed to learn that the hired chaise had been dismissed and Lady Whitton, always hospitable, had invited Sir Aubrey to stay at Milford Manor. However, his annoyance at the prospect of enforced intimacy with the demi-beau was tempered with amusement at Miss Delia's rapture. The Lost Heir had evidently eclipsed the Absent Guardian as a figure of romance, and the baronet played the part of hero much more convincingly. Delia, ignorant of the ways of the Polite World, found no fault with his foppish dress and swallowed indiscriminately his tales of high adventure in the Spanish Main.

Lord Iverbrook caught his hostess's eye. The twinkle in it told him that she, at least, was not taken in. Whether Miss Whitton would be as full of admiration as her sister remained to be seen.

Selena came down to afternoon tea, looking much better. She curtseyed politely to her cousin and bade him welcome, but her mind was elsewhere.

"Is Iverbrook still out, Mama?" she asked.

"Yes, he rode out again after lunch. He left a message for you, that the reaping you had ordered was nearly done and he awaits your instructions as to what comes next."

"I must go and see what he has been doing."

"Miss Whitton—Cousin Selena, if you will permit—I had hoped to have a private word with you on a serious matter of some import." The baronet, having inspected his intended through his quizzing glass, was relieved to find that she had no greater defects than excessive height and slenderness and a hint of a snub nose. He wondered why the viscount had mentioned broad shoulders.

"You will have to excuse me, Cousin. Nothing can be more important than the farm at present, for there is no knowing when this dry spell will break. Where is Peter, Mama?"

"Delia took him with her to the Russells'. She wanted to see Jane."

"To gossip about our new cousin, no doubt. You will be a nine days' wonder in the neighbourhood, Sir Aubrey. I shall see you at dinner. Now don't fuss, Mama, I assure you I am right as a trivet, as Peter says. Your prescription worked wonders, as always."

Selena found Jem in the stables.

"His lordship di'n't need me this arternoon," explained the groom, "and I c'd see Orion wou'n't come to no harm with him."

"He's riding Orion? How dare he!"

"Well now, miss, that's the only horse up to his weight. You can't expect a lordship to ride a carriage horse, and Miss Delia's Lyra is too small."

"I suppose so, but doubtless I shall have to ride her. I hope Delia walked to Bracketts!"

"Yes, miss. I'll saddle Lyra and Pippin in a jiffy."

"You need not come, thank you, Jem."

"The gypsies is still about, miss."

"I'll watch out for them. I expect Lord Iverbrook will protect me against all the perils of a summer afternoon in Oxfordshire."

"If he don't, miss, he'll have me to reckon with, lord or no lord!"

Tom Arbuckle was sitting nearby, polishing a harness. "Miss ain't going to come to no harm," he said scornfully, "no more nor her horse, you young nodcock."

Foreseeing a battle royal, Selena intervened. "Saddle Lyra, Jem, and then you may go at it hammer and tongs, when I am well away."

She trotted down the lane on her sister's mare till she came upon the viscount, leaning on a gate, while Orion nibbled at the hedge beside him. Lyra's hooves made little noise on the dusty track, but his lordship looked up when Orion whickered a welcome.

"Good afternoon, Miss Whitton. I have been puzzling over this meadow. Unlike the rest of your land, it seems to be in a state of disgraceful neglect."

If he had expected to provoke her, he missed his mark.

"It is not mine," she said. "It belongs to Lord Alphonse Sebring and he will neither lease nor sell it to me. That is, he has never deigned to answer when I have written with offers."

Iverbrook shouted with laughter.

"You plainly do not know Addlepate Sebring if you propose to do business with him. It is common knowledge that he tosses all his correspondence in the fire without opening it, even invitations. He just turns up at whatever function his bosom-bows are gracing with their presence, invited or not. Being the younger son of a duke, he is rarely refused admittance, except at Almack's when he turns up in pantaloons."

"What am I to do then? These fields have been a thorn in my flesh for years. All they need is drainage and regular mowing, and they would soon be excellent pasture."

"Addlepate's brother George is a friend of mine. I'll see if he can do anything in the matter. At the least I will find out who handles his affairs and you can address yourself to him."

"Thank you, Iverbrook. And also thank you for helping with the harvest, though I mean to see for myself what has been done before I sing your praises! Shall we go on?"

He swung himself into the saddle and they rode side by side up the lane. Queen Anne's lace grew tall on either side, and honeysuckle perfumed the air; overhead swallows darted and swooped, catching insects to feed their insatiable young.

Selena decided that her companion was not, after all, without redeeming features. He guided her precious Orion with a gentle hand, and in spite of his casual dress she could find no fault with the way he sat the black gelding. She herself had put on a new habit of russet cloth, and had darkened her eyebrows with walnut dye. It would not run in the cool of the evening, she hoped.

"I owe you an apology too," she admitted. "I ought not to have snapped at you this morning when you offered me sympathy."

"I think you were too unwell to be held responsible, though I confess I was hurt when you called me a fribble!"

She looked at him in surprise. "Is it not true?"

"Tell me how you define 'fribble.' "

"Oh, a man-about-town. Someone who has no useful occupation and lives only for amusement. A Bond Street beau."

"No, *that* I am not!" he said in revulsion.

"Perhaps not. I do not precisely know what a Bond Street beau is. You cannot deny, however, that your life has been spent in the pursuit of frivolity."

"I have sowed my share of wild oats," he acknowledged, "nor do I promise that I am an entirely reformed character. But I do intend to embark upon an occupation generally considered useful. In the autumn I shall take my seat in the House of Lords."

"And add your mite to the weight of Tory repression!"

"Far from it, Miss Whitton. I am going to join Mr. Wilberforce in his fight against slavery in the colonies. After the sights I saw in the West Indies, I can think of no endeavour more worthy of support."

Again Selena looked at him in surprise, but this time her face, always a tolerably exact mirror of her emotions, showed respect as well.

"Was it so very dreadful, then?"

Since she neither berated him, like his lawyer, nor hushed him, like his friend, Iverbrook elaborated.

"What decided me that freeing my own slaves was not enough was a trial I attended in Tortola, in the Virgin Islands. A man called Arthur Hodge had settled there on an estate some twenty years ago. In 1803 he owned a hundred and forty slaves. Since then it seems he murdered over one hundred of them, in the most hideous ways, until a free negro woman who had worked for him laid information with the local justices."

"No one had tried to stop him?"

"His overseer, and even his sister, were witnesses against him. One must suppose they had thought that since he owned them he could do with them as he wished."

"And the justices?"

"They sentenced him to be hanged. Had the letter telling of my brother's death not reached me at that time, after long delays, I'd have stayed to see the hanging, though it is not a spectacle I find edifying."

"A horrible story." Selena's voice trembled. "I perfectly understand why you will join the struggle against slavery. I had never considered that it might lead to such crimes, never thought on the subject at all, in fact."

"Nor I, nor most people. Perhaps I was wrong to tell you. I hope you do not suffer from nightmares!"

"My nerves are not so delicate, I assure you. Very well, when you make your maiden speech I will withdraw the word 'fribble'!"

"I thank you, ma'am. And now you may pass judgment upon my abilities as a farm bailiff."

They turned in at an open gate. Before them lay a field patterned with stooks of corn in neat rows. Already gleaners with rush baskets foraged for spilled grain, the kerchiefs of the women bright against the pale yellow stubble.

Selena studied the scene as Lyra and Orion picked their way up the slight slope. There was a dip in the ground near the top of the hill that was difficult to mow. If the viscount had managed to persuade the men to do it properly, then he was of more use than she had thought possible.

The hollow was clean cut.

"Beautiful," she said with satisfaction. "Thank you, Iverbrook." She held out her hand and he raised it to his lips.

"Delighted to be of service, ma'am. Now if you will just explain to me what is to go forward tomorrow?"

"I cannot suppose that you wish to concern yourself any further, sir."

"But I have been enjoying myself immensely. I was used to go harvesting with my father when I was a child."

"Yet you have chosen not to occupy yourself with running your estates."

"I had little choice in the matter, Miss Whitton! My father died when I was sixteen. Mama would not hear of my leaving school to learn how to manage Iver, and before I was of an age to decide for myself, she had remarried. Mr. Ffinch-Smythe having turned the place into an excessively profitable pig farm, I set foot in the place as rarely as possible thereafter."

"Does not your step-papa own his own land? Surely he and Lady Lavinia could remove thither and you could return Iver Place to mixed farming."

"It is obvious you are well acquainted with neither Iver nor my mother. It is poor land, with sour soil, better suited to raising swine than to anything else. The first viscount bought it to be near Windsor. He and his son and grandson made their fortunes at Court, and it was not farmed at all until my father tried. He spent a fortune on enclosures, to no avail."

"And Lady Lavinia?"

"Lady Lavinia has palpitations at the thought of removing even to the Dower House. Her health is not strong, has never been strong, and her nerves are easily overset."

"And you were brought up always to give in to her, lest she become seriously ill. I see how it is."

"No, you do not, Miss Whitton! You cannot possibly guess at the depth of my aversion for pigs!"

Selena laughed and dropped the subject. They were approaching the fields she wanted to inspect, some barley, some wheat, and some clover for fodder. She decided in what order they should be cut, and they turned homeward.

"Do you really mean to oversee the rest of the harvest?" she asked anxiously. "I am sure there must be a hundred things you had rather be doing."

Lord Iverbrook thought of Amabel Parcott and Brighton, but neither seemed as attractive as before. He consigned them to oblivion.

"Nothing," he assured her. "Besides, I could not reconcile it with my conscience were I to allow you to make yourself ill again. What I do not understand is why you employ a bailiff like John Peabody, who is so ineffectual he cannot control your labourers."

"John is extremely knowledgeable about farming. He and Mr. Russell taught me all I know, for Papa was never in the least interested. Papa hired him, not I. In fact, they were very alike in a way, knowledgeable but not practical. My father was a brilliant Classicist and an amateur astronomer of some renown. Hence our names."

"Names? Selena, Phoebe, Delia—ah, Greek names for the moon goddess! Artemis, Diana—you must consider yourself lucky not to be Hecate or Trivia, if I remember my mythology aright."

"Yes, and also that Papa had no son. I could not bear with equanimity a brother called Apollo!"

"True," he said, much struck. "Sir Apollo Whitton does not even bear contemplating! Selena suits you well, however, for one might suppose your hair spun from moonbeams."

Selena blushed. "That is the prettiest compliment I have ever received," she said, then looked at him with laughing eyes. "But I think any compliment from a Bond Street beau must be taken with a pinch of salt."

"Since we agreed that I am *not* a Bond Street beau, you may accept it as sincere, Miss Whitton. Fribble though I am, I do not offer Spanish coin." His eyes laughed back at her. "At least, not to young ladies as accustomed to plain speaking as you are!"

=== 6 ===

"MY LADY, MY lady, come quick! Mrs. Tooting's fallen into a fit and there's a blackamoor in the kitchen asking for his lordship!" Polly, her pretty face scarlet with excitement, burst into the peaceful dining room.

Bannister surged forward.

"Now what is this, my girl? You just beg her ladyship's pardon for interrupting dinner and I'll have a word with you outside."

"Nonsense, Bannister," said Lady Whitton firmly. "Polly is quite right to tell me at once about Tooting, though her manner might be improved upon. I'm coming, child. Delia, pray go to the stillroom and fetch me the vervain. And Hugh, dear boy, you had best come and deal with this blackamoor. One of your Jamaicans, I expect?"

Selena jumped up. "Stay here, Delia, and entertain our cousin. I will fetch the vervain. I have been longing all week to meet one of Hugh's blackamoors and I'd not miss it for the world."

"It must be Joshua," said Iverbrook, puzzled. "I wonder what brings him here."

In the kitchen two housemaids clutched each other hysterically while the housekeeper lay on the floor drumming her heels, her eyes rolled back into her head. Cook, a tall, spare, phlegmatic woman, was standing at the stove, calmly stirring her sauces.

"I couldn't let the custard burn, my lady," she explained. "Mr. Arbuckle took the African outside, seeing as how he was causing such a commotion. That Polly's the only one with a grain of sense, and she don't have much."

The viscount left Lady Whitton to deal with her staff and went to the back door. Outside, in the dusk, his servant was talking to a tired-looking young black man, watched from a safe distance by Jem and the gardener.

"Mr. Joshua's come to see you urgent, m'lord," said Tom. "He took the stage to Oxford but he's walked all the way from there."

Limping badly, the ex-slave approached his lordship.

"I must speak to you, my lord." He spoke perfect English in a sonorous voice, with just the hint of an exotic accent. "But I do not wish to frighten the good people within."

"Yokels!" snorted Tom Arbuckle, from the vantage point of a world traveller.

"A moment, Joshua. Let me consult the lady of the house." Iverbrook turned back to the kitchen just as Selena entered it, carrying a brown glass jar.

"Mama, here is the vervain. What is the matter, Iverbrook? Is it Joshua?"

"Yes," he said in an undertone. "He has some urgent news for me but will not come in lest your people take fright again."

"Fools! Bring him in through the side door, to the library. I will go and light some candles there."

She was just finishing this task when the viscount and his protégé came in.

"Have you eaten, Joshua?" she asked, turning from the candlestick on the mantelpiece. "Oh, you have hurt your leg! My mother will be able to help it, I am sure."

"An old injury, ma'am. I thank you for your kindness."

"Made worse by your walk from Oxford. And no, he has not dined, Miss Whitton."

"I shall have a tray sent in. Should you like the rest of your dinner on a tray, Iverbrook? I doubt Mama will return to table."

"I am very sorry, ma'am, to have caused such consternation."

"Our local people are anything but cosmopolitan, I'm afraid. Few of them have ever been farther afield than Oxford and the next county seems like a foreign country though it is just the other side of the Thames. Iverbrook, a word with you and then I shall leave you to your business."

"Sit down, Joshua," said his lordship, following her out.

"I shall have a room prepared for him," she said. "He looks to be tired and in pain. How very gentlemanly he is! I had thought he must be an ex-slave."

"He belonged to that Arthur Hodge of whom I told you, but now he is articled to a solicitor in London. If you have a truckle bed that may be set up in my chamber, that will do very well. We shared a cabin from Jamaica and I know that, unlike Tom, he does not snore!"

"We have another room, though it is small. Persuade him, if you can, to let my mother look at his leg. You know her abilities."

"Yes, and that she is as kind as her daughter. Thank you, Selena." He took her hand and dropped a kiss on the palm, then went back into the library.

For a moment she stood there, her hand pressed to her hot cheek. In the past few days she had felt that they were becoming friends, but this was the first time she had heard such warmth in his voice. Why should it make her heart beat faster? If she welcomed his Joshua, it was small return for all he had done for her. All the barley was cut and stacked, and she had been able to catch up on her accounts for the first time in three months. For once she would have a free Sunday, and they planned to take a picnic on the river after church.

Smiling in happy anticipation, she went to see if she could find a servant capable of carrying out her orders.

Lord Iverbrook turned to Joshua, who gasped with pain as he tried to stand.

"Sit down, man! What's the trouble? Are you at odds with Mr. Crowe? Or come to cuffs with the other clerks?"

"No, sir, they treat me very well. Mr. Crowe was good enough to allow me two days off to come here when I explained. It's Mr. Hubble, my lord!"

"Hubble? What the devil have you to do with that old shyster?"

"He has a clerk, James Goodenough, with whom I have become friendly. When James heard your name from me, when I told him what you have done for me, he said he had been given the task of preparing papers to enter suit in your name against your brother's will. Since you confided in me that you had not yet decided to go to law, I asked if this was usual when the suit might not be pressed. Sir, James told me the decision had been made and the papers were to be ready for Chancery by Monday!"

"The blackguard! I'll wager he aims to make a pretty penny off me.

You were quite right to come, Joshua, and I'll make it all right with Crowe."

"I asked James if he could delay the matter, and he said he might find some error that required recopying, but he dared not stretch it out beyond Tuesday."

"I shall post up to London tomorrow and wait on Hubble's doorstep on Monday morning. No, I'll send for him to come to Dover Street. He will take me more seriously if I stand on my dignity. And what is more, I shall set things in motion to transfer my affairs to your old Crowe's hands."

Pondering ways and means, Iverbrook paced up and down the library. It was a long, narrow room, its walls lined with books ranging from rare editions of Horace's *Odes* to a *Manual of Modern Methods of Raising Cattle*. The ceiling was painted dark blue, relieved by gilded stars arranged in their constellations as nearly as possible in a sky with the wrong dimensions. Orion's belt caught his lordship's eye and he swung round.

"Don't tell Miss Whitton! It can only worry her. I'll just say I am called away on urgent business. Shall you be fit to travel tomorrow?"

"Yes, sir, of course, if you do not mean to make me walk to Oxford again." Joshua smiled at the viscount's indignant denial. "Though it is not so very far if you do not lose your way."

"Ha! So you lost it too, did you? These damned country lanes with never a signpost had me going round in circles."

There was a knock on the door and Polly peeked in. "I brung some dinner for Mr. Joshua, my lord," she announced. "And her la'ship says she'll take a look at his leg after, him being willing, that is. You oughta, sir, honest. My lady can cure anything." She deposited a loaded tray on the huge mahogany desk that filled one end of the room. "Can I getcha anything, my lord? That Sir Aubrey, he's at the port in the dining room."

"A glass of brandy, please, Polly. I won't join Sir Aubrey though."

"He's a naughty one that, and no mistake," she giggled, and seemed ready to proceed to further revelations, but Bannister's entrance sent her flying.

"A good girl, but chattersome, my lord," apologised the butler. "A glass of brandy for your lordship? At once! Is everything as you like it, Mr. Joshua?"

"Perfect," said Joshua, lifting the dish covers and releasing clouds of fragrant steam.

Later, on his lordship's orders, he allowed Lady Whitton to examine his bad leg. She bustled into his chamber and closed the door firmly behind her.

"I can't see you blushing, young man," she said, "but judging by the look on your face you are embarrassed enough without half the world peering in as they pass by. I have seen legs before, dear boy, though not of this colour. I daresay they are all alike inside. Tell me when this hurts."

She sat down on the edge of his bed and gently manipulated his knee. He said nothing, but looking up she saw his eyes closed, brow furrowed, and lower lip caught between his teeth. She took one of his clenched hands in both hers.

"You must tell me when it hurts, child. Otherwise I cannot find out what is amiss."

"Sorry, ma'am," he burst out. "Mr. Hodge, when he hurt you, he like hearing squeals. More you squeal, more he hurt, so I learn to be silent."

She stroked his hand till it uncurled and he lay back on his pillows.

"Mr. Hodge did this to you?" she asked quietly. "He was your master?" With a lace handkerchief that smelled of rosemary she wiped the sweat from his brow.

"Yes, my lady. My owner. This was nothing. He killed many slaves. Too many in the end. He was arrested and brought to trial for murder."

"How did you come to meet Hugh?"

His face lit. "I was a witness at the trial. Many people came, Lord Iverbrook among them. He talked to me and I told him how I admired the lawyers who were fighting for the rights of slaves against their owners. I remember his exact words. He said, 'You seem to be a clever chap, how should you like to be one of them?' Then he bought me, and freed me. On the way here from Jamaica he shared his cabin with me and taught me to speak properly. In London he found me lodgings, gave me money to live on, and paid for me to learn to be a lawyer. At first I thought he was a god, one of our African gods, but now I know he is a very good man, and my friend."

"Your friend indeed! I am happy to hear that Hugh has so much practical compassion, for the one without the other is useless. And now, let us be practical and try if we can find what is the matter with your leg."

While her mother was thus occupied, Selena was receiving Iverbrook's apologies for his proposed abrupt departure on the morrow.

"I wish you success in your business," she said. "And I hope you will not quite abandon us in future?"

"By no means! I shall return as soon as I can, no later than Tuesday if all goes well. There is still the wheat and clover to be cut."

"You must not feel obliged to return for that! I cannot express my gratitude for your help, but I have done the harvest before and will do it again. It will not kill me, you know."

"No, but it makes you excessively uncomfortable, and then you are cross as a bear at a stake."

"How odious of you to put me to the blush! At least you need not be present to suffer my megrims."

"Oh, but I must. There are certain matters between us that have not been settled, and I have not forgot if you have."

"Peter!" The twinkle in her hazel eyes was extinguished. She bit her lip. "You are persistent, my lord. I assure you that I shall not give him up, and if you continue to press me, you will not be welcome here, harvest or no harvest."

"I shall rely for a welcome on your amiable mother, Miss Whitton. I mean to obtain custody by hook or by crook, and if you fight me it just makes it more difficult for both of us. Come, let us cry friends, and discuss the matter calmly for once."

Selena turned on her heel and walked out.

Going in search of her mother, to try to persuade her not to invite the viscount to return, she found her in the stillroom.

"Have you found out what is wrong with Joshua's leg?" she asked.

"It is an old injury that never healed properly, and rheumatism has set in. I am making up some oil of wintergreen liniment and white willow tea for the poor boy to take back to London with him."

"Was it caused by his owner? Iverbrook told me a little about him."

"Yes, that dreadful Hodge. Dear Hugh behaved just as he ought, bought him and freed him." She told Selena the story. "The dear boy would die for Hugh," she finished.

It did not seem a propitious moment to request that the paragon be refused admittance to the Manor. Her feelings utterly confused, Selena went to bed.

She was woken in the night by the sound of water dripping through the elm outside her window. It was raining steadily; there would be no harvesting tomorrow. She decided to stay a-bed late and miss the viscount's departure, thus solving the problem of how to bid him farewell.

The heavy drizzle was still falling when Tom Arbuckle shook his master awake. His lordship yawned and stretched and sat up. Then he saw the clock on the mantelpiece.

"Seven o'clock? What the devil do you mean by it, Tom? I distinctly remember saying eight for today. No farm work and we've not so many miles to cover."

"'Tis sixty mile to London if it's a score, m'lord, and the lanes will be like a hasty pudding." He pulled back the draperies at the window. "We've a ways to go afore we reach the post road."

"Oh lord!" groaned Iverbrook, "and we've only the curricle. We can't let Joshua get wet, with his leg the way it is. I wonder if we might borrow the Whittons' carriage, just till we get to a posting-house and can hire a chaise."

"Better ask her ladyship," advised Tom with a grin. "Miss Whitton 'd likely say no."

"You servants are gabblemongers, one and all. Now how did you know Miss Whitton and I are at outs? No, don't tell me, you impertinent clothhead. Give me some clothes!"

Still grinning, Tom went to the wardrobe.

Though half expecting it, my lord was disappointed when Miss Whitton did not put in an appearance at the breakfast table.

"I expect she is sleeping in," said Lady Whitton placidly. "She rises so early as a rule, but in this weather there is not much to be done about the farm."

"It's raining, Uncle Hugh," Peter explained. "Do you like rain? Lots of grown-ups don't like it. Me and the ducks do, 'cept when I'm not 'lowed to go out." He clapped his hands across his mouth in dismay, but his grandmother neglected to issue the expected prohibition.

"I wonder what Sir Aubrey is doing?" said Delia. "He retires when we do but he is never seen below stairs before noon. He cannot still be sleeping."

"I expect he is trying to decide what shade of red to wear today," said Lord Iverbrook acidly. "I gather he brought no servant, and a fop without a valet must spend the greater part of his time dressing himself. Nor dare he entrust the care of his wardrobe to mere maidservants, and I'll wager Bannister has better things to occupy his time."

Delia looked reproachful. "Just because he is a gentleman of fashion and you do not care how you dress . . . " She flushed at her mother's shocked glance. "I beg your pardon, sir," she stammered.

"Very true, I do not," he said cheerfully. "My friends frequently roast me on my unmodishness. Lady Whitton, pray advise me. Will Joshua come to much harm travelling in this weather?"

"I have already told Jem to set your horses to our barouche, Hugh. You will send for your curricle whenever it suits you. Try to keep Joshua warm and dry and rested. I had Bannister take him his breakfast in his chamber so that he could keep the leg up as long as possible. In a day or two, God willing, he will be as well as ever, though I fear the leg will always pain him."

"Thank you, ma'am. If you please, may I come for the curricle myself? I have no intention of abandoning Miss Whitton in the middle of the harvest."

"Are you coming back soon, Uncle Hugh?" Peter bounced up and down in his seat. "Will you bring me one of your gentleman's horses for my own, like you said? Please will you?"

"You are much too little for a gentleman's horse," said Delia scornfully.

"Timmy Russell says he's going to get a gentleman's horse and he's only a little bit bigger'n me."

Lady Whitton intervened before Delia could animadvert on the general untruthfulness of small boys.

"If you are done with your breakfast, Peter, go up to Nurse now," she said. "You may come down to say good-bye to Uncle Hugh later."

However, Lady Whitton was the only one to wave good-bye as the carriage rolled down the drive half an hour later, with Tom on the box, Iverbrook and a bundled-up Joshua within. It turned down the lane and she hurried back to her stillroom.

She did not see the rest of the family until lunch time, when she found both Delia and Selena in the dining room. Sir Aubrey made a grand entrance, spectacular in crimson and pale pink. He apologised for his late appearance and blamed it on the exigencies of his toilette. Selena hid a giggle, but Delia thought the effect well worth the effort and looked at him in awe.

"Where is Peter, Mama?" asked Selena, helping herself to raspberries and cream. "Is he coming down to lunch?"

"I'm sure dear Aubrey will not mind if he joins us as usual. I expect Nurse has not noticed the time. Bannister, send Polly for Master Peter, if you please."

Bannister returned moments later. "Master Peter is not with Mrs. Finnegan, my lady," he announced. "It seems she has not seen him since just after breakfast. She thought he was with your ladyship."

"No, not since breakfast. Selena? Delia?" They both shook their heads. "I expect he went to see Jem in the stables, the naughty child."

"I'll send Polly, my lady." They heard him shouting, "Polly, run quick now and see if Master Peter's in the stables!"

With a hollow feeling in her stomach, Selena realised what must have happened.

"No use, Mama," she whispered. "He swore he would do it by hook or by crook. Iverbrook has abducted Peter!"

— 7 —

THERE WAS A stunned silence.

"Nonsense!" said Lady Whitton, recovering. "Hugh would not dream of running off with the child."

"Besides, he left his curricle here," pointed out Delia.

"I expect that was a ruse to divert suspicion," said Sir Aubrey. "To a gentleman as plump in the pocket as Lord Iverbrook, the loss of a carriage is nothing. I have seen a thousand times its worth wagered in a single evening's gambling. By heaven, I shall call the dog to account!"

"Nonsense," said Lady Whitton again.

"He is quite determined to take Peter from us, Mama," Selena repeated. "He has told me so in no uncertain terms."

"But you cannot suppose that he would act in such a surreptitious fashion. It is underhanded, and quite illegal I am sure."

"Possession is nine tenths of the law," said Sir Aubrey with relish. He had no wish to have the child on his hands when he married Selena.

"I expect he wandered off across the fields," said Delia. "Mama, you remember how he said at breakfast that he likes the rain. We must organise a search."

Lady Whitton paled. "The river! Surely he would not go down to the river?"

Her daughters joined in soothing her. Peter had been told time and time again that he must not go near the river on his own. He was a sensible, obedient little boy and understood the dangers. His grandmother herself had forbidden it, and though he might occasionally rebel against the dictates of his aunts, or of Nurse, he had never been known to disobey Grandmama.

Bannister came back. "He's not in the stables, my lady. Jem's not seen him this morning."

"The gypsies!" Delia exclaimed. "Do they not steal children?"

"They moved on, Miss Delia, two or three days past."

"Thank heaven!" said Lady Whitton.

"We must organise a search," insisted Delia. "Mama, you send out the house servants, and Selena must gather the farm workers."

Selena smiled at her hollowly. "How practical you are of a sudden," she said. "We'll do as you suggest, but I am afraid it is useless. They will be half way to Iver by now."

Delia, feeling unusually helpful and competent, donned pelisse, bonnet, and boots and slipped out of the house to join the search. She was determined to find her nephew and show Selena that she was not merely a pretty widgeon, as her sister had been known to describe her.

Undeterred by the rain, now slackened to a damp, grey mizzle, she crossed the lane, climbed a stile, and took the footpath across the meadow. The long grass soon soaked her skirts but she pressed on eagerly, now and then calling, "Peter!"

By the time she had crossed several fields of grass and skirted one of ripe wheat, Delia realised that she had unthinkingly taken the way to Bracketts, her favourite walk. Peter had come this way with her just a few days ago, to play with Jane's little brothers. She decided to go on and see if Jane and Clive would join the search.

A copse straddled the boundary between the Russells' land and the Manor's. As Delia entered the shelter of the trees, she remembered that Peter had wanted to climb one of them. A tall larch, she thought, that seemed easy for a small boy. She had hurried him past, and he had been in the mopes about it for quite five minutes. She looked about: there it was. Pushing through clutching brambles she made her way to it and peered up through the dripping green needles.

Half way up, a good twenty feet over her head, hung a damp blue bundle. Peter had hooked his arms and legs over the branches. His eyes were shut, and since she could see no way for him to have hurt himself, she assumed that, unable to climb down, he had fallen asleep.

She was about to shout his name, but a horrid thought came to her. Startled, sleepy, he might relax his grip and fall. If she went for help he might fall before she returned. The only thing to do was to climb up and help him down.

Selena would have done it without a second thought. Mama said Selena had been a real tomboy, and even Phoebe had liked climbing trees. Delia had been a delicate child, often ill, and by the time she grew stronger she was a young lady, too old for such tricks. Besides, Jane Russell would have stared to see such hoydenish conduct.

But Jane was not here. Peter was in danger. Taking off bonnet and pelisse, tucking up her skirts as best she could, Delia started climbing.

Several breathless minutes later, she reached him. One arm around the swaying trunk, resolutely not looking down, she put the other arm about Peter and whispered his name.

Angelic blue eyes opened. "'Lo, Auntie Dee." He blinked, and shifted a little, to her alarm. "Oh! I 'member. I got stuck. Did you come to get me?"

"Yes, Peter. I'll go down first and help you find places to put your feet. You'll see, it will be easy."

"All right. You look funny with wet hair."

"So do you. Hold on tight now while I start down."

Clinging to the trunk with both hands, Delia felt below with one cautious foot. She found a branch, stepped on to it, and moved her other foot. As the branch took her full weight it snapped with a noise like a pistol shot. For a heart-stopping moment she hung by her arms, then pulled herself back up.

"Auntie Dee? Are you all right?" For the first time Peter sounded frightened.

"Yes. Yes, I'm fine." She forced herself to open her eyes and smile at him. "I'll try again, more carefully!"

Again she felt with one foot and found a branch. This time she tested it before trusting it with her weight. It felt solid enough, but she held on tight as she lowered herself. Then suddenly she couldn't move.

"I'm stuck," she said in horror. "It's my dress." The jolt when she nearly fell had loosened her skirts. Behind her, unreachable, the fabric had caught on a dead branch. Her walking dress was made of good, strong kerseymere and showed no sign of ripping when she daringly let go with one hand and tugged on it. "Oh Peter, now I'm stuck too!"

"We'll sing songs," he suggested stoically. "Aunt Sena will come and get us soon."

"There are lots of people looking for you. We must shout for help."

It seemed a long time that they alternated singing and shouting. Delia was growing hoarse when at last they heard an answering hail and Clive Russell appeared, leading his mount.

"Delia! What the deuce are you doing up there?" Even soaked to the skin, his dark hair dripping, the young man was extremely good-looking. For once Delia had no thought for romance.

"Having a picnic! We are stuck, silly, and if you dare to call me a featherhead for climbing up, I shall . . . I shall . . . well, I'd like to know what you would have done and oh, Clive, please get us down quickly!" Delia burst into tears.

"Now stop crying, Dee, and tell me what the trouble is. Are you too scared to move?"

"No!" Indignantly she explained. "So you will have to climb up and unhitch my skirt," she said, "and then you can go away and I will help Peter down."

Clive crimsoned. "I can't climb up underneath you," he stammered. "It wouldn't be decent."

"Fustian! If you think I care a farthing for propriety when I am in this fix, then you are a numbskull! Now hurry up because my hands are getting cold and if I slip and fall I hope I land on you!"

Stunned to hear such language from a delicately bred female of a romantic disposition, Clive gulped and climbed.

Half an hour later, he led his horse up the drive to Milford Manor. On its back, Delia held Peter before her, hugging the shivering child. Lady Whitton and Selena rushed out to greet them.

"So Iverbrook did not take him!" cried Selena thankfully. "Where did you find him, Dee?" She lifted Peter down, and Delia slid down into Clive's arms.

"Come inside and get dry, children," said Lady Whitton. "You can tell us all about it when you are warmed. Bannister, pray call off the hounds."

"At once, my lady!" said the beaming butler.

All in dry clothes, with Clive looking thoroughly embarrassed in the late Sir William's emerald silk dressing gown, they met before a roaring fire in the drawing room.

Sir Aubrey, still immaculate in crimson and pink, examined Clive through his quizzing glass and tut-tutted. Delia eyed her cousin with dislike. He had stayed at home in comfort, and all the romance of his heroic Caribbean adventures was undermined. Clive might be just a farmer, and a shocking tease besides, but he was there when one needed him. He looked splendidly Oriental in Papa's dressing gown. She patted the sofa beside her and he sat down.

"It was Delia who rescued him," he said, setting the seal on her approval.

They told their story, with Peter chiming in. Selena listened in silence. Happy as she was to have Peter back safely, she felt guilty for misjudging Lord Iverbrook. What a ninny she was to believe that he had done anything so dishonourable! When he returned, she would discuss Peter's future with him calmly and sensibly, as he had requested. He was a reasonable gentleman; once he had heard her arguments, properly presented without flying into the boughs, he must agree that she had the right. Then he would come often to visit Peter and perhaps . . . and that would be delightful. For all his toplofty manner, he could be charming when he chose. Thinking of the smile that wrinkled the corners of his eyes, she smiled herself.

Lord Iverbrook returned to a royal welcome.

After three days of rain, the sun shone once more and a strong but warm breeze was rapidly drying out the fields. Selena had been to inspect them and was trotting home on Orion, followed by Jem. She met the carriage as it reached the gates of the Manor. It pulled up and the viscount jumped down, to stand looking up at her with a glad light in his eyes.

"Miss Whitton."

"Welcome back, Iverbrook." She felt oddly breathless. "Help me down and I'll walk with you."

He caught her with strong hands at her waist and released her reluctantly. She smoothed down the skirts of her habit, then took his proffered arm.

They walked up the gravel drive. Selena was very conscious of her fingers on the smooth sleeve of his coat, and of his enquiring look bent upon her face.

"Are you well, Miss Whitton?" he asked at last.

"Very well, I thank you. You are come back just in time to resume the harvest."

"Hence the warm welcome!" he laughed. The moment of awkwardness was past.

"Did your business prosper? I hope poor Joshua was much improved before you left him?"

"Very much. He was able to take up his duties again yesterday, thanks to your mama's skill. I spoke to Crowe, who is a very good sort of fellow for a lawyer, and he will watch that Joshua does not overtax his strength."

"The case must have been desperate indeed to bring him all the way to the wilds of Oxfordshire."

"Desperate indeed, but I have dealt with that, I trust. I also went to see Wilberforce, hoping to ask his advice about my maiden speech in the Lords. He was not there, but I arranged to meet him this day fortnight."

"And you will stay here until then? That is famous!"

"I dare to hope that Lady Whitton will not throw me out," he admitted with a grin. "And even if the weather holds fine, I daresay it will be that long before the harvest will be finished, so that *you* will be forced to tolerate my presence!"

Before Selena could retort, Peter raced down the steps and threw himself into his lordship's arms.

"Uncle Hugh, Uncle Hugh, I seed you from the window. Finny said I can come. Me and Delia got stuck up a tree and Mr. Russell had to rescue us. I drawed you a picsher, will you come and see it right now? I'll draw one for you too, Aunt Sena. It's teatime and I told Finny to save you a bixit, Uncle Hugh, so will you come and have tea upstairs?"

"Calm down, young man," said Hugh, laughing and hugging him. "You are getting your words all mixed up. I must make my bow to your grandmother before I begin to think about bixits."

Lady Whitton appeared at the front door.

"Hugh dear! Just in time for tea. Now no nonsense about changing your clothes first, pray. Peter, you may stay down and have a jam tart if you like."

"Yes, please, Grandmama. Finny can have my bixit."

In the drawing room, Delia was pouring tea for Sir Aubrey. She greeted Iverbrook with pleasure and gave him the first cup. Peter picked up the plate of jam tarts, warm from the oven, and carefully handed it round, informing everyone that he liked the red jam best. Thus warned, everyone but Sir Aubrey chose yellow, and he retired happily to a corner to get red jam all over his face in peace.

Iverbrook sat back and sipped his tea. *What a delightful place,* he thought. The French doors stood open to the garden, and from the river beyond came the quacking of ducks and the occasional shout of a boatman. He stretched out his long legs and regarded his booted feet. Lady Whitton had no objection to boots in the house, and how she would have stared to see him in kneebreeches at dinner. He even managed to cast a benevolent eye on Sir Aubrey's mulberry coat. The man was without doubt a fop and a demi-beau, but harmless withal. Miss Whitton had by far too much sense to consider his suit.

And how charming she looked! The riding dress of russet cloth became her to perfection, roses bloomed in her cheeks, her eyes sparkled. Unconscious of the disarray of her pale curls, she told him all about the state of the various fields, and watching her, he heard not a word.

"If you are not tired," he suggested, "we had best ride out before dinner and you can show me. I have brought a riding horse with me this time so you will not be dispossessed of Orion, nor Miss Delia of Lyra."

"How very thoughtful," said Lady Whitton approvingly.

"Did you bring a horse for me?" asked Peter. "A gentleman's horse?"

"No, I brought you a pony."

Peter's mouth dropped open and his eyes shone. "For me? A really truly pony? Where is it, Uncle Hugh? What's its name? When can I ride it?" He launched himself at the viscount and generously shared the jam on his hands and face with that gentleman's shirt before he was removed by his giggling aunts.

During the next two weeks, Iverbrook found that his presence was only occasionally required in the fields. His authority was sufficient to keep things running smoothly even in his absence.

He taught his nephew to ride the pony, a shaggy-maned sorrel promptly christened Leo.

He walked with the young ladies and Sir Aubrey, and more often rode with the young ladies, since Sir Aubrey had never found it necessary in Kingston to learn that art. Nor could he drive a carriage. Delia was thoroughly disillusioned.

They dined at Bracketts. Mr. Russell, a stout, hearty gentleman of no pretensions, still showed signs of the handsome features now inherited by his son. His wife, Lady Anne, a severe matron with an aristocratic nose, was quick to make sure Iverbrook knew her to be the daughter of an earl. She was distantly acquainted with his mother, a fact that did not recommend her to him, but he liked the rest of the family.

The Russells joined them for a picnic on the river. Iverbrook had the unspeakable satisfaction of seeing Sir Aubrey dangling from the end of a swaying punt pole for a good thirty seconds before it finally deposited him in the murky water. His carmine velvet coat was ruined, and even Lady Anne was seen to hide a smile behind her gloved hand.

"Most unsuitable dress for a picnic," she observed acidly.

Two weeks passed, and Lord Iverbrook left for his appointment with William Wilberforce.

"I shall not be gone for long," he promised. "After all, there is still the clover to be mowed."

As Selena waved good-bye, she realised that not once in the whole fortnight had they talked about Peter's future. Had he come to accept, without words, that Peter belonged here? Had he avoided the subject, as she had, because he did not want to spoil the growing accord between them? Or was he biding his time, cozening her into believing he had given up, only to return to the attack when he was sure she had changed her mind about him?

For she was no longer so certain that he was unfit to have charge of his nephew. Watching them together, she could not imagine him abandoning the boy to the care of servants and his hypochondriacal mother.

Restless, she wandered down the garden to the river. A bright-painted barge was floating downstream with the current. On the bows an elderly man smoked his pipe, and the young fellow at the tiller waved his hat at her.

"Fine mornin', miss!" he shouted.

Selena waved back. Peter would be growing up, she thought. She could send him to school, but then he should take his place in Society and she could not guide him through the shoals and rapids of the Polite World. His uncle's help would be indispensable; Hugh must not be alienated. But surely he would not insist on taking the child away while he was so small?

A fish jumping after flies plopped back into the water and roused her from her revery. There were bills to be paid, accounts to be made up, and even though her constant presence seemed no longer necessary she must ride out to the fields before luncheon. She climbed the steps to the house.

An hour later, dressed in her old habit, Selena descended the stairs. Seeing the butler crossing the hall, she called out, "Bannister, I am going out. Pray tell Mama I shall return for luncheon, if she should ask for me."

"Certainly, Miss Selena. Her ladyship is in the drawing room, miss. Lady Anne Russell has called with Miss Russell and Mr. Clive."

"Oh dear, I suppose I had best make my curtsey. Thank you, Bannister."

Selena found Delia and Sir Aubrey in the drawing room with her mother and the Russells. She paid her respects to Lady Anne and stood for a moment making polite conversation. She was about to excuse herself and escape when the door opened and Bannister appeared.

"Lady Gant to see you, my lady," he announced, "and Mrs. Amabel Parcott."

— 8 —

A STOUT ELDERLY lady in a regrettable puce carriage dress trotted into the room, followed by Mrs. Parcott, an opulent vision in her favourite rose pink.

Lady Anne's nose, always haughty, rose several degrees.

"Jane, my reticule!" she said sharply to her daughter. "My dear Lady Whitton, we must be on our way. Perhaps Delia would care to return to Bracketts with us if you can spare her? Come, Clive." Urging her offspring and their friend before her like a sheepdog with an unruly flock, she gave Lady Gant a cold nod in passing and left.

Lady Whitton jumped up. "Lady Anne is always so anxious to return to the children," she suggested hopefully. "How delightful to see you, Lady Gant. It is an age since you called and I fear I rarely have the leisure to drive so far as to Cowley. And you have brought dear Amabel with you. I expect London is far from pleasant at this season."

"Mama insisted that I not spend the summer in town," drawled Mrs. Parcott. "The country is so charmingly refreshing, is it not, Selena? Oh, I beg your pardon! Since you rusticate here year round I daresay it seems quite ordinary to you."

"I much prefer the countryside, Amabel," said Selena, feeling more than usually dowdy as she eyed the other's dark, shining ringlets and modish bonnet trimmed with silk roses. "And you prefer the city, I imagine, since we have not seen you in Oxfordshire for quite two years!"

"La, you are right! But I declare I am quite worn down with all the bustle and gaiety. Though it is excessively flattering to have so many suitors, one must needs escape them all now and then."

"Lady Gant, Amabel, let me present Sir Aubrey Whitton," Lady Whitton intervened. "Sir William's nephew and heir, you know. He has been residing in the West Indies and is staying with us for the present."

"How vastly odd!" cried Mrs. Parcott. "Why, I have never before given a thought to the West Indies, I vow, and now here are two gentlemen but just arrived from there. I suppose Iverbrook visits here often, since his brother was wed to your Phoebe. He is a very dear friend of mine, you know. On his return he came to see me even before his mama. Is it not shocking how a gentleman will put his beloved before his own mother? I feel sure you would not do such a thing, Sir Aubrey."

"Pray excuse me . . . farm business," muttered Selena, and fled, leaving her mama uncharacteristically flustered.

"So quaint," murmured Amabel to Sir Aubrey.

The baronet had inspected Mrs. Parcott through his quizzing glass, and apparently found her appearance inviting, for a look of admiration spread across his handsome face. "Iverbrook and I are old friends, ma'am," he claimed. "He has been staying here and left but an hour since, for London."

The widow looked chagrined. "La, I am sorry to miss him, Sir Aubrey. However, I do not plan to stay more than a few days with my parents. I shall see Iverbrook in town next week."

"I fear not, ma'am. His lordship said most particularly that he expected to return here at no very distant date."

"Well, my own plans are flexible, I vow. Since dear Mr. Parcott passed away, I have been able to please myself. 'Pon rep, I cannot but wonder what is the attraction that brings a fashionable young gentleman to such an out of the way spot."

"He is fond of his nephew, I believe," responded the baronet cautiously, looking round to be sure that Lady Whitton and Lady Gant were safely engaged in conversation. "I have sometimes thought that he may hold Miss Whitton in some affection also, for which I am heartily sorry since he is bound to be disappointed."

"Indeed?"

"I daresay you are unaware of the shocking muddle in which the late Sir William left his affairs? While I inherited the title, the property went to his eldest daughter. It must be plain to a person of the meanest intelligence that he intended to make a match between me and my cousin Selena."

"I am to wish you happy then?"

"I must confess that I have not yet actually requested my cousin's hand, though she must certainly be aware that such is my intention. I have thought it best to allow our acquaintance to ripen."

"Let me urge you, my dear Sir Aubrey, to lose no more time! I am sure Selena is much impressed by your modish appearance and elegant address, but alas! the attractions of a viscountcy may in the end outweigh any personal superiority."

"I believe you are right, ma'am, though I am loath to think that worldly considerations might prevail over Miss Whitton's natural duty to obey her father's wishes. I will press my suit before Lord Iverbrook's return."

"I wish you every success, sir," said Mrs. Parcott warmly. "Mama, we must not outstay our welcome. I hope, Lady Whitton, to call on you again while I am fixed in the country. Such a shame that Selena had to leave before we could enjoy a good cose."

As the widow swept out with a rustle of skirts, Lady Gant trotting at her heels, Lady Whitton collapsed into a chair and fanned herself.

"Oh dear," she said, "oh dear. Lady Anne is a trifle high in the instep, to be sure, but I have seen her on terms of perfect amity with Lady Gant these thirty years. Now why did she cut Amabel in that unkind way, and insist on taking Delia along with her? Oh dear!"

"I thought Mrs. Parcott charming," said Sir Aubrey with a simper. "I suppose she is left in easy circumstances?"

"Lady Anne must have heard some spiteful tale about Amabel. A young and pretty widow living alone is bound to become the butt of scandalmongers. What a pity that she does not choose to return to her parents, though I must say that to be obliged to listen constantly to Lady Gant's chatter would try the soul of the most patient of mortals. Poor Amabel!"

"If she were purse-pinched she would have to return home. However, the settlements may be tied up in such a way that she is forced to remain single. Dear Aunt, I can no longer restrain my feelings. May I have your permission to address my cousin?"

"Address your cousin? Whatever do you . . . oh, you mean to propose marriage! To Selena?" Lady Whitton looked at him in astonishment and doubt. "Selena is her own mistress, you know. I confess I have seen no more sign of an attachment in her than I have in you,

Aubrey, but for what it is worth, you have my permission to approach her."

Four days passed before Sir Aubrey ventured to avail himself of Lady Whitton's permission. Not only did Selena show no sign of attachment, she treated him with nothing above common courtesy. Often, in fact, she carelessly ignored his presence in a way he found rather daunting. However, the viscount might return at any moment, so when the perfect opportunity presented itself, he seized it.

He was admiring his reflection in the antique mirror over the fireplace, a favourite occupation, when Selena came home from the fields and entered the drawing room. Swinging round, he bowed with a flourish.

"Cousin!" A suspicion of a frown marred his brow as he noticed that she was clad in her working clothes, most unsuitable for receiving an offer of marriage. "May I beg the favour of a word with you in private?"

Selena looked around the room. "It would appear so, sir, since no one else is present. Where is my mother?"

"Surely, being cousins, we may dispense with a chaperone."

"Third or fourth cousins, but by all means. I merely enquired as to Mama's whereabouts. If you do not know, pray tell me and I shall ask Bannister."

"I understand my aunt went out gathering herbs, attended by Polly. I cannot conceive why she should, since the gardens grow little else. But, Selena, allow me to express . . . "

"There are certain plants that will not flourish under cultivation. Is Delia not returned from Bracketts? She spends half her time there, I vow."

"No!" the baronet shouted. "I beg your pardon, cousin. You must make allowances for the emotions of a man half crazed by love!"

"Did you fall for Amabel? I had not realised it. I must admit she is as beautiful as ever, and as catty!"

"Certainly not! I mean, Mrs. Parcott is beautiful but though I did not think her—ah—catty, I have not fallen. Selena, my adored one, have you not guessed how I admire you?"

"To tell the truth, cousin, I thought you had little admiration to spare for anything but your own countenance. Oh, I beg your pardon, that was as catty as anything Amabel ever said. I am very flattered, sir, by your kind words. Now I had best go and change my clothes."

"Do not leave me! You look charmingly in that . . . in that particular shade of blue, which matches your eyes to perfection."

Her hazel eyes cold, Selena said scornfully, "You are unobservant, Sir Aubrey. Pray excuse me."

He seized her hand.

"Selena, cousin, let me speak. You have so bewitched me that I do not know what I am saying. All I ask is the honour of offering you my hand; my heart you have already. Marry me, Selena!"

"Thank you, sir, but I think we should not suit." Not without a struggle, Selena disengaged her hand and stepped back.

"Indeed we should. I shall relieve you of the burden of running Milford, and you will be Lady Whitton, like your mama. It is what Sir William undoubtedly intended when he left the farm to you, knowing the title would be mine. It was his way of saying, 'Marry my daughter, Aubrey, and take care of her for me.'"

"Poppycock! Insofar as Papa had any say in my upbringing, he brought me up to take care of myself. *And* the farm. And what is more, I do not believe he even knew of your existence. So accept my refusal, if you please. I do not wish to hurt you but I cannot suppose that I should ever have for you those feelings which a wife ought to have for her husband."

"I shall not abandon hope," he said sulkily. "Pray believe that your maidenly reserve does you no disservice in my eyes. I took you by surprise, I fear, but I shall give you time to consider my offer. After all, no female wishes to dwindle into an old maid."

He went out through the French doors into the garden. What a gapeseed the man was, thought Selena, to suppose she might be won over by an insult! She had a thousand times rather "dwindle into an old maid" than marry a posturing fool more interested in her land than herself. Baronet Whitton he might be, but he would never add "of Milford Manor" to his title.

She changed quickly for dinner that evening, donning a gown of bronze silk that accentuated the true colour of her eyes. Throwing a Paisley shawl about her shoulders, for there was a hint of autumn chill in the air, she went to her mother's room.

Lady Whitton was seated at her dressing table, tying the ribbons of her *crêpe lisse* capote under her chin. Polly was brushing the grass-stained walking dress her mistress had been wearing, and Peter, already in his nightshirt, bounced on the bed.

"Hello, Aunt Sena," he said. "I comed to say goodnight to Grandmama. Her bed bounces better'n mine does but why because has it got dragons on the curtains?"

"To guard Grandmama when she is asleep, of course. Actually, I think they are supposed to be peacocks; the brocade is so old and faded it is hard to make them out."

"Your Grandpapa always said they had guarded three generations of Whittons, from draughts at least!" said Lady Whitton. "He never would let me replace them."

"You shall have new ones tomorrow, Mama, if you will do but one thing for me."

"Oh no, I have grown accustomed to them and I should miss them. But what would you have me do, dearest?"

"Give Sir Aubrey his marching orders!"

Polly drew a quick breath and stopped brushing. Peter, hearing the note of wrath in his aunt's voice, decided not to ask what marching orders were. In her reviving indignation at her cousin, Selena forgot their presence.

"What has he done to put you in a tweak?" asked her mother resignedly.

"He had the gall to tell me he considers the Manor to be rightfully his, and that he intends to gain possession by marrying me!"

Polly dropped the brush with a clatter and, red-faced, bent to retrieve it.

"I don't like Uncle Aubrey too," said Peter. "He always pats my head and tells me to run along. Timmy Russell says . . . "

"Polly, pray take Master Peter to Nurse," requested Selena sharply, suddenly aware of her audience. "Goodnight, Peterkin. Give Grandmama a kiss now and off you go."

The child obeyed, reluctantly. At the door he turned and, peeking past the maid's skirts, said with a wicked grin, "I'll tell Uncle Aubrey to run along for you, Aunt Sena."

"Ooh, you're a cheeky one, Master Peter!" exclaimed the maid, and ushered him out.

"Now, what did Aubrey actually say?" asked Lady Whitton. "Admittedly his understanding is not superior, but I cannot credit it that he is so lacking in address as to tell you such a thing without wrapping it up in clean linen."

"Oh, he swore that he adored me, admired my *blue* eyes, and claimed that Papa had wished him to offer for me else he'd not have left me the Manor. He wants to relieve me of the burden of running the farm, just like Iverbrook with Peter. Men," said Selena bitterly, "are all the same."

Her mother refrained from pointing out that most females *wished* to be relieved of their burdens. "It sounds as if he expressed himself with propriety. Have you taken him in dislike because he mistook the colour of your eyes?"

"Of course not, Mama, though if he truly loved me he'd have been a little closer! No, that was bad enough, but when I refused him he said he'll not despair because I shall not like to dwindle into an old maid! You cannot expect me to meet him with complaisance after such an insult!"

"Oh dear, I am sure you must have misunderstood him. Even Aubrey could not be such a nodcock as to say such a thing to a young lady he wishes to marry! Selena, how can I ask him to leave? He has no home, no friends in England, and no other family."

"Do you know why his father was sent abroad?" Selena's curiosity momentarily overcame her resentment.

"I believe he ran off with a gypsy girl. And from the family's point of view made things worse by insisting on marrying her. No great sin, you see."

"Cousin Aubrey has nothing of gypsy looks about him."

"No, luckily he took after his father. He was always paid an allowance, your papa told me, but he has certainly not the means to put up at an hotel."

"So he is to live here at rack and manger, hanging upon my sleeve, while he insults me with impunity?"

"As heir to Sir William's title, he certainly has a claim to our hospitality, my love. Doubtless when he discovers that you are adamant in your refusal of his offer, he will look about for some suitable occupation, or perhaps return to Jamaica."

"Jamaica is not far enough. I wish him at Botany Bay!"

"You will, however, continue polite to him, Selena. No guest in this house shall be treated with discourtesy."

"Oh very well, Mama. I daresay there may be other young ladies in the world who are forced to reside in the same household with a rejected suitor! It is fortunate indeed that he never appears at the breakfast table, for I don't believe I could face him with equanimity at that hour!"

Selena found it difficult enough to bear with Sir Aubrey that evening. She did not experience the anticipated embarrassment; she had too little regard for him to feel concern for his feelings. But mannerisms that had previously seemed laughable now irritated her unbearably: the way he called her mother "dear Aunt"; his habit of checking his appearance in the mirror every ten minutes; the hare's foot with which he dusted the snuff from his shirt front; his crooked little finger when he sipped his tea.

Every time he spoke, she wanted to contradict him. He ventured a remark concerning the weather in the West Indies. Selena immediately recalled that Lord Iverbrook had said the precise opposite. He lavished effusive praise on Delia's performance upon the pianoforte.

"I must suppose," retorted Selena, "that you had little opportunity in Jamaica to indulge your taste for music. Delia's playing is nothing above the ordinary. Indeed, her friend Jane plays better."

Delia cast her a hurt glance and launched into a long and involved Haydn sonata.

Before she retired to bed, Selena went and tapped on the door of her sister's chamber.

"Delia!"

"What is it?" Dressed in a white cotton nightgown, Delia was brushing her long blond hair.

"Let me do that. Do you remember when you were little and Phoebe and I used to quarrel over who should brush your hair? You were the best doll we ever had."

"I wish my hair would curl, like yours. When I go to London in the spring I shall have to put it in papers every night, and use curling tongs before balls and parties."

"Before grand parties, perhaps, but it is beautiful as it is, so smooth and silky. Dee, I'm sorry I was rude about your music. Your playing is perfectly unexceptionable and gives me much pleasure, though I admire your singing more. Only I could not listen to Cousin Aubrey flattering you in that odious way."

"I play like an angel in heaven!" She giggled. "I ought to have studied the harp. I don't heed Cousin Aubrey, Selena. Clive says he is a toad-eater and a rasher-of-wind."

Selena laughed. "Young Clive has a discerning eye. Do you like him?"

"Clive? Why yes, when he does not try to come the high and mighty.

He is even handsomer than Cousin Aubrey, is he not? But I do not mean to wed him. Somewhere, there is a man who *is* as romantic as he *looks,* and next year, when I make my come-out, I shall meet him and we will fall in love and marry and live happily ever after."

"I hope so!" said Selena. "Goodnight, and sweet dreams."

Suppose it had been Hugh, not Aubrey, who had asked for her hand. Selena lay gazing into the darkness, wishing she had asked her mother for some chamomile tea. She heard the clock in the hall below strike one.

Would Hugh expect her to live at Iver Place, or in London? Or would he want to move into the Manor, take over her farm, just like her cousin? For the umpteenth time she told herself it was useless to speculate. He had not asked her, and doubtless never would. He enjoyed his gay and carefree life as a bachelor, and if he ever decided to marry there must be dozens of beautiful, rich, and aristocratic damsels waiting to pounce on the handkerchief when he dropped it.

Not to mention Amabel Parcott.

She woke to a damp morning. A mist hid the river; when she looked out of her window, the big oak at the bottom of the garden seemed to be growing on the edge of the world. Dew dripped from leaves and eaves, flowers hung their heavy heads, and the smell of woodsmoke permeated the still air.

At breakfast, Delia announced that she was going to spend the day with Jane.

"We're going to the old quarry to pick blackberries," she said. "Clive has a friend staying and they will both ride with us."

"Can I go too?" begged Peter.

"No, it's a grown-up party. Besides, I took you last year and you ate so many berries you got a tummyache. And Nurse cut up stiff because you stained your clothes."

"You can come with me if you like, Peter," said Selena. "I must choose which lambs to send to market next Monday. I wish I had more pasture, so that I could enlarge the flock."

"Can I ride Leo, Aunt Sena? Can I, please? Leo likes sheeps."

"He looks more like a sheep than a lion," Delia remarked thoughtfully. "A sort of cross between a sheep and a horse."

"That's enough!" said Lady Whitton hastily, seeing Peter about to rise to the bait. "Delia, 'cut up stiff' is *not* a ladylike expression. Pray mind your tongue, child."

"Clive says it!"

"Clive is not a lady," Selena pointed out unanswerably. "Peter, I have some letters to write before we go, so you will have time to learn your lessons. Tell Finny you are to be dressed for riding by ten o'clock."

Selena retired to the library, mended her pen, and set to work. Half way through the second letter, there was a knock at the door.

"Come in."

"The post, Miss Selena." Bannister deposited four or five missives on her desk.

The first one she opened necessitated rewriting the letter she had just finished. That done, she read a long epistle, full of complaints and grievances, from the cousin with whom she had shared her one London season. Setting it aside to be answered later, she turned with relief and interest to the third in the pile, addressed in an unknown hand. She broke the seal, and as she unfolded the sheet a small slip of paper fell to the floor unnoticed.

She looked first at the signature: Archibald Hubble. Hubble? Wasn't that the Carricks' lawyer?

> *"Madam,*
>
> *"Whereas you, Miss Selena Whitton, Spinster, of Milford Manor in the County of Oxford, were appointed by the Last Will and Testament of the late Honourable Gilbert Carrick to be Sole Lawful Guardian of his Son and Heir, Peter Carrick;*
>
> *"I have the honour to inform you, madam, that on this day, the Fifth of September, in the Year of Our Lord eighteen hundred and eleven, a Suit was entered in Chancery in behalf of Hugh Carrick, Fourth Viscount Iverbrook, of Iver Place in the County of Buckingham, challenging the said Last Will and Testament of his Brother, the heretofore mentioned Gilbert Carrick, now deceased, with regard to the said Guardianship of the heretofore mentioned Peter Carrick, Son and Heir of the heretofore mentioned Gilbert Carrick*

and Heir Presumptive of the heretofore mentioned Hugh
Carrick, Viscount Iverbrook;
  "Hereby be it known, madam, that . . . "

Selena sat stunned, staring unseeing at the letter. He had done it! He had gone to law to take Peter away from her. Strip away 'whereas' and 'heretofore,' and there it was in black and white.

Iverbrook was a faithless traitor!

— 9 —

IN SPITE OF the dank weather, Lord Iverbrook strode up the front steps of Milford Manor with a light heart.

His business in London had prospered. William Wilberforce was delighted to welcome him to the ranks of the anti-slavery forces. He had given him several good ideas to work on for his maiden speech.

"Your experiences will be the most telling argument," the MP had said. "Describe what you saw in the Indies. To the majority of them 'tis a mere abstract matter but that will bring it home. Apropos, I should like to meet your Joshua. Doubtless he can provide ammunition for my campaign."

The viscount and the ex-slave had spent a pleasant and productive evening in Clapham, finding their host as charming and amusing as he was dedicated.

Consulting his new lawyer, Mr. Crowe, Iverbrook learned that the transfer of his affairs from Hubble, Blayne, and Hubble was proceeding smoothly. Mr. Crowe was also able to direct him to Lord Alphonse Sebring's man of business, and he had made the first steps in the acquisition of those long neglected water-meadows that so distressed Miss Whitton's sensibilities.

Miss Whitton—Selena—ah, there was the chiefest cause of his lordship's lightheartedness. "Marry her!" Mr. Hastings's recently repeated words rang in his ears. From a practical point of view, as a way of obtaining his nephew while avoiding a lawsuit, they had always been sound advice. Advice he had once soundly rejected, to be sure, but he had not then known Selena.

He had not known those changeable hazel eyes, that face that eloquently expressed every emotion, the moon-pale hair so often ruffled in glorious disarray, the slim, strong, upright figure—in his mind Iverbrook waxed rhapsodic. How competent was his love, and how firm of purpose! How reasonable and enchanting her conversation and how enchanting the sparks that flew from her eyes when . . . The door opened.

"Welcome home, my lord," bowed Bannister. "I should say, welcome back."

"Hello, Bannister!" He tossed the butler his hat and drew off his gloves. "Welcome home will do nicely, thank you. Where is Miss Whitton?"

"In the library, my lord. Shall I announce your lordship?"

"No, don't bother. I had rather surprise her. She is alone?"

"So I believe, my lord. Some refreshments, perhaps, for your lordship?"

"Thank you, no. I slept last night at Watlington and have made only a short stage this morning."

"Very good, my lord. I shall inform my lady of your arrival."

With eager steps Lord Iverbrook approached the library, flung open the door, and entered.

"Marry me, Selena!" he cried.

Pale and tight-lipped she rose behind the desk.

"How dare you!" she hissed. "How dare you show your face here, you mean, despicable, treacherous monster!"

Completely taken aback, his lordship stammered, "Bu-but I only asked you to marry me! Perhaps I might have approached the matter with more delicacy but really, Selena . . . "

"Don't call me Selena! I'd as soon marry Aubrey as you. Sooner! At least his motive is straightforward greed, while you sneak around behind my back, plotting to ruin half a dozen lives to gratify your own vanity. And for all I know you want my land too, since you have allowed yourself to be dispossessed by pigs. Pigs! Suitable companions indeed for a so-called gentleman who visits his *chère-amie* in London before his poor, neglected mother!"

Bewildered now, the viscount concentrated on the most recent attack.

"You don't even know my mother, and I don't see how you know about Bel. And I went up to town direct from Southampton to see my lawyer, not Bel anyway."

"As I know to my cost, having just received from him proof of your perfidy! And it is 'Bel,' is it? I had thought she was merely boasting, for Amabel Gant always was an odious little sycophant!"

"Selena, that's all . . . "

"Go away!"

" . . . over now, and what do you mean, you have just received proof from my lawyer?"

"Here, read this and deny it if you can!" Selena thrust the letter at him. Watching him read it, his face set, she felt the blind fury draining from her, leaving her exhausted. She sat down.

He finished reading. Leaning on the desk he regarded her with hard eyes, and when he spoke there was a steely note in his quiet voice that she had never heard before.

"You are by far too ready to jump to conclusions, Miss Whitton. That is forgivable. You might, however, have seen fit to request an explanation before pouring insults on my head. I do not choose to justify my actions now, nor to disabuse you of your ill-conceived notions. I shall leave at once, as you requested. Good-bye, Miss Whitton!"

The viscount stalked from the room and, with meticulous care, closed the door softly behind him. Selena laid her head on her arms and wept.

Half an hour passed before she regained her composure sufficiently to notice the time. It was nearly ten o'clock. Her tears had blotted the two letters she had completed and they would have to be rewritten, but she had promised to take Peter out at ten.

As she tidied the desk, she saw a piece of paper on the floor and bent to pick it up. There was writing on it, in the same hand as the letter from Iverbrook's lawyer. Curious, she sat down to read it. It seemed to have been scrawled in a hurry, for though similar to Hubble's letter it was hard to make out.

"Miss Whitton," it began, "his lordship knows Nothing of this. Mr. H. acted against his express Instructions. I shall tell Joshua of it and he will tell his lordship. Pray do not Divulge this to Mr. H. Yr humble and obed't servant, James Goodenough."

Selena was aghast. Her accusations had been false, and she had said such things to the viscount as made her blush to think of. Little wonder that he had been so coldly angry!

Perhaps he had not left yet. If the horses had been unharnessed, his bags carried up, Tom Arbuckle sat down to a mug of ale in the kitchen, then he might still be within reach. She rushed from the library, calling, "Bannister!"

Her mother was crossing the hallway.

"Mama, is Iverbrook here?"

"He left ten minutes past, dearest."

"Then I am too late. By the time I could catch up he would be on the post road. I cannot chase him down the public highway!"

"What happened, Selena? He said only that you had ordered him to leave and he would not disobey you."

"He asked me to marry him, Mama." Selena's voice was very soft. "I was so angry with him I did not listen, indeed I scarcely heard him. I told him I had rather marry Cousin Aubrey."

"Come into the drawing room, my love, and tell me all about it."

"I cannot, not now. I cannot bear to repeat the things I said. Besides, it is time to inspect the lambs and I am surprised Peter is not yet here to remind me of it." She tried to smile.

Bannister appeared.

"You called, Miss Selena?"

"Yes, but it is no matter now. Oh, send one of the maids to fetch Master Peter down, if you please. Mama, I must go and put on my hat. I promise I will tell you everything later."

When Selena descended the stairs, pulling on her gloves, Polly was hovering in the hall.

"Master Peter's not with Mrs. Finnegan, miss," she announced. "And I went and asked my lady in the stillroom and he's not there neither, and Jem's in the kitchen taking a bite so I 'spec's he's not down at the stables."

Selena sank down on the stairs. This time it *must* be Iverbrook, and she had no one but herself to blame. She had given him no reason to suppose she was capable of discussing their nephew's future calmly. She had denounced and abused him and this was his revenge.

"Has that vexatious child run off alone again?" enquired her mother, appearing in her apron, pestle in hand. "Polly, what exactly did Nurse say?"

"She said as how Master Peter told her he were a-going to pick blackberries, my lady. And she knowing Miss Delia were going, so thought no more but dressed him up in his riding clothes. Right after breakfast it were, my lady."

"Thank you, Polly. I expect he wandered farther than he had intended. Selena, you are very pale. Are you unwell?"

"No, Mama, quite well. Polly, are you sure he has been gone since breakfast?"

"Mrs. Finnegan says so, miss. 'Bout ha' past eight, she said."

"Thank heaven! Bannister? Bannister! Did Master Peter go out with Miss Delia?"

"No, miss. They all came by to fetch her, Miss Russell and young Mr. Russell and another young gentleman, and I watched them ride off, thinking what a merry party they was. Master Peter was not with them."

"I suppose since she would not take him, he went to find some berries on his own. He has not been gone so very long. I expect he will hear the church clock strike ten and run home. I will wait a few more minutes before I go to look for him."

Overjoyed to find her suspicions of Lord Iverbrook once again unfounded, Selena went back to the library to copy out the letters she had spoiled. She sat down and took a fresh sheet of paper. Then she remembered that nothing had changed, that she had quarrelled irrevocably with him. She gazed down the long room at the grey river beyond the window. Mist still floated patchily above it and the eaves still dripped.

Peter must be wet through. She had best go and look for him at once. She laid down her pen and was rising to her feet when a sudden commotion in the entrance hall startled her.

Surely that urgent voice, that rose above the others in tones of command, was Iverbrook's?

"Don't stand there gaping, you fools! Fetch my lady, quick!"

When Lord Iverbrook stalked out of the library after the quarrel, he had every intention of going straight to the stables and departing on the instant. Lady Whitton, coming to greet him on his arrival, met him in the passage.

"Hugh dear, how lovely to see you again. I hope your affairs in London go on well?"

"Very well, thank you, ma'am. I hope I find you in prime twig?"

"Yes indeed, if that means what I think it means! Have you seen Selena already? Bannister said you had gone to her in the library."

"I have seen her." Iverbrook's attempted cheerfulness vanished. "Miss Whitton desired me to remove myself from the premises at once. I am returning to London immediately."

"Hugh, do not say that you two have quarrelled again? If I ever knew such a pair! Come and sit down and tell me what it is this time."

The viscount followed her ladyship into the drawing room, and when she patted the sofa invitingly he sat down beside her. He had grown very fond of Selena's mother, and he felt a great urge to disburden his soul to her. He resisted it.

"What a miserable day it is," he said lightly. "In weather like this I almost wish I had stayed in Jamaica."

"Enough to give anyone the dismals," she agreed. "Now what is this nonsense about leaving when you are scarce arrived?"

"You had best apply to your daughter for details, ma'am. She ordered me to go, and I'll not disobey her, in this at least."

Lady Whitton sighed. "Selena is so efficient and so collected where the farm is concerned that one is apt to suppose that she has equal dominion over her own sensibilities. Yet when her feelings are involved she is often impulsive, even hotheaded. Perhaps I ought to have tried harder to teach her to command her emotions, but so much was expected of her in other ways. No demure young lady of unimpeachable propriety could have succeeded as she has."

"Miss Whitton is certainly no bread-and-butter miss. You must, however, allow me a modicum of pride. A gentleman of breeding does not stay when he has been dismissed! Dare I hope that this will not cause a breach between us? I should be sorry indeed to lose your friendship."

"You will always be welcome, Hugh."

He stood up and bowed low over her hand. His resolve wavered as he looked at her sorrowful face, but Selena's words still sounded in his ears. A mean, despicable, treacherous monster, was he? Who plotted to ruin lives to gratify his own vanity! Such an abominable creature would certainly not make the first step towards reconciliation.

He almost ran to the stables. If he should meet Peter now, he could not answer for his steadfastness.

Tom Arbuckle had just finished hanging up the harnesses. He groaned when ordered to set the horses to again, but after a single glance at his master's thinned lips and abstracted eyes, he did not protest.

"Got to get the luggage out again, m'lord, and tell Cook, as was preparing a nice hot toddy for me," he said. "It'll be ten-fifteen minutes if Jem here'll lend a hand wi' the horses."

Jem was willing, glad to see his rival depart so rapidly. Anxious to be gone, Lord Iverbrook helped to buckle the harness and was waiting with the reins in his hands when Tom reappeared with the bags and slung them into the carriage.

"Shall I drive, m'lord?" he enquired, climbing up.

"No!" said the viscount through gritted teeth, and they swung out of the stable yard and down the drive at a pace that made Tom clutch at his cap.

The muddy lane and tired horses soon moderated their speed. Iverbrook drove in grim silence, broken only when he said abruptly, "You'll get your toddy when we reach Watlington, Tom."

"Thank you, m'lord."

Iverbrook recognised the deep disapproval in his voice. He was beginning to wish he had not acted so precipitately. Deuce take the wench! She made him as impetuous as she was herself! Still, it was too late now. He could not creep back to the kennel like a whipped cur. How sorry she would be when she found out he was not going to law! Only, that might now be his one possible course of action.

What a Godalmighty mess he'd made of it, dashing in there and demanding her hand without any preparation, without any of the compliments and flowery language women set such store by. And when she had just received that letter, too. It was all his fault. No, by God, it wasn't! he thought savagely. It was Hubble's fault, and he'd wring the man's neck, if he hanged for it!

"M'lord!" Tom reached over and tugged on the reins. "My lord, been't that Master Peter? Stop, my lord! Whoa there; whoa!"

As the horses came to a standstill, Iverbrook saw a small, muddy figure staggering towards them. For a moment he could not believe it was his nephew. Then he recognised the brass buttons on the green riding coat he had given him. He leaped down into the mire, ran to the child, and picked him up.

Peter shrieked and struggled.

"No, no, no!" he screamed. "I won't go and live with the pigs. I won't, I won't!"

"Of course you shall not, if you don't want to. We'll take you home right away. Tom, turn around in that gateway. However did you get so filthy, Peter?" Besides the mud, the boy's flushed face was smeared with purple. His eyes were huge and dark, glazed, and he fought his uncle with silent desperation.

Iverbrook put him down. He sat down, quite calmly, and said, "Can I have a drink, Cook? *Please,* dear Cook, I'm so thirsty. Finny, I want my milk. *Run, quickly,* Timmy, the big bad wolf is coming to gobble you up!"

"He's ill, Tom. Hurry!"

"Hello, Uncle Hugh. I'm glad you comed back but I have to run along now. Timmy's waiting. I'll see you at tea time. Bye bye." Peter got up and started running down the lane.

His uncle caught him in three quick strides and picked him up again. He went rigid, teeth bared in a horrible grimace, and shuddered all over.

The carriage pulled up beside them.

"Here, get him aboard quick, m'lord. Here's my jacket to wrap him up in, poor little tyke. We'd best get him to my lady on the double."

"Drive fast, man! Don't overturn us, but you can kill the horses for all I care. I think he's eaten poisonous berries. Fast!"

Peter lay quiet in his arms now. His pulse was rapid, tumultuous, his dilated eyes staring at nothing.

"I'm thirsty," he moaned. "I'm thirsty, Uncle Hugh. Where's Grandmama? Tell her to put blue flowers in my lemonade 'cos I'm hot all over. Why won't you let me sit up? I want to see out."

"Hush, Peter, hush," said Iverbrook helplessly. "You'll be with Grandmama soon and she'll take care of you."

Peter pulled away from him and knelt up on the seat.

"I can see the house now. Let me out so I can run to Aunt Sena and give her a surprise." He was fumbling with the door catch when another seizure took him and he fell back into Iverbrook's arms, his small body convulsing violently.

For the first time in his life, the viscount knew terror.

"Faster, Tom!"

"We're almost there, m'lord. Hold on, Master Peter, your granny'll make you better, all right and tight."

They turned into the drive with screeching wheels and the horses reared as they pulled up at the front door. Tom jumped down, jerked on the bellpull and, not waiting for a response, had his hand on the latch when the door was opened from the inside by Bannister.

Iverbrook carried Peter in, the boy shrieking again and waving his arms. Mrs. Tooting appeared, and one of the housemaids, open mouthed.

"Don't stand there gaping, you fools!" he shouted. "Fetch my lady, quick!"

— 10 —

"CARRY HIM TO the stillroom, Iverbrook." Selena took in the situation with one glance. "All Mama's medicines are there."

"My lady's there too." Bannister suddenly looked ten years older. He put out his hand to brace himself against the wall.

Mrs. Tooting had fallen into a fit. As the viscount strode past her, Selena took charge.

"Bannister, sit down. There is nothing you can do for Peter. Doris, fetch Polly to Mrs. Tooting, then go and warn Nurse to put a warming pan in Master Peter's bed. You had best tell Cook to make plenty of barleywater, too."

"Oh miss, is he going to die?"

"I don't know what is wrong with him, Doris. We must put our trust in God and in my mother's skill. Hurry now. Bannister, are you feeling stronger?"

"Yes, Miss Selena. It's right sorry I am to be another trouble to you, when I know Mrs. Finnegan won't be much help neither. It was just the shock."

"Of course. I rely on you to see that the servants do all that is necessary. Tom, tell me what happened."

Tom Arbuckle was standing by the door, twisting his tweed cap in his hands.

"Terrible it were, miss," he said. "We drove down the lane—his lordship were driving, that is, but I could see as his mind weren't on it. Then I seen the little tyke, all covered with mud, which ain't to be wondered at, only he walked kind of funny, like he couldn' see where he were going. So we stopped and my lord jumps down and tells me to turn the carriage, the which I does, and all the time I can hear Master Peter hollering. And my lord gets him in the carriage and says he's ate poison berries, drive like the devil. Begging your pardon, miss. So I does, and if the nipper up and dies I'll always think I could of drove faster."

Selena laid her hand on his arm. "Don't say that, Tom. You did your best and I thank you for it. I expect his lordship's horses need your care. Will you see to them?"

"O'course, miss, and bless you. His lordship's hard hit, miss. I never seen him look like that."

"Thank you, Tom." As Selena turned to go to the stillroom, she recalled Hugh's white, agonised face. She had scarcely noticed it before, her attention concentrated on Peter. Yes, his lordship was hard hit. She had not supposed him to have so much sensibility.

Poison berries, Tom said. The stains about Peter's mouth were purple. That could be from blackberries, but she shuddered at the thought of the alternative: deadly nightshade!

The door of the stillroom was open. She stood there a moment, forcing herself to remain calm. Her mother was stirring a blackish powder into a glass of water. Iverbrook sat on the room's only chair, holding Peter in his lap, but when the boy saw her he slid down and ran to her, talking excitedly. His voice was slurred and she could not make out his words. She picked him up and sat down on the chair, vacated by the viscount.

"It's belladonna, Selena," said her mother, voice shaking but hands as steady as ever. "Nightshade, deadly nightshade. He had some berries in his hand. The first thing is to bring it up. Black mustard seed to make him vomit. You hold him, keep him still, while I make him drink it. Hugh, there's a basin under the table. Come, Peterkin, drink this for Grandmama, like a good boy."

Peter took a sip. .

"It tastes nasty," he said clearly, then stiffened, his arms and legs flailing wildly. One arm escaped from Selena's grasp and knocked the glass from Lady Whitton's hand. It smashed on the floor and she stood for a moment looking blankly at the shards of glass and the wet spot on her skirt.

Iverbrook put his arm round her shoulders. "I shall mix some more," he said. "Tell me exactly what to do."

The seizure weakened Peter and he drank the second potion docilely.

Its effect was immediate and Iverbrook was only just in time with the basin.

As the worst of the retching passed, the child lay back limply in his aunt's arms. Lady Whitton felt his forehead.

"Another dose, Hugh. I will prepare willowbark for the fever and powdered charcoal to absorb the poison." The sound of her own voice steadied her. She took down several jars and began to pound and stir their contents in her mortar. "Centaury as a stimulant, and some say vinegar is efficacious against belladonna. He must be kept warm."

Selena unbuttoned his wet coat and took it off. She had his shirt half off when Iverbrook approached with the second dose of mustard and water. Peter began to struggle again.

"I won't! I won't! It makes me hurt in my middle. Don't make me, Aunt Sena. I'll be a good boy, I won't eat any more berries."

"Peter, be still!" said Iverbrook sternly. "This is no way for a gentleman to behave. Drink!"

Cowed, he obeyed, and the dreadful spasms began again. They so exhausted him that he swallowed without protest the murky liquid his grandmother next pressed upon him. Iverbrook stripped off the rest of his damp clothes, wrapped him in his own coat and, hugging him close, looked enquiringly at Lady Whitton.

"To bed?"

"To bed."

"Mama, you look worn to the bone. Hugh and Nurse will settle Peter. You come and lie down and tell me just what we must do for him, and what to watch for. I'll join you shortly, Iverbrook."

The viscount carried his slight burden up the stairs. He was half way up the second flight when Peter twisted in his arms and cried out.

"I'm stuck, Auntie Dee! I can't get down. You'll get stuck too if you climb up. Help me! I'm going to fall!"

"It's all right, Peter. Hush. I shan't let you fall. You're quite safe."

"You're not Mr. Russell. Go away. Mr. Russell will help me down. Auntie Dee, come quick!" His words began to slur again, and he lapsed into lethargy.

Mrs. Finnegan had his nightshirt warming by the fire. A tiny, wrinkled old woman, she started up as Iverbrook entered the nursery. Between them they quickly put him to bed. Nurse tucked him in and felt his flushed forehead.

"Oh my dearie!" she moaned. "My poor precious lamb!"

Peter muttered and opened his eyes.

"You promised, Aunt Sena. You said I can go with you to see the lambs. But Leo is turning into a sheep! I can't ride a sheep. Leo, stop it! You're not a sheep, you're a pony. Uncle Hugh, don't let Leo turn into a sheep. Please! If he gets all woolly, he won't be a gentleman's horse when he's growed up."

Mrs. Finnegan sank onto a chair, crossed herself, and flung her apron over her head.

"My baby's lost his mind!" she wailed, rocking back and forth.

"You have lost yours, woman!" said Iverbrook harshly. "Peter, *Peter,* Uncle Hugh won't let Leo turn into a sheep, I promise. You must get well quick, for he is waiting to take you for a ride."

"Leo's waiting. I have to go." Peter strained to sit up. "Jem says you must never keep a horse waiting. Let me go. Let me go! I'm so thirsty."

Iverbrook looked around helplessly. Not even an empty cup met his eye. The old woman was sniffling to herself beneath the apron and it seemed useless to ask her for help, nor would he leave the child alone with her. Selena seemed to have a lot of incompetent servants, he thought angrily. Still she had explained her bailiff to him, and doubtless she had reasons as good for employing the others. In general, the household ran perfectly smoothly.

But now Peter was crying out for a drink and there was none in sight. Selena came in.

"How is he, Hugh?" she asked, casting an exasperated glance at Nurse.

"Hallucinating again, and very thirsty. He's so hot, Selena. Must we keep him covered?"

"Mama says to keep him warm. He is to drink as much as we can persuade him to, and I'm sure we might bathe his forehead. I shall fetch barleywater, and a cooling lotion for his head. Can you manage alone here?"

"Yes, but hurry back. I am an unpractised sickroom attendant."

"You have contrived to admiration so far. I'll be back in no time."

Selena hurried down to the kitchen, where Cook, impeturbable as ever, had barleywater ready. Polly was hovering there, so Selena asked after Mrs. Tooting.

"Me and Mr. Bannister took her to her chamber, miss, and I give her the medicine like my lady done last time. She's much better now. How's Master Peter, miss?"

"Much the same, I fear. Bless you both. What should I do without you?"

"Oh miss!" Polly crimsoned and her eyes filled with tears. Cook grunted and turned back to her stove.

"Polly, since you were so handy with Mrs. Tooting's physic, can you find me the lovage and rosemary lotion, and bring it to the nursery? I must take Peter his drink."

"Oh yes, miss. I know where my lady keeps it. I'll get it right away."

Selena sped back up the stairs. She found the viscount sitting by the bed, holding Peter's hand, his eyes fixed on the small, hot face. Peter lay motionless.

"He is in a stupor," said Iverbrook. "At least, it does not seem to me like a natural sleep."

"We must rouse him to drink. Feel how dry his skin is! Peter, here is some barleywater Cook made specially for you. Wake up, darling. It will make you feel better."

The child half opened his eyes and reached out weakly. Iverbrook raised his shoulders and Selena held the cup to his lips. He gulped thirstily till it was all gone, but would not take more. His uncle laid him down and covered him carefully with the blue counterpane.

"What now?"

"Polly is bringing some lotion which will make him feel cooler, I hope. Finny . . . oh, she is gone!"

"I sent her away."

"I hope you were not too harsh with her. She is not a great deal of help in sickness, and Mama always cared for us when we were ill, but she has so many other good qualities. We all love her dearly, Peter too."

"At all events, she is not needed while you and I are here. Is there nothing else we can do for him?"

"He must drink some more in a while, and Mama will bring him another draught when it is time for him to take it. Patience is often the hardest part of nursing."

"Is Lady Whitton recovered from the shock? How I admire her! She was plainly much shaken, yet she had the remedy to hand in a moment."

"How else should she act? If there is something one can do, one does it. But of a sudden she looked so old. Is it not painful to watch one's parents age?"

The viscount thought of his mother, who had not noticeably changed since he could remember, and who had fallen into hysterics if one of her sons appeared with a scraped knee or a bloody nose.

"Is she well?"

"I gave her her own sedative tea and made her promise to stay abed for two hours. I shall call her if anything changes in the meantime. Oh, here is Polly. Thank you, child. He is resting quietly now."

The maid curtseyed and tiptoed out. Selena poured a little of the lotion onto her handkerchief and a fresh herbal scent filled the air. She wiped Peter's face gently.

"If nothing else, it is cleaning off the mud," said Iverbrook, trying for a light tone.

"Yes, and even the purple stains are fading a little."

All too soon there was nothing left to do but wait. Peter lay alarmingly still, with only bouts of muttering to suggest that the hallucinations continued. Selena and Iverbrook sat on either side of the bed, drained, yet alert to any change in his condition.

"There was a note inside the letter," said Selena, after a long silence. "I found it later. From a James Goodenough; one of Hubble's clerks, I suppose? It said you knew nothing of the lawsuit."

"It's not important."

"No, but I'm sorry."

He looked at her, saw a glint of tears in her eyes, and stretched his hand across the narrow bed between them. She clasped it briefly, felt forgiven, felt the warmth of his strong fingers renewing her energy.

"Time for barleywater," she said.

Delia burst into the room, her face tearstained.

"It's all my fault!" she wailed. "If only I'd let him come with us!"

"Hush!" said Selena sharply. "Of course it is not your fault, little nodcock." She hugged her sister tight. "But if you want to help, I wish that you will look after Mama and see that the household does not come to a standstill. And ask Cook to prepare some luncheon, for I declare I am positively famished."

After a few more words and a peep at Peter, Delia went away cheered and reassured.

"I had not thought I could touch a morsel," said Iverbrook, pouring barleywater, "but since you mentioned luncheon, I find I am sharp-set after all."

"I only said that to give Delia something to do," Selena confessed, "but I too am suddenly ravenous. Come, little boy, let me help you sit up. Uncle Hugh has a drink for you."

Peter peered at her drowsily; his eyes were still dilated, his skin hot to the touch. His pulse seemed to have slowed, but it was also weaker so that was no comfort. He drank gluttonously, liquid dribbling from the corners of his mouth. There was no sign of perspiration, and as Selena laid his limp form down again she began to despair.

Luncheon arrived, and they both found they were not as hungry as they had imagined.

"Thank heaven Cook is not temperamental," said Selena as Polly carried out a tray of barely touched food. "I think I will go and ask Mama for the medicine, Hugh, unless you wish to go?"

"I ought to have a word with Tom, perhaps. You don't mind staying here alone? I'll be as quick as I can."

"I am sure you need to stretch your legs. A sickroom is no place for a gentleman. Indeed, you have more than exceeded the bounds of duty, and Mama or Delia can keep me company now."

He took both her hands in his and smiled at her lovingly.

"It is not a matter of duty. A gentleman has as much right here as a young girl or an elderly lady, if you will have me. Peter needs both aunt and uncle."

She looked up at him, trying to read his eyes. They baffled her. She dropped her gaze to his mud-smeared neckcloth, then turned away as he released her hands.

"Yes, and also his medicine."

"I'm on my way," he bowed.

He met Lady Whitton on the stairs, carrying a vial full of a most unappetising grey-green liquid. He almost turned back to watch the effect of the draught, but it was already mid-afternoon, and Tom must be on his way. If Peter died, the lawsuit begun by the unscrupulous Hubble would be irrelevant. That alternative was unthinkable. Peter would survive and the suit must be stopped.

In the library he wrote a quick note to his new lawyer. Crowe was the best person to deal with the matter. As an afterthought he added a commendation of one James Goodenough, with a suggestion that Mr. Crowe might look into hiring the young man next time he found himself in need of an honest clerk.

Tom Arbuckle was in the kitchen, talking quietly and seriously with Cook. He jumped to his feet, took the letter, and listened to his instructions.

"Be back termorrer evening, God willing, m'lord," he said. "Don't let the little master die."

He kissed Cook good-bye and was off.

Iverbrook pretended not to notice. He was about to leave when Bannister entered, sighing heavily.

"Summun ought to rescue poor Miss Delia from the Bart, Cook," said the butler. "It's a sin and a shame the way he . . . Oh, I beg your pardon, my lord. I didn't see your lordship."

"Nor should I be intruding on your domain, Bannister, only with the house all at sixes and sevens I did not want to disrupt things further when I needed Tom. Where are Miss Delia and, er, the Bart? Devil take him, I'd forgot the man existed!"

"In the drawing room, my lord. And he's telling her dreadful stories of people as died of poison fruit and snakes and such in the Indies. It sounds like a very dangerous place," he said severely, adding, "How's the lad, my lord?"

"No change. Lady Whitton is physicking him now. I'll try and rescue Miss Delia before I go up again."

Iverbrook had just reached the drawing room when the front door bell rang. He heard Bannister's hurrying steps and turned back to help the butler dissuade any visitors from entering.

The door swung open to reveal a liveried groom. Beyond him in the drive stood an elegant landau, from which emerged a vision of loveliness, clad in rose pink.

"Good God!" said his lordship. "Go away, Bel!"

$==11==$

UNPERTURBED BY THE viscount's hostility, Mrs. Parcott trod daintily up the steps, leaving Lady Gant to struggle out of the carriage behind her.

"Good day, Iverbrook. I see your manners are become as rustic as your attire." She looked with disfavour at his besmirched coat, then smiled sweetly as her mother panted up beside her. "I think you have not met Mama, Iverbrook. Mama, this is Lord Iverbrook who, I must suppose, is visiting the Whittons. Iverbrook, my mother, Lady Gant."

"La, sir, I have been hearing about you forever, I declare. Such a good friend as you have been to my poor, widowed little girl," simpered her ladyship.

The viscount was forced to bow over her pudgy hand with a semblance of politeness, but he shot a darkling glance at Amabel.

"I fear you are arrived at an inopportune moment, ma'am," he said. "There is sickness in the house." He sensed Bannister standing firm behind him, barring the way.

Lady Gant began to splutter apologies, condolences, and excuses in equal measure, and turned to go. Her daughter was not so easily ousted.

"We are not afraid of illness, are we, Mama?" she said brightly. "Lady Whitton will be glad of a distraction from her cares, I vow. La, it is our duty to visit the sick, is it not?"

Negating Iverbrook's and Bannister's efforts to stop her by simply ignoring them, she swept into the hall.

The viscount saw that the butler was about to essay a final protest. He shook his head infinitesimally and jerked it towards the drawing room. An idea had come to him for killing two birds with one stone, and from the light in Bannister's eye he saw that the elderly man had understood him.

Lady Gant and Mrs. Parcott were ushered into the drawing room.

Delia made a despairing face at Iverbrook and curtseyed to the visitors. She moved to stand beside him as Sir Aubrey made his bow and began a flowery speech of welcome.

"Mama said I must keep Cousin Aubrey occupied," she whispered.

"No longer necessary," he whispered back, then said aloud, "Delia, your mother was looking for you not five minutes since."

"I'll go at once," said Delia obediently, twinkling at him.

Mrs. Parcott tittered. "You are grown positively paternal, Iverbrook." She fluttered her eyelashes. "I think the country does not agree with you. Do you return soon to town?"

"Not, at least, until my nephew is out of danger, ma'am," he responded harshly. "You will excuse me, I must see how he does." He left without a backward glance.

Hurrying up the stairs, he arrived in the nursery at the same time as Delia.

Selena and Lady Whitton were trying to persuade the little boy to swallow his medicine. Though half conscious, he had set his lips in a firm line and refused to open them.

"Peter, here is Uncle Hugh," said Selena gently. "Will you not take it for him? Show him how good you are."

There was no response.

"Peter, do as your aunt bids you," Iverbrook ordered.

The mouth opened.

Selena sighed with relief and poured the medicine down before she voiced her indignation.

"Well, really! I have been coaxing for quite twenty minutes."

"We gentlemen must stick together," explained the viscount, and was rewarded with a tiny smile that faded all too soon.

Lady Whitton took Peter's wrist in her fingers.

"His pulse is slower, but weaker," she confirmed Selena's fears. "Unless the fever breaks soon . . . The willowbark is usually so efficacious but it does not seem to have helped. I will prepare an infusion of yarrow."

She went off, returning a quarter hour later with a new potion.

"Bannister tells me Amabel Parcott is here, with her tiresome mother,"

91

she said as they roused Peter once more. "Would you not expect them to have enough tact to leave at such a time?"

"I had quite forgotten them!" Iverbrook exclaimed. "I trust Sir Aubrey is entertaining them?"

"If he is, it will be the first time he has done anything the least bit useful in this house," said Selena. "Peter, love, just swallow this last drop, my poor darling."

"He is too weak to resist," whispered Delia in horror. "I've never seen him take medicine without a fight."

Iverbrook led her to the fireplace and sat down beside her, talking quietly. Selena and her mother took up their posts on either side of the bed, Lady Whitton holding one of her grandson's hands. Outside, the grey day merged into dusk. Polly came in to light the candles, draw the curtains, and build up the fire. She cast a frightened glance at the still figure under the blue counterpane, and slipped out again without speaking.

A few minutes later Lady Whitton raised her head.

"Selena, feel his forehead," she said, her voice so strange that Delia and Iverbrook started to their feet and approached the bed.

"He is still very hot, Mama. Oh, but his face is damp! He is sweating at last!"

"I was afraid I had imagined it. Thank God! The fever has broken."

Delia asked the question Iverbrook was afraid to utter.

"Does that mean he is safe, Mama? He will recover?"

"He is not yet out of danger, and at best he will be weak for some time, but the worst is past, my loves. With care, he will recover!"

Iverbrook insisted on standing watch that night. When Selena went in early the next morning, he greeted her with the news that Peter had slept well, waking only once or twice to ask for water.

"I think he is much better," he said anxiously. "At least, he feels cooler and his pulse seems strong and steady."

Peter opened cornflower blue eyes.

"Hello, Aunt Sena," he said in a tiny voice. "I had a bad dream."

Selena ran to him and hugged him.

"I know, sweetheart, I know. You were very ill but now you are going to get well quickly. Cook has made you a milk jelly for your breakfast, and Grandmama will come and help you eat it. It will make you strong again.

Say goodnight to Uncle Hugh now. He has been sitting with you all night so now he is going to bed."

" 'Night, Uncle Hugh." Peter's eyelids drooped and he drowsed off.

"There's breakfast in the dining room, Hugh, if you can stay awake long enough to eat it, and Mama is having water heated for a bath, should you care for one. I must advise you to take advantage of it. Are you aware that you are still wearing your muddy clothes?"

He looked down at himself and smiled ruefully. "No, I was not aware. How very shocking! Now what can have made me forget such a thing?"

"I shall certainly never again describe you as a Bond Street beau! Sleep well, Hugh. Your presence has been a great comfort to all of us."

His lordship flushed, muttered something indistinct, and fled.

In the mysterious but inevitable country way, news of Peter's mishap had spread far and wide. Throughout the morning a series of grooms and maidservants arrived with enquiries, gifts, and messages of sympathy.

"Lady Anne Russell's compliments, Mr. Bannister, and how does Master Peter go on? Her la'ship's sent this bunch of grapes from her greenhouse."

"Oh sir, Miss Pauley sent me to see if the little boy's a-goin' to live and here's some beef tea made by her own hand an' ever so strengthening, she says."

"Mr. Brightwell, greengrocer of distinction, begs acceptance of a dozen fine lemons, brought from Spain, and how's the lad?"

"Blackcurrant cordial" . . . "a receipt for honey gruel" . . . "a tame thrush in a cage" . . . "a hop pillow to help the poor mite sleep" . . . The neighbours, great and small, rallied round to repay Lady Whitton for the care she had lavished on them for so many years.

Even Mrs. Parcott had the good sense, that day, to send a groom rather than appearing in person. If she feared a reprise of the humiliation of the previous day, she was justified. She would have found Lady Whitton occupied with her grandson, Selena out on farm business, and the viscount sound asleep.

Lord Iverbrook was woken by a ray of afternoon sun, which broke through the clouds, squeezed between the curtains, and came to rest on his face. He lay for a few minutes feeling warm and comfortable and happy, not remembering why. Then he sat up and swung his long legs out of bed. Peter was on the road to recovery and Selena had forgiven him! Was it true? He scrambled into the nearest clean clothes and ran up to the nursery.

Delia had taken her mother's place with Peter and was singing to him. Iverbrook paused in the doorway, admiring the picture they made. The sunlight on Delia's hair made it shine with gold lights. It was just the same shade as Selena's, the prettiest colour hair could be.

She finished her song and noticed him.

"Peter, it's your Uncle Hugh. He's much better, sir. He just drank a whole cup of veal broth, didn't you, Peter?"

" 'Lo, Uncle Hugh. Auntie Dee's singing to me till I go to sleep. She knows lots of songs."

"And sings them beautifully. How are you feeling, young man?"

"Under the weather. Jem says that means sort of wobbly and maybe sleepy and like not doing nothing. Will you stay till I go to sleep?"

"If you close your eyes right now and Auntie Dee sings a lullaby. I'm so hungry I could eat a horse."

That made Peter laugh. "Don't eat Leo," he said. "He's only a pony."

Weak and tired, he was soon asleep.

"I'll watch him," said Delia. "You go and have something to eat, but don't you dare eat Lyra!"

"I won't. Do you know where your sister is?"

"I don't know if she's come in yet; I expect not, because she would have come to see Peter. She went to choose the lambs to send to market."

"The market in Abingdon? I found myself tangled up in it the first day I came to Milford."

"Yes, it's held every Monday. It's one of the things she hates doing, dickering with the buyers and all that, but she can get a better price than John Peabody does."

"Not so good as I can, I'll wager! I wonder if she would let me do it for her?"

"Ask her. I wish you lived here always, to bring in the harvest and go to market and geld the bull calves. Those are the things that throw Selena into high fidgets, though in general she is the most amiable sister in the world."

"Geld the calves! I hope Selena does not do that herself!"

94

"Not precisely, I believe, though she has never let me see it. In fact, she will not even tell me just what they do. Will *you* tell me?"

"I will not!"

Delia sighed. "Well, she has to make sure that it is properly done, and that the men do not hurt the poor little things more than is necessary."

The viscount shuddered. "I'll offer to take the lambs to market, but I make no promises about the calves! And now I go in search of food. Take good care of our nephew."

Heading for the kitchen, Lord Iverbrook passed the butler's pantry. He heard voices within, Bannister's and Lady Whitton's, and knocked on the door.

"Do I interrupt?" he asked. "I was going to try and coax something to eat out of Cook, but methinks propriety demands I consult my kind hostess first."

"Nonsense, Hugh. You know you are more than welcome to raid the larder, with or without Cook's permission. Bannister has been recounting to me all the messages people have sent about Peterkin. What delightful neighbours we have! And only look at the presents. A singing thrush from old Mrs. Garfield! I'm sure I don't know what to do with the poor bird."

"Set it free. I will do it for you. Whoever sent the port? Peter will be drunk as a wheelbarrow for a week!"

"It's from Mr. Liddell, my lord, the landlord at the Royal Oak in the village. There's a message for you, my lord. Mrs. Parcott sent her groom over to ask after Master Peter, and he was very particular you should be told of it."

The viscount grimaced. "Thank you, Bannister. I'm off to the kitchen now, ma'am, to tell Cook I have your blessing for my depredations on her larder."

Iverbrook was seated at the kitchen table, attacking a large beefsteak, when Tom Arbuckle arrived.

"Young Jem says Master Peter's getting better!" He gave Cook a hearty kiss and a squeeze.

"Which is more nor you'll do, an his lordship sees you," she retorted, waving a wooden spoon in the viscount's direction.

Tom started and blushed. "Beg pardon, m'lord, I'm sure."

"That's all right, Tom, go ahead. After all, I am an intruder in Cook's territory. Just let me know when you are done."

Tom's face deepened to beetroot red. "All done, m'lord," he assured his master. "Is it true, then, about Master Peter?"

"True enough. He is not yet in prime twig, but goes on as well as can be expected. What news from London? Sit down, man, and ask your sweetheart for something to eat."

Tom flushed again, but he sat down at the table. Cook drew him a mug of ale and set another piece of beef to fry.

"I give your letter to Mr. Crowe, m'lord, and he says as how he's had his eye on that Hubble for many a year and he'll fix it up all right and tight."

"Good. Did you see Joshua?"

"Aye, m'lord, and that's another thing Mr. Crowe said, that Mr. Joshua'd be the best clerk he ever had and he'll give a tryout like to the other young man you recommended. Mr. Joshua and Mr. James Goodenough kindly invited me to dine with them, m'lord, and we was joined by Mr. Hastings's man. Mr. Dimbury that is. And one thing leading to another, Mr. Hastings come down with me and he's putting up at the inn in the village."

"Hasty's here? Good heavens! I must go and see him right away."

"I hope I done right, m'lord, to bring him?"

"Of course, though how the devil you could stop him if you'd wanted to I'd like to know. I suppose he has Dimbury with him?"

"What do you think, m'lord?"

"Now, Tom, don't be cheeky to his lordship!" put in Cook.

"Don't worry, Cook, Tom is almost as necessary to me as Dimbury is to Mr. Hastings. Mark that 'almost,' Tom."

"Yes, m'lord!"

The viscount finished his meal and went in search of Lady Whitton. He found her in the stillroom, making up a dose for Peter.

"What are you giving him now?" he asked with interest.

"He is still somewhat feverish, so here is more yarrow. Then a general tonic, made from betony, pennyroyal, St. John's wort, and agrimony."

"Ugh. No eye of newt and blood of bat?"

" 'Eye of newt and toe of frog, *Wool* of bat . . . ' "

" ' . . . and tongue of dog.' Was Shakespeare acquainted with a witch or two, do you suppose, or did he invent the whole?"

"I suspect he made it up," said Lady Whitton with a twinkle in her eye. "At least, many of the country folk hereabouts think me a witch, and I have certainly never used such ingredients."

"What, no scale of dragon? No tiger's chaudron? You disappoint me. Perhaps only wicked witches use them, for you are certainly a good witch. Do you wish me to help you pour your potion down Peter's throat?"

"Not unless you choose to. Now that I have time, I sweeten it with honey and anise, and he takes it without trouble."

"Then I will leave you to it. My servant is just now come from town and he tells me a very good friend of mine is staying at the Royal Oak, so I shall walk down to see him. My legs need stretching. Can I perform any errands for you in the village?"

"I think not. Mrs. Tooting sent one of the maids earlier. But Hugh, I cannot allow a friend of yours to put up at the inn. You will invite him to stay with us while he is in the neighbourhood."

"Have I ever told you that I adore you?" he asked, kissing her cheek. "You are quite the nicest person I know."

"Silly boy! You will tell him that we do not entertain a great deal, but he is to treat the Manor as his home and come and go as he pleases."

"You do not even know his name! Besides, I must tell you that he is very much attached to his valet and will not go anywhere without him. You are already housing and feeding an extra servant, and cannot wish to take on another."

"Fustian! Perhaps his valet would consent to help with Aubrey's clothes, for if I have heard him complain of Bannister's attentions once I have heard him a hundred times. And I'm sure poor Bannister cannot be expected to learn the business at his age, besides having his own duties."

His lordship grinned a wicked grin. "I look forward to hearing Dimbury's reaction to Sir Aubrey's wardrobe," he said. "Never fear, I shall advise Hasty of your kind invitation."

"Hasty?"

"Mr. Lennox Hastings, known to his friends as Hasty because of his tendency to speak before he thinks. He will amuse you, ma'am. I'll not fail to bring him back with me to pay his respects at least."

As Iverbrook left the house, he heard the church clock in the village striking five. It was a pleasant evening, sunny and warm for the time of year. The lane was still muddy, so he walked along the grass verge, shuddering involuntarily as he passed the spot where he had met Peter.

A flock of rust and blue chaffinches was gorging on the crimson berries in the hawthorn hedge. At his approach they rose, flashing the black and white bars on their wings, then quickly settled again behind him. A cock pheasant, its plumage even gaudier, ran ahead of him for a few yards, then forced its desperate way through the hedge as if it knew the shooting season was no more than a fortnight away.

The viscount reached the crossroads and turned left to Kings Milford. A couple was strolling towards him arm in arm. One glance at the man's mulberry coat told his lordship his identity, and the pair was not much slower to recognise him.

"My lord!" exclaimed Polly, pink faced, and pulled away from her companion. "I come across Sir Aubrey in the village and he up and offered to carry me parcels." Nervously she smoothed her black stuff gown, then snatched a basket from the baronet and fled, showing a very neat ankle as she passed Iverbrook.

Sir Aubrey's face clashed abominably with his jacket.

"I suppose you will tell my aunt," he growled.

"You are foolish beyond permission," said his lordship gently. "What sort of despicable wretch do you take me for?"

"Then I can count on your discretion, my lord? She's a pretty piece, is she not? But reluctant, I must admit, very hesitant. Not like those hot-blooded wenches in the Indies, eh?" He smiled and winked.

"You mistake me, sir. I will not tell because I mislike bearing tales, not because I have any sympathy with your conduct. The girl's unwillingness serves to raise *her* in my estimation, but not *you,* sir, most certainly not you. Have a care what you are about."

A shade of grey entered Sir Aubrey's complexion, so that it nearly matched his coat. He muttered something and hurried round the corner after the maid.

Lord Iverbrook strode on into the village. At the Royal Oak, a low brick building with a gilt sign proclaiming the proprietorship of Jacob Liddell, Esquire, he enquired for Mr. Hastings.

"Where'd ya put the gemmun, Maisie?" roared Jacob Liddell, Esquire.

"In the front room, Jacob!" roared back his wife, an enormous woman presiding at the bar in the taproom.

"Alf, take the gemmun up to the front room," bellowed the landlord at a tired-looking waiter.

Alf scurried up the stairs in front of Lord Iverbrook, tapped timidly at a door, and announced in a high, squeaky voice, "Gemmun to see you, sir." He then twitched past Iverbrook and scurried down the stairs again.

"Come in?" said Hasty's voice, uncertainly. "My dear fellow, how good to see you! I thought I heard that wretched waiter scratching at the door."

"Pour me a glass of brandy, Hasty," said his lordship, sinking into a chair. "I think I must be entering my dotage. Can you imagine *me* in the rôle of defender of virtue?"

== 12 ==

"INDEED I CANNOT, sir," said Dimbury tearfully. "His coats are all different shades of red. It makes me bilious only to look at them. And the waistcoats!"

"They cannot all be as devilish as that green and pink affair he wore last night." Mr Hastings, sitting up in bed with a cup of chocolate, had never seen his correct manservant so nearly succumbing to emotion.

"Oh, can't they!" My lord Iverbrook lounged in a chair in the corner of the narrow chamber. The scene was providing quite as much amusement as he had foreseen. "Still, never mind, Dimbury. Lady Whitton will find a prescription to settle your stomach."

The valet eloquently ignored him.

"Sir, if you saw his linen! Ready made, I am certain of it."

"The exigencies of life in the Indies. It is your duty to remedy the defects in his wardrobe," said his inexorable master.

"That will not be easy," said the viscount. "Sir Aubrey, or 'the Bart' as the servants call him, is purse-pinched if not quite at point-non-plus. His intention is to marry Miss Whitton and allow her to feather his nest."

"Tallyho, a villain, a money-grubbing villain! In that case, Dimbury, it is your plain duty to make the Bart look ridiculous."

"Sir, there is nothing I can do which can possibly make him look more ridiculous than he makes himself."

The quiet conviction of his tone silenced Mr. Hastings momentarily, but he made a quick recover.

"Then, Dimbury," he sighed, "since you will not do this small thing for our kind hostess, we shall have to return to the inn."

The valet blenched. His ears still rang with the boom of the landlord's voice, not to mention his wife's.

"Sir!" he said reproachfully.

His master took this for capitulation.

"All you need do is keep his things clean and in order, and you have my permission to filch the worst of the waistcoats."

Iverbrook laughed, and let the subject drop. "When are you getting up, Hasty?" he asked.

"My dear Hugh, it cannot be a moment past nine o'clock! This is unconscionably early, even for the country."

"Gammon! I want to introduce you to my nephew this morning, and later I must ride out with Selena so that she can explain the lambs to me."

"Explain the lambs? Lambs, Hugh, are baby sheep," Hasty said kindly. "You know, mutton? Wool? Baa, baa."

"*These* lambs are going to market, whither I have offered to accompany them. Hence Miss Whitton is to tell me what prices she expects to get, as I have wagered that I can do better."

"So Miss Whitton inflates her price and you lose. You have been rusticating too long, my lord. Your wits are wandering."

"Selena is incapable of deceit. I'd as soon distrust you, Hasty."

Mr. Hastings raised his eyebrows and directed a speculative look at his friend. He swallowed the last of his chocolate, pulled off his nightcap, and announced, "I'll come with you."

"Do! Perhaps Delia will join us. Her mother was saying at breakfast that she ought to go out today, having watched Peter most of yesterday."

"You have breakfasted already? Heaven help me, I am fallen among heathen! Really, my dear chap, this is going too far. I suppose next you will invite the Bart to go along?"

"Certainly not. Like yourself, the Bart does not appear before noon. Besides, the man is such a flat he can neither ride nor drive."

This news so startled Mr. Hastings that he was deprived of speech, and in that condition Iverbrook left him, with a parting admonition to Dimbury to bustle about.

He went up to the nursery, where he found Selena reading to Peter from a book of fables.

"Why because did the fox want the grapes?" Peter asked disapprovingly. "Foxes eat chickens and rabbits, not grapes. Hello, Uncle Hugh. Do you know any foxes which likes grapes?"

"I don't believe so, but next time I meet one I'll ask him."

"That's a silly story, Aunt Sena. I want to get up."

"You know Grandmama said not today, darling."

"But I'm right as a trivet. And I won't go out alone and I won't eat berries and climb trees and go near the river. So why because can't I?"

"Grandmama will come and sit with you in a little while and you can ask her."

"Coward!" said Hugh with a grin.

"*You* see if you can find a story this wretched child will not argue with!"

"I'm not a wretched child."

"Peter, if you will hush a minute, I shall tell you about Robin Hood. Selena, I invited Hasty to ride with us. I hope you do not object?"

"Of course not. Mr. Hastings seems to be a most gentlemanly person, and his manners are such as must please the most exacting critic."

"Lady Anne Russell, for example. Do you think Delia will like to go too?"

"I'll ask her. Now do tell Peter your tale before he bursts with curiosity. Be good, Peterkin."

A gusty wind was blowing when the four riders set out. Cool but refreshing, it tore a few yellowed leaves off the still green trees and tossed them at the horses' hooves. Clouds of swallows swooped and darted over the river, collecting the last of the summer's gnats before departing to winter in warmer climes. A solitary grey heron rose among them on stately wings and flew upstream, mournful in its aloneness.

Mr. Hastings soon learned more about lambs than he had any desire to know. Delia found the subject equally tedious. She suggested that they should ride into Abingdon to see if the Circulating Library had any new novels, and the gentleman accepted with alacrity.

Delia had quickly decided that Mr. Hastings's restrained elegance made her Cousin Aubrey look like a crow in peacock's feathers. Perhaps that was somewhat less than accurate, since Aubrey was undeniably handsome while Hasty's round, good-natured face bore no marks of distinction. Nor was there anything romantic in his style and bearing, but he looked every inch a gentleman of fashion, and behaved likewise, and she was proud to be seen with him.

As they rode over Abingdon Bridge, Mr. Hastings noticed ruins on the opposite bank. Nearest the bridge nothing was left of the buildings but scattered blocks of stone, surrounded by grass where a flock of coots grazed. Beyond, built right onto the water, the remains were in better repair.

"A castle?" he enquired.

"No, the abbey," breathed Delia, eyes shining. "Is it not sinister? I have always wanted to explore but Selena is not interested in such things."

"I shall arrange an expedition," said Mr. Hastings promptly. "We will drive over, I shall treat you to luncheon at the Nag's Head, and you shall explore all afternoon."

"Not the Nag's Head," objected Delia, unexpectedly practical in the face of such a treat. "It is a common tavern, though its situation in the middle of the bridge is excessively romantic. The Crown and Thistle would be better."

"The Crown and Thistle let it be. On the next fine day . . . "

"After the apple harvest. Selena says they must be picked next week."

"The next fine day after the apple harvest," agreed Mr. Hastings nobly, wondering how long that would be. He had come into the country on a whim, and had scarcely looked to stay more than a few days. "And now, show me your lending library and let us see whether the latest works of Mrs. Meekes and Kitty Cuthbertson are on the shelves."

"Do you like Mrs. Cuthbertson's novels? I had thought gentlemen read only Latin and Greek histories, and books about farming. Is not *Santo Sebastiano* the most delightful thing in the world?"

A twinkle in his eye, Mr. Hastings realised he had hit the mark.

"Certainly," he assured her. "My sister and I read it together and I shall never forget Lord St. Orville swooning at Julia's feet!"

"I have never swooned," regretted Delia, "and I cannot imagine Clive swooning at my feet, or even Cousin Aubrey, let alone Gilbert or Hugh. Have you ever swooned, sir?"

"No, no, indeed I have not! That sort of thing is best left to romances!"

Delia had to agree that it would be most inconvenient if gentlemen were to make a habit of falling into faints.

Selena and Lord Iverbrook finished discussing the marketing of lambs and went on across the fields. Some were being ploughed for winter wheat or root crops, in others crows, seagulls, and pheasants quarrelled over the last gleanings from the harvest. They rode for the most part in silence, enjoying each other's company.

"We are not far from Bracketts," said Selena eventually. "I ought to go in and report on Peter's progress. Will you dare Lady Anne with me?"

"If you will protect me, though I think I have not yet had the misfortune of falling under her absolute censure."

"If you had, you would know it, though in general she is more tolerant of the failings of gentlemen than of mere females. She cannot approve of me, for it is excessively unladylike to be a farmer, yet as I am beyond redemption she no longer frowns on me. With poor Delia it is otherwise. Lady Anne has hopes of her becoming a demure, well-bred young lady like Jane, so every slightest backsliding from the highest standards of propriety calls forth reproof."

"Your mother does not take snuff at such interference?"

"Can you imagine Mama taking offence, for I collect that is what you mean? I doubt she knows how. She and Lady Anne are not close, for their characters are so very different, but the Russells were a great comfort when Papa died, and Phoebe too, and Mama sees only her kindness."

When they reached Bracketts, a lovely old Tudor mansion, they left their horses in the care of a groom in the stables, where they met Clive.

"Is Delia not with you?" he asked. "I hope she is well. Oh, I ought to have enquired after Peter. I beg your pardon."

Selena rescued him from his confusion, informed him of Peter's progress, and said that Delia had ridden into Abingdon with Lord Iverbrook's friend.

"Indeed!" Clive frowned. "I was going that way myself, but I will take you into the house first, if you like, so that you need not go round to the front door."

"No, hurry after them. I expect your mama will forgive us for entering by the back way, since we bring good news."

"Good news?"

"Peter," Selena reminded gently, and bit her lip to hide her smile. "Off you go."

"Mooncalf!" snorted his lordship as the youth dashed off.

They found the Russell ladies in an elegantly appointed salon. Crocodile-legged occasional tables in the latest style displayed bibelots of delicate

Limoges porcelain, and the lacquered bamboo furniture looked too fragile to support a full-grown man, let alone the stout and hearty master of the house.

Miss Jane Russell was engaged in embroidering a slipper, while her mother read to her from a volume of sermons.

Lady Anne regally pronounced her delight in Peter's recovery, firmly dismissed the viscount ("Mr. Russell will be happy to see you in the gun room."), and sent Jane on an obviously fabricated errand to the nursery.

"And now, Miss Whitton, we may enjoy a comfortable cose," she declared. "I do not like to see you ride alone with Lord Iverbrook, but I expect you will say that I am a trifle old-fashioned."

Since Selena did not dare say anything of the sort, she continued after a pause.

"After all, he is practically a member of your family, poor Phoebe's brother-in-law. And though it would not do for Delia, you are of an age where it may not be considered *utterly* compromising."

Selena thought of Delia going to Abingdon with only Mr. Hastings for escort. How could she have let her go? At the time it had seemed unexceptionable.

"I have been hoping for several days to see your dear mama, but since she is undoubtedly occupied with her grandson, I venture to speak to you, Miss Whitton. I fear I was shocked, yes, I must say shocked, to meet with Amabel Parcott in your house!"

"But why, ma'am? You and Mama have been acquainted with the Gants since before Amabel and I were born, have you not?"

"I cannot possibly tell you why, my dear Miss Whitton. It is not the sort of thing one repeats to an unmarried girl. You may tell Lady Whitton that I shall not permit Jane to visit Milford Manor while this unfortunate intimacy persists, and I advise her to send Delia to Bracketts if the woman shows her face again. Knowing your mama, I place no reliance on her denying the creature entry."

"You must also know, ma'am, that Mama does not listen to gossip and scandalous rumours!" Selena rose to her feet.

"I washed my hands of you, Miss Whitton, several years past." Lady Anne's dispassionate voice changed not a whit. "Delia, however, is not beyond hope of making a respectable alliance. I beg you will ask Lady Whitton to heed my advice."

"I shall report your concern, ma'am. Pray excuse me now. We are expected at home." She curtseyed unsteadily.

"Good-bye, Miss Whitton. I hope you will not come to regret your stubbornness."

Selena fled. Outside the door she paused, leaning against the wall, unsure whether she was angrier with Lady Anne or with herself. Why had she defended Amabel Parcott, when what she really wanted to do was to scratch the cat's eyes out?

She wished she had not brought Iverbrook with her. Whatever the relationship between him and 'Bel,' she could not tell him of Lady Anne's vague accusations, and he would most certainly want to know why he had been blatantly excluded from their conversation!

He did. He was in a teasing, charming mood, and as they rode homeward he tried to trick Selena into revealing the secret. He made her laugh in spite of herself, though she managed not to give anything away. By the time they reached the Manor, she had resolved to tell her mother what Lady Anne had said and then to put it out of her mind. She had enough reasons to avoid Mrs. Parcott without giving credence to the latest *on dit.*

They entered the house by the side door.

"I must change," said Selena. "I do not know what possessed me to present myself to Lady Anne in my riding dress. It is the sort of rag-manners she abhors and I should have remembered it."

"I shall go straight up to Peter, since I think it unlikely that he will object to my attire."

"Uncle Hugh can do no wrong. I'll join you in a few minutes."

Selena stepped into the entrance hall and came face to face with Lady Gant.

"My dear Miss Whitton, so pleased you have returned, we have but now arrived and your butler was saying that he will see if Lady Whitton is at home, we are come to ask after the poor little boy of course such a dreadful pity no permanent nervous damage I trust?"

Half listening, a polite smile frozen on her face, Selena watched out of the corner of her eye as Amabel sailed forward, ravishingly beautiful in buttercup yellow silk. She did not see the hunted look on Lord Iverbrook's face, or his stiff bow, only the way the widow raised her glowing eyes to him, and her full, inviting lips.

"*Dearest* Hugh," she crooned, "how delighted I am that your nephew is better. You must have been quite distraught with worry! I have been thinking of you constantly."

Selena did not want to hear the viscount's reply. "Won't you come into the parlour, ma'am?" she invited. "I expect my mother will be down in a minute."

"And where is dear Sir Aubrey such a charming gentleman and so good-looking what a delightful addition to the family, I knew his father but I never did find out perhaps you know?"

Selena barely heard the question, and certainly had no intention of unveiling her cousin's gypsy mother. Lady Gant was not in the least discomposed by the lack of response but rattled on.

Why am I always wearing my oldest clothes when she arrives? wondered Selena.

Mrs. Parcott took the viscount's hand and half led, half pulled him to the French doors, where she stood close beside him, pointing out something in the garden or on the river. Lady Whitton came in and freed Selena from the chatterer. Tentatively she moved towards the pair at the window, dreading to overhear, longing to interrupt. Sir Aubrey arrived and waylaid her with an endless description of something he had seen in the village, she could not tell what. Iverbrook laughed; he found Amabel amusing; he must be in love with her.

"No, Bel," he was saying, but Selena could not hear him, "it's no use playing off those tricks on me. I shall not escort you to the assembly in Oxford. I have no intention of going at all. What an impudent minx you are! I beg you will cease to visit here while I am here."

Selena watched her looking up at him saucily.

The fifteen minutes proper to a courtesy call stretched into half an hour. At last the visitors rose to take their leave.

"I shall come on Monday to enquire after your grandson, ma'am," said Mrs. Parcott, glancing sideways at the viscount.

"What a pity that Lord Iverbrook will not be here," put in Sir Aubrey. "He is to go to Abingdon market."

The widow flashed him a look of gratitude.

"Or perhaps Tuesday, if that is more convenient," she went on smoothly.

"On Tuesday we begin the apple harvest," said Selena.

"I adore picking apples, I vow! 'Tis the only country festival I can abide. I shall come and help you without fail. Good-bye, Selena, and thank you for the invitation!"

Defeated, Selena retired to her chamber to change.

Iverbrook went up to the nursery, annoyed with Selena, annoyed with Sir Aubrey, and above all annoyed with the Merry Widow.

Peter took one look at his face.

"Are you in a miff, Uncle Hugh?" he asked.

"Not with you, at any rate. How are you feeling?"

"I want to get up. Timmy Russell says only girls stay in bed when they're ill."

"What does Grandmama say?"

"Tomorrow. That's the day after today. Tell me about Robin Hood? Please, Uncle Hugh?"

Uncle Hugh complied, dredging details from the depths of his memory and making up the bits he could not remember. After the new story, Peter wanted to hear again the one he had told before. Not unnaturally, it emerged somewhat differently this time. Peter did not hesitate to voice his disapproval.

"Stories is s'posed to stay the same," he insisted. "You said Maid Marion has long black hair."

"I made a mistake," said his uncle firmly. "Her hair was most definitely short and fair and curly."

"Like Aunt Sena's?"

"Like Aunt Sena's."

Before Iverbrook could err again, Delia bounced into the room, followed by Mr. Hastings at a more sedate pace.

"Guess what!" she crowed. "There's going to be a subscription ball in Oxford next Saturday."

"It was advertised in the bookseller's in Abingdon," confirmed Mr. Hastings.

"And Mr. Hastings has bought tickets for us all! Even for Jane and Clive! And Cousin Aubrey! And Mama!"

"Lend me fifty guineas till quarter day, my dear fellow?" murmured Hasty.

— 13 —

MR. HASTINGS WAS persuaded, much against his will, to accompany the lambs to Abingdon.

"Or rather, to follow them," said Iverbrook, "for I understand they leave at dawn. The shepherd and his dogs can get them there without our assistance."

"Thank heaven!" Hasty shuddered. "Why the deuce can't the shepherd sell the beastly creatures?"

"He has a vocabulary of approximately twenty words, ten of which are comprehended only by sheep and dogs. Besides, I told you of our wager."

With that reminder, Hasty ceased to object. A wager was sufficient justification for virtually any activity.

Lord Iverbrook soon discovered why Selena disliked going to market. Around the edge of the marketplace a few women had stalls selling butter, eggs, and great yellow cheeses; others patronised a couple of peddlers hawking ribbons and buckles; but the main business of the day was exclusively male.

Stock pens built of withy hurdles held bleating sheep, rambunctious bullocks, and one evil-looking Hereford bull. Underfoot, the glutinous mud gave off a penetrating stench. Buyers and sellers, pushing through the narrow walks between the enclosures, had to shout to make themselves heard over the animals.

Hasty at once escaped to the Crown and Thistle, with a promise of ordering a neat luncheon.

It was quieter and slightly less smelly under the arches of the town hall, where stout farmers in homespun retired to dicker with butchers in blue and white striped aprons and straw hats or sharp-faced drovers down from London and Birmingham. Here the viscount began to enjoy himself. He discovered a hitherto unused talent for bargaining, and by the time he joined his friend at the inn he had a very inflated idea of himself and a bank draft in his pocket for considerably more than Selena had expected.

The panelled coffee room of the Crown and Thistle was dark and quiet after the noise and bustle of the street. Mr. Hastings was sitting on a settle in the chimney nook. Opposite him, a lady warmed her hands at the fire. From the doorway, everything but those hands and a corner of a sapphire blue cloak was hidden by the high side of the seat; nonetheless, Iverbrook had a very good idea who it was.

He made his way between gateleg tables and Windsor chairs, for the most part unoccupied as it was still early, and found his guess correct. Amabel jumped up, flung her arms around his neck, and kissed him full on the lips.

Taken by surprise, Iverbrook put his arm about her waist and returned the kiss—she was after all a cosy armful—then disentangled himself and firmly sat her down.

"Hugh, darling, what a delightful surprise!" Amabel cooed. "I happened to meet Mr. Hastings in the street and he invited me to join you both for luncheon. Such charming friends you have, I vow!"

Resignedly, cursing the Bart under his breath for giving away his whereabouts, Iverbrook seconded the invitation. He put his foot down when a private parlour was suggested. Over luncheon he described his triumph in the marketplace, which Hasty ascribed to shopkeeper ancestors. Amabel was certain it was due to his personal charm and address, and the innate genius of the nobly born.

"I am surprised to hear that Selena usually does it herself," she added. "Such a very masculine business. La, I'm sure I should have no more notion how to set about it than a babe in arms!"

"Doubtless," said the viscount drily.

After the meal they escorted the lady to her carriage, handed her in, and watched as it drove off.

"What the devil do you mean by asking her to eat with us?" demanded Iverbrook.

Mr. Hastings was taken aback.

"I can see no harm in it," he protested. "You are not known here and she resides in London."

"I am certainly known to be staying with the Whittons, especially after this morning's work. And she will regard it as encouragement to come to Milford Manor."

"Good Lord no, my dear fellow! Your *chère-amie* to call on your . . . ahem, on your brother's family? Even the Merry Widow would not do such a thing."

"Would she not! She has done so already, and more than once, since I came into the country. I'd forgot you were out on Saturday when she was there."

"Oh no, I say, my dear Hugh! Can't have that. Very bad *ton,* very bad indeed. It simply won't do."

"How am I to stop her? She has known the Whittons forever, it seems. I can scarcely be expected to ask Lady Whitton to refuse her on the grounds that she used to be my mistress. *Used to be,* mind you, Hasty. I told her in London that all was over between us."

"Don't think she believed you, dear boy. It's my belief she still has her eye on the banns, for it's a title she's after, mark my words."

"She won't get mine! Hasty, you won't mention this meeting to Miss . . . to the Whittons. Though I daresay she will herself when she turns up for the apple harvest tomorrow," the viscount concluded gloomily.

"The Merry Widow picking apples?" said Hasty, incredulous. "Never!"

Mr Hastings's skepticism proved well-founded. Mrs. Parcott arrived at noon wearing a pink and white striped carriage dress of Circassian cloth, a pink cachemire spencer, a Leghorn straw bonnet with roses (pink), and a striped parasol. Nothing could have been more charming, nor more unsuitable for any exertion beyond a stroll in formal gardens.

Sir Aubrey, fortunately dressed in a crimson which complimented her pink, spread a rug on a wooden bench by the orchard gate, where stood a cart half loaded with baskets of apples. He seated her there, and begged permission to join her.

"I was never more shocked in my life," he remarked, "than when I discovered that the family intended actually to help in the picking."

"Indeed," she murmured, "I had thought it rather an occasion for a picnic or something of the sort. Is not that Mr. Hastings in that tree? La, it is no place for a Tulip of the Ton to be seen!"

"My cousin Delia persuaded him to it. No true Dandy would so compromise his principles."

"They say Brummell turns back from the hunt after the first field lest the white tops to his boots be splashed. Of course, Iverbrook is careless in his dress, and subject to odd enthusiasms, so I am not surprised that he has not yet noticed my arrival."

At that moment his lordship passed down a basket of pippins to Selena and Delia, saying something that made them laugh and nearly drop it. With merry faces they turned to carry it to the gate, and caught sight of Amabel, a vision of rustic beauty.

"Why has Mrs. Parcott come here again?" demanded Delia. "You were not used to be so intimate with her. In fact, I thought you disliked her excessively."

"I do!" said Selena through gritted teeth, immediately conscious that she was hot and tired and grubby, that her cotton dress was not only faded but stained, and that her hair was tousled and probably full of leaves. Iverbrook was climbing down the ladder behind her and could not fail to be struck by the contrast.

"Put that down, Selena," said the viscount. "I shall carry it, or one of the men. I have been enjoying myself so, I had not realised how hard we have made you work."

Amabel came to meet them, her pink kid half-boots and dainty ankles revealed as she raised her skirts to clear the grass.

"Poor Selena, you do look tired," she said brightly. "And the sun is so hard on a delicate complexion, is it not? I can see that that is no occupation for a lady."

"Which is why you have arrived just in time for luncheon, no doubt," said Iverbrook. "Selena, take my arm as far as the house."

"Yes do," agreed Mrs. Parcott, "and I shall walk on your other side, Hugh, for I declare your sleeve is so soiled I hardly like to touch it."

"I must tell the men it is time to eat their dinners," said Selena, turning away. "Delia, pray call Mr. Hastings down from his tree, since you talked him into it. Jem! Where is the keg of ale I bade you bring? It is time to broach it. Has Carter kept a count of the baskets, as I asked?"

Willy-nilly, his lordship escorted Amabel back to the house.

Luncheon was not a cheerful meal, especially after Amabel mentioned how kind Hugh had been to treat her to a fine spread in Abingdon on the previous day. Even the urbane Mr. Hastings lost his tongue, and only Lady Gant and Sir Aubrey seemed unconscious of restraint.

Selena returned to the orchard, rejecting any further assistance. Iverbrook escaped to the nursery and Lady Whitton, called away by Mrs. Tooting, remembered Lady Anne's obscure warning and bore off Delia with her. Mr. Hastings, far too gentlemanly to run away, was left to entertain Lady Gant, no arduous task as he merely had to school his features into an expression of interest and murmur, "Indeed!" now and then.

"How very vexatious!" said Mrs. Parcott in a low voice to Sir Aubrey. "Selena is as close to pulling caps with Iverbrook as I could have wished, but Iverbrook is at outs with me. You must make a push to win her. Have you proposed marriage to her yet?"

"Yes," admitted the baronet sheepishly. "She said she did not feel for me as a wife ought towards her husband."

"Missishness! And most unbecoming at her age. However, you must not expect her to proclaim undying love at first asking. It will take some effort on your part to engage her affections, you know! She will not drop into your hand like a ripe apple."

"Why should she not? At her age! It is an excessively suitable match and I think she cannot have taken a dislike to my person." He smoothed his thick, wavy golden hair and presented his profile for the widow's inspection.

"You ought to wear blue," she said, "or green."

"Henry Cole of Brighton is said to wear nothing but green. His fame has reached even to Jamaica. I do not wish to be a mere imitator."

"Blue then. Red is such a trying colour."

He frowned. "I was under the impression," he said haughtily, "that red became me to perfection."

"Certainly. A complexion such as yours, my dear Sir Aubrey, looks superb in any hue. But think of Selena. Her face is pale, and freckled too; red makes her positively haggard."

The baronet looked sulky. "I don't know that I want to marry her after all. Neither her appearance nor her manners are more than tolerable."

"You must not let her intimidate you!" said Mrs. Parcott in alarm, involuntarily raising her voice. Mr. Hastings regarded her with surprise, and she went on in a near whisper, "Only think of the fine property you will own! I can see I shall have to help you. You say you are all going to the ball in Oxford on Saturday?"

Mrs. Parcott's plans for assisting Sir Aubrey to a bride appeared to please the gentleman, for he sniggered once or twice and Mr. Hastings heard him say, "'Pon my soul, you're a clever woman." When after half an hour, neither Iverbrook nor Lady Whitton had reappeared, Sir Aubrey escorted the ladies to their carriage in a high good humour.

Lord Iverbrook, with Grandmama's permission, had carried Peter down to the orchard, bundled in a rug. Selena would willingly have ignored the viscount's presence but she could not ignore her nephew when he waved and called to her.

She offered him an apple.

"I want to climb up a tree and pick one," he said. "If I get stuck, Uncle Hugh will help me down, won't you, Uncle Hugh?"

"I think you had better not, Peterkin. You are still convalescent."

"Grandmama said I may. Uncle Hugh asted her. Long as I don't get cold or hot or wet."

"Or tired," confirmed Uncle Hugh. "Which tree would you suggest, Selena?" He smiled at her over the child's head.

She looked away quickly. "Phoebe and I always used to climb that winesap over there. It is easy because it grows at a slant, and the apples are sweet."

They stood beneath the tree, watching Peter climb, Iverbrook ready to catch him if he slipped.

"Is . . . " Selena's voice sounded strange and she cleared her throat. "Is Amabel gone already?"

"I neither know nor care." Iverbrook turned to her and took both her hands in his. "Selena, I knew Amabel in town before I went to Jamaica. She had any number of admirers, the sort of court collected by any beautiful and fashionable young widow living on the fringes of Society, and I was one of them. That life is past. I have a mission now, and a nephew, and soon, I dare to hope . . . "

"Uncle Hugh, look at my apple. Isn't it big, Aunt Sena? It's the biggest one on the tree. I can't climb 'cos I have to hold onto it with my hand. Come and get me, Uncle Hugh."

Uncle Hugh went.

On Saturday evening, Lord Iverbrook was loitering in the hall when Selena descended the stairs, dressed for the ball. She seemed to float in her gown of amber sarcenet, trimmed with Honiton lace, and the topaz necklace at her throat sparkled no more brightly in the candlelight than did her eyes.

She read admiration in his face and a delicate flush tinted her cheeks.

He bowed low over her hand.

"Madam, allow me the pleasure of driving you to the ball. I wish to be seen to arrive with the most elegant lady in the place."

She dimpled. "Why thank you, kind sir. I shall be happy to go with you, if Mama permits."

"I have already consulted Mama. At first she did not think it quite the thing for a young lady to drive alone with a gentleman at night, but I pointed out that since it will be dark, no one will see us, and she is altogether won over."

"I do not believe you even broached the subject! However, I mean to tell Mama I am going with you, not to ask her if I may, and I doubt she will object. You are, as even Lady Anne was forced to acknowledge, practically one of the family."

" 'Practically' will not suffice for long," he said, a gleam in his eye.

The door bell rang and Bannister admitted Jane and Clive Russell, who were to dine at the Manor before they all set out for Oxford. Clive had promised his mother to see that Jane danced only with gentlemen of their own party.

"For she is not yet out, ma'am, you know," he explained to Lady Whitton. "And she is to ride with me in our own carriage. Will you go with us, ma'am? Our coachman is very safe and steady, I promise you." He glanced wistfully at Delia, who was looking very pretty in pale blue muslin, her silk-smooth hair wound in a knotted, grown-up style. She was laughing with Mr. Hastings and had scarcely acknowledged his arrival.

Mr. Hastings, Delia, and Sir Aubrey were to travel in the Whittons' barouche. Selena thought of suggesting that it was not quite proper for her little sister to go alone with two gentlemen, but she was too happy in her own arrangement to risk upsetting it. Her mother seemed oblivious of any possible impropriety, and she decided that Lady Anne's strictures must be preying on her mind. After all, if Iverbrook was nearly one of the family, Cousin Aubrey was not only a family member but actually the head of it. She dismissed her qualms and prepared to enjoy the evening.

Delia was already enjoying herself. She had noticed Clive's pleading look and deliberately ignored it. Handsome as he undoubtedly was, next to Mr. Hastings's sartorial splendour he looked a country bumpkin. Not that Mr. Hastings was flamboyantly dressed—far from it. His fastidious black and white made Sir Aubrey's vermilion ridiculous.

Sir Aubrey seemed unaccountably nervous. He jumped when spoken to, and had a tendency to look behind him in a hunted way. He insisted on conferring with Jem, on the box of the Whitton carriage, for several minutes while the others disappeared down the drive and out into the lane. Delia was biting her nails with impatience by the time they set off at last.

It was a moonlit night, and once they reached the post road they proceeded at a good pace for several miles. Delia had been to Oxford any number of times, and she chattered about shopping expeditions and concerts and the hordes of dashing young gentlemen who swarmed about the city during the university terms.

"I have never been to an Assembly, though," she confided, "for though I was old enough last year, we were in mourning for poor Phoebe. Is it not vastly exciting?"

She scarcely noticed when they left the main road at Cowley and drove a short way down a bumpy lane, but as they turned in between gateposts of ornately carved stone, she exclaimed in surprise.

"Wherever are we?" she said, puzzled. "The ball is in the Assembly Rooms at the Blue Boar, not at a private house. Jem has made a mistake."

"You are sure?" queried Mr. Hastings. "Let me stop him before we disturb the residents."

"It's all r-right," stammered Sir Aubrey. "I t-told him to come here."

Before they could demand an explanation, the carriage reached the end of the short drive and pulled up before an elaborately Italianate house. The front door swung open at once, and there stood Amabel Parcott, resplendent in a daringly diaphanous, peach-coloured ball gown, already hatted and gloved. A servant was placing a cloak about her exposed shoulders as Sir Aubrey let down the step of the barouche, and a moment later she seated herself beside him.

"G-go on!" he called to Jem.

Unlike the baronet, Mrs. Parcott was perfectly composed.

"So kind of you to stop for me," she said, pressing his hand, then turned to the others. "When I told Sir Aubrey that my parents would be absent for several days, taking our carriage with them, he insisted on fetching me on the way."

Delia was too young, and Mr. Hastings too proper, to do anything but accept the situation with what complaisance they could muster. As they left Cowley behind and started down Headington Hill, the former wondered what Selena would say, while the latter had a very good idea of what to expect from Lord Iverbrook!

When they arrived at the crowded Rooms, a cotillion was in progress. The viscount was dancing with Jane Russell and Clive with Selena. Lady Whitton had met several acquaintances among the chaperones and was enjoying a comfortable cose. It was too late for the newcomers to take their places on the floor, so Mr. Hastings escorted Delia to her mother's side and begged the honour of the next dance.

The cotillion came to an end. Lord Iverbrook left his demure and rather speechless partner in Lady Whitton's care and went in search of Selena. A glance flashed between Delia and Mr. Hastings. He must have missed Mrs. Parcott's arrival: best not to mention it.

Sir Aubrey appeared and with a flourishing bow requested Miss Russell's hand for the country dance, which the musicians were just striking up. Clive came up just in time to watch both his sister and Delia being led onto the floor. With a disconsolate face he wandered away, but his circle of friends in the neighbourhood was large, and he was soon provided with a partner.

Lord Iverbrook danced with Selena. He found it hard to take his eyes off her, but the figures of the dance sometimes separated them and during one such moment, glancing about the room, he noticed Bel. She was standing at the side of the room, talking to a pair of gentlemen who seemed to be old acquaintances.

The viscount groaned, eliciting a surprised look from the lady standing next to him. He had not enjoyed a ball so much for years and the wretched female had to come and spoil it for him. He made a silent vow that he would not ask her to dance, no matter what wiles she employed against him. His neighbour's elbow nudged him back into the dance, and he found himself promenading arm in arm with Selena.

"You are looking very fierce," she whispered.

"Am I? I am minding my steps, you see. It takes a deal of concentration, for I renounced country dances years ago!"

"Had you rather sit it out?"

"No; it would spoil the set. Besides, I think I am doing splendidly."

She laughed. "Unlike Clive, you have not yet stepped on my feet!" She gave him a slight push and skipped to the left, so he hurriedly skipped to the right.

Amabel did not approach him all evening. She danced only three times, once with Sir Aubrey, once with a stranger and once, Iverbrook was amused to note, with young Mr. Russell. Clive seemed very much *épris;* the typical callow youth with an older, experienced woman, he thought wryly. As the night advanced and she did not seek to speak to him, he relaxed his guard.

He took Selena to supper, and later stood up with her for a waltz. It was the first time, he confided, that he had found a partner tall enough to waltz with comfortably. As a result, he did not have to watch his steps but surrendered to the music and to her hazel eyes, and drifted round the floor in a dream.

Still dreaming, he gave her up to her next partner and sought out Lady Whitton.

"I am glad to see you, Hugh," she said. "I think we had best leave after this dance, for we have a long drive ahead of us. Do you not agree, Aubrey? That we must leave soon?"

The baronet, who came up just then, acquiesced. "As you w-wish, Aunt." His stutter seemed to be growing worse. "B-but I have been meaning to ch-challenge Lord Iverbrook to a hand at picquet. Will you p-play, my lord, before we go?"

Iverbrook had no desire whatever to play cards, but he was in an amiable mood. He followed Sir Aubrey into the card room, sat down, and watched benignly as the Bart made inept efforts to attract the attention of a waiter. At last Sir Aubrey stood up and went to fetch some cards.

He returned bearing a tray with a fresh pack and two glasses of brandy. While he shuffled, the viscount sipped at his glass. They settled the odds and began to play. Sir Aubrey proved as inept at picquet as he was at calling for service, and Iverbrook wondered why the devil he had issued the challenge if he meant to discard at random.

His lordship took the first rubber without difficulty. He took a swallow of his brandy and was about to suggest that they return to the ballroom to find the ladies when a wave of nausea swept through him.

Unsteadily he stood up. The room whirled about him and he sank insensible to the floor.

Two waiters rushed over, but Amabel was there before them. She laid her hand on his forehead and felt his pulse.

"Too much of your odious brandy!" she diagnosed. "He should not be moved far. Surely you have an unoccupied chamber here?"

The Blue Boar's landlord bustled in, tut-tutted, and directed the servants to carry the inert viscount above stairs. Sir Aubrey accompanied them into the lobby and watched as they carried him up, Amabel following and urging them to take care. Then he returned to the ballroom.

The dance was over and Lady Whitton had gathered her party together, Delia hotly protesting that it was too early to leave.

"Oh there you are at last, Aubrey," she said. "Who won your game? And where is Hugh? We are all ready to go."

"I do not think we should wait for Lord Iverbrook," said Sir Aubrey solemnly. "I saw him not five minutes ago going upstairs with Mrs. Amabel Parcott!"

=== 14 ===

LORD IVERBROOK DID not return to the Manor until midday on Sunday.

There was no one in the stables and the barouche was missing. He entered the house by the side door. Bannister emerged from his pantry to greet him frostily with the information that the family was at church.

"They'll be back soon, my lord," he added more kindly, noting the pallor of his lordship's face. "Oh, a letter came for you last night; brought by a special messenger, it was, my lord. Here, I'll get it."

He popped back into his room and returned with a sealed paper.

Iverbrook leaned against the wall, opened it, and read it. He closed his eyes for a moment and ground the heel of his hand into his temple, as though to still a throbbing headache.

"I have to go to London at once," he said harshly. "Where is Tom?"

"He went to church with Cook, my lord."

"I cannot wait. It is past noon already. I must write a word to Lady Whitton."

"There's paper in the library, my lord."

The viscount's note to his hostess was brief:

"My lady, I am called away urgently to London on legal business. I hope to return on Tuesday. You will not, I know, judge me without a hearing. Hugh."

He folded it, wrote her name on it and, after a moment's thought, took another sheet of paper.

"Hasty," he scribbled, "I know not what you saw or were told. I fell into a dead faint after drinking some brandy and when I came round it was morning and Mrs. P. was at my bedside. She said bad brandy but I suspect foul play. I must go to London to put a stop to this damnable suit against Miss W. Tell them what you see fit. I."

"L. Hastings, Esquire," he wrote on the outside, and left both letters on the desk.

Mr. Hastings was acutely uncomfortable. He had entered the Whitton household under the auspices of his friend. His friend was now in disgrace, a disgrace so deep as to be unmentionable. Mr. Hastings's lifelong *savoir faire* deserted him and he had no idea how to extricate himself from the situation. He went to church.

He returned from church none the wiser. The butler met the family at the door and handed him a letter. He retired to his chamber to peruse it, dismissing Dimbury who was waiting to rid his master's coat and boots of any speck of dust or lint inadvertently picked up during the morning's devotions.

The reading took a few seconds. It took him the better part of half an hour to decide what to do. He emerged from his chamber into a house as silent as a tomb and went in search of Lady Whitton.

Her ladyship was in her stillroom, not usual on the sabbath but the place to which she invariably escaped when troubled in spirit. Mr. Hastings had not previously penetrated this sanctum and he was startled to find his hostess enveloped in a stained apron, grinding something aromatic with her pestle and mortar in a way which suggested that she wished it was Iverbrook's bones.

"Ahem," said Mr. Hastings weakly.

She looked at him with uncharacteristic severity and went on grinding.

"Iverbrook's letter," he went on. "He said to tell you what I think fit." She put down her pestle and, regarding this as encouragement, he continued. "I've known Iverbrook forever, ma'am, and I've never known him run sly. He wouldn't have done it, I'd stake my last farthing on it. He seems to think he was drugged."

"Drugged?" Lady Whitton was intrigued.

"In the brandy. He didn't wake till morning, and the Merry Widow was there."

"The Merry Widow?"

"Mrs. Parcott. That's how she is known in town. She was Iverbrook's light-o'-love;" here Mr. Hastings paused, horrified to find that his unruly tongue had once again escaped his control. He rushed on. "But that's all over now, of course. At least, it is as far as he is concerned, but she is fishing for a wedding band and a title and it's my belief she's caught on he's in love with your daughter."

"Do you think so? I own I have suspected it."

Mr. Hastings was relieved to find his unintentional revelation met with such composure. Perhaps my lady had suspected that too. He hurried to reassure her about his friend's present feelings.

"Why, it's as plain as the nose on your face. Positively mooning over her, I'd say. So Mrs. P. wants to put a spike in his wheel and it looks as if she's succeeded!"

"He suspects her of drugging him? I wonder what she used. Though I find the whole story hard to credit, I confess."

Mr. Hastings drew himself up in superb indignation.

"Iverbrook," he stated flatly, "does not tell lies." He spoiled the effect by adding, "I'm not saying he don't have his faults, mind, but I would take his word against any gentleman in the land." He pondered. "Except my father. Have to take my father's word, you know."

"Of course. Thank you, Mr. Hastings, for being so frank with me. I shall have to consider what to tell Selena, for I cannot possibly reveal all that you have said. I think she had best await Hugh's story from his own lips, since we know so little. She has misjudged Hugh by jumping to conclusions before now, so perhaps this time she will give him the benefit of the doubt. Only it does look so very damning, his running off to London like this."

"He has done it for her!" Mr. Hastings placed his hand on his heart and declaimed, " 'I must go up to London to halt this devilish suit against Miss. W.' His very words, ma'am."

"I must suppose it was of the utmost urgency. He hopes to return on Tuesday, he says."

"On Tuesday? Then I have a suggestion to take Miss Whitton's mind off her griev . . . off her sorrows. I promised Miss Delia to get up an expedition to Abingdon Abbey so, if you do not object, we will go tomorrow. I do not think Hugh will regret missing the ruins."

"You mean to invite the Russells?"

"I suppose Delia will expect me to," sighed Mr. Hastings.

"Then you had best go and propose your outing at once, or it will be too late to warn them. In fact, I think it an excellent scheme, and I will come with you to support you. They are all in the drawing room, I believe."

Delia greeted the scheme with delight, Sir Aubrey with a return of his extraordinary nervousness, and Selena with a listless refusal that she changed to a reluctant acceptance on meeting her mother's eye.

Mr. Hastings penned a polite note to the Russells in which he begged the pleasure of their company on the morrow. Sir Aubrey, expressing a desire for exercise, offered to carry it down to the stables for Jem to take to Bracketts.

"I should not call the walk to the stables exercise," said Delia scornfully, as soon as he shut the door behind him.

Judging by the excessive length of time that passed before the baronet returned, the distance was more than sufficient for him. Jem also was unusually dilatory, taking more than two hours to run the errand, but when they read Clive's reply to the invitation Delia thought she knew the reason.

"Jane's mama will not let her go!" she said in disappointment. "I expect Jem had to wait while they tried to persuade Lady Anne. I am glad that you are not such a fussbudget, Mama!"

As always when Lady Anne disapproved, Lady Whitton had qualms. After due consideration, however, she could see no harm in a party of young people lunching at a respectable hostelry and exploring ancient ruins. Though "fussbudget" was not precisely the phrase she would have chosen, Lady Anne Russell was undoubtedly a high stickler.

Clive was expected at eleven the following morning, but the half hour passed and there was no sign of him, nor had Sir Aubrey yet put in an appearance. Mr. Hastings requested Lady Whitton's permission to go ahead in the barouche in order to arrange their luncheon.

"I had forgot that it is market day," he pointed out. "The inns will be busy and I would not have my guests forced to wait, or worse, ill fed."

Delia insisted on going with him, "to be sure he orders good things to eat."

Mr. Hastings drove off with every intention of demonstrating his prowess as a first-rate whip.

When Clive arrived at last, it was plain to Selena that he was far from happy to find that half the party, or rather that particular half of the party, had already departed. He seemed to be in two minds whether it would be preferable to follow as fast as possible or to abandon the expedition, but he was by far too polite to suggest the latter course. Selena herself had no wish to go, though a long talk with her mother had left her feeling less despairing. However, she could not disappoint her sister and Mr. Hastings, and Sir Aubrey was anxious to go. They set out at noon and were soon enjoying a delectable repast in the coffee room of the Crown and Thistle.

Clive devoted himself to entertaining Selena, glancing now and then at Delia to see if she was aware of his defection. If she was, she gave no sign of it. She and Mr. Hastings were discussing the romances they had read in which sinister abbeys, ruined or otherwise, played a part. Neither Clive nor Selena had even heard of most of the titles they mentioned, and Sir Aubrey did not attempt to join in either conversation. He seemed to be trying to watch the door of the coffee room, no easy task as he was sitting with his back to it.

It was after two by the time Mr. Hastings called for the reckoning. While he paid the shot, the ladies donned their pelisses, bonnets, and gloves, for though sunny the day was distinctly chilly.

As they left the inn, they came face to face with Mrs. Parcott. Selena paled and nearly turned her back, then remembering what her mother had said about misunderstandings and premature judgments she nodded frigidly.

Mrs. Parcott was not in the least dismayed.

"What a charming surprise!" she cried gaily. "Are you walking down to the river? I will go with you, I vow, for I have finished my errands in the town and I cannot leave for some hours yet."

Sir Aubrey was clearly delighted to see her; Clive was torn between disapproval and admiration; the others found it impossible to tell her outright that she was not welcome; so she accompanied them to the abbey.

They quickly discovered that the ruins were far more extensive than was visible from the road, stretching along the river bank for several hundred yards in various stages of dilapidation. Delia bemoaned the sunshine. A storm, she said, or a thick fog would provide a far more mysterious atmosphere. She and Mr. Hastings wandered off, deep in their literary discussion.

Clive watched them go, then turned and offered his arm to Mrs. Parcott. Selena declined to take Sir Aubrey's arm.

"I prefer to trust to my own feet," she said coldly, wishing with fervour that she had not come.

They strolled across the grass, among tumbledown walls. Clive, who had been there before, explained that the stones nearest the bridge had been used for building elsewhere in the town after Henry VIII's dissolution of the monasteries. He pointed out the area where the chapel had supposedly stood, and told a story of a young monk who, having been reprimanded for missing matins, had killed himself at the altar and whose ghost was said to haunt the place.

"Naughty boy!" exclaimed Amabel with a giggle. "I shall never be able to pass by at night without a shiver."

"Come and see the monks' cells," he said. "They were in here, right on the river. They were tiny, and must have been fearfully cold and damp."

They followed him into a building which seemed once to have had an upper story, of which little remained. The ground floor was in comparatively good condition, though well lit by holes in the ceiling. There was a wide, stone-flagged corridor running parallel to the river, with evenly spaced doorways along each side. In several places the remains of heavy oak doors still hung.

They picked their way around fallen beams, black with age, some of them leaning against the walls in a most precarious fashion.

"I wonder why the doors opened outwards," said Selena, puzzled. "The monks must have all left their cells at once to proceed to services, and the doors would have blocked the corridors."

"I told you the cells are tiny," Clive reminded. "There would have been no room at all for furniture if they had opened inwards."

"Let us go into one with a door and close it," suggested Amabel. "Then we will see how it felt to be a monk."

"This door is very well preserved." Clive paused in a doorway. "I wonder if it will move." He pushed on it. The rusted iron hinges creaked but the door moved quite easily. He went in.

Selena went after him, but Amabel hung back and spoke softly to Sir Aubrey. Then she said aloud, "La, it makes me quite nervous. I suppose there are no skeletons in there?" She and Sir Aubrey joined the others inside.

The cell was crowded with four people in it. While Clive pulled the door shut, Selena and Sir Aubrey stood by the small high window. Sir Aubrey peered out, and remarked that the wall rose directly from the river, eight or ten feet below.

The ceiling of the closetlike room was unbroken, so with the door closed they were plunged into a dim twilight. Mrs. Parcott emitted a ladylike shriek and clutched at Clive's arm.

"Let me out of here," she moaned. "Open the door, quickly!"

Before it was half open she slipped out, pulling Clive after her. Selena would gladly have followed, but Sir Aubrey had embarked on an endless, stammering disquisition in which medieval building methods and religious liberty figured largely. He seemed to be equally uninformed on both subjects. When she stepped towards the doorway he said, "D-do you not agree, Cousin?" so she turned back and murmured in agreement, though far from sure what he had asked.

Pretending to listen, she leaned against the cold stone wall, gazed out at the river, and thought her own thoughts.

What was Iverbrook doing in London? He had left so suddenly, with no effort to explain. What had happened in Oxford on Saturday night? Mama said all was not as it seemed; she must not jump to conclusions but wait to hear what he had to tell. Which was all very well, only after Cousin Aubrey's announcement at the ball, it was difficult to imagine how Iverbrook could vindicate his disappearance.

Cousin Aubrey's announcement: she looked at him in sudden suspicion. If it were not for that, they might have gone in search of the viscount. Until that moment it had been a wonderful evening. Hugh had been charming, amusing, attentive. When they were apart she had felt his eyes on her, had believed that he longed to be at her side. Then Cousin Aubrey's voice shattered her dream.

Cousin Aubrey's voice was abruptly cut off as the door crashed shut. A loud thud followed, the heavy sound of wood striking wood. The monk's cell suddenly seemed to shrink.

Selena reached the door in two strides and pushed, then threw her weight against it. It did not move.

Nor did Sir Aubrey.

"Come and help me!" she demanded.

He joined her and half-heartedly leaned against the solid wood, to no result.

"It's stuck," he said inanely. "The wind must have b-blown it."

"It's not windy."

"I expect a beam f-fell against it. The ceiling is quite rotten in p-places."

She looked up. "Not in here," she noted, then shouted, "Clive, help!" No answer. "Clive! Mr. Hastings! Help, somebody!"

The dank stone absorbed the sound, giving in return only the gurgle of water outside and the distant quacking of ducks.

Selena went to the window. The thickness of the wall made it hard to see out except straight ahead, where only the wide, green-brown river and the far bank with its towpath were visible. Standing on tiptoe she could see further. It was not easy, for the opening was small. Too small, she thought, to squeeze through, even if the river did not wash the base of the wall, just as her cousin had described it.

Downstream the river divided, to flow on each side of a small island. One pier of the bridge rested on this island, and a tavern stood there, the Nag's Head, the upper story of which opened directly onto the bridge. It blocked Selena's view of the far end of the bridge, but she could see the near end. The current sped slickly under the arches with a violent swirl. Above, she could see a cart, a horseman, and two people on foot.

"Help!" she cried; none of them looked around, or even paused. "They are too far off. If we keep shouting, Clive and Mrs. Parcott, or Delia and Mr. Hastings, are bound to come. Even if they do not hear us, they will look for us when they are ready to leave. What an excessively ridiculous situation to be in!"

It was not only ridiculous, it was tedious. Sir Aubrey had no conversation beyond mere commonplaces, and she could not listen to his lecturing with any show of complaisance. Alternately pacing up and down, four steps one way and four steps back, or huddling in a corner, she shouted from time to time. No one answered.

The afternoon passed and dusk brought swift darkness to the gloomy cell. As Selena grew more and more anxious, the baronet became calmer, lost his stutter, and began to look smug.

The last gleam of evening light faded from the river. Selena leaned by the window, looking into blackness, listening to the water lapping at the rough stones of the wall, the sound of voices floating across the river from the Nag's Head.

She heard Sir Aubrey moving, and suddenly he was beside her, breathing heavily.

"No one will come now." His voice was triumphant. "We will have to spend the night here, alone together!" He put his arm around her waist.

She pulled away. "Don't touch me!" she snarled. "If you come near me again I shall scratch your face!" It was a pitiable threat, but remembering his vanity she hoped that it might suffice.

"You will sing a different tune in the morning, Cousin. Your reputation will be ruined unless you marry me."

"Believe me," said Selena with calm deliberation, though her heart was beating wildly, "I should not marry you if my life depended upon it! I had rather live in the utmost disgrace than have you for a husband."

"We shall see." Sir Aubrey sounded sulky.

"Did you plan this? Did you arrange beforehand to shut us in here?"

"I've never been here before. How should I plan it? Besides, I could not shut the door from inside."

"I suppose not." Selena, though unconvinced, asked no more questions, turning her mind to the more important business of finding a way out. She had been so sure they would be rescued that she had not seriously considered the possibilities before. But despite her bravado, she was afraid that if she was indeed forced to spend the night with her despicable cousin, she would have little choice but to give him her hand in marriage.

There was no hope of opening the door. Sir Aubrey had not exerted himself to help her before and would not do so now. The window was the only chance of escape.

If she took off her pelisse, perhaps she might wriggle through and drop into the river. Her dress would weigh her down; that must come off too. There was no way to tell how deep the water was. She could wade downstream past the building and climb ashore, but if it was too deep to stand, swimming in that direction would put her perilously close to the bridge with its rushing, swirling currents.

She peered out into the darkness. The island stood out, a blacker black on the starlit river. Lamplight gleamed through a crack in the tavern's shutters, illuminating the bridge's parapet. A sudden memory came to her: on the other side of the tavern, steps led down from the road to the island—she had seen them a hundred times.

Swim straight out to mid-channel (thank heaven Papa had made her learn to swim!); drift with the stream to the island; run across the bridge to the towpath on the other bank; then the long, slow, probably painful, barefooted trudge home in her shift.

Anything was better than marrying Cousin Aubrey!

The moon had been nearly full on Saturday. Selena was not sure when it would rise but it would make things so much easier that she decided to wait.

Huddled in a corner, she felt unbearably imprisoned, so mostly she stood at the window in spite of the cold draught. Aubrey had fallen silent some time ago, sulking no doubt, but now he began a monologue detailing exactly what he would do with her money once they were wed. Selena tried not to listen.

At last the sky paled in the east. She returned to her corner and started to strip, praying that Aubrey would not guess what she was doing, that she could climb through the window quickly enough not to give him a chance to stop her. She bundled her clothes together, shivering as the clammy air caressed her skin.

In one smooth motion she reached the window, threw the bundle out, and pulled herself up.

The baronet shouted. She kicked out, knocking him backwards and propelling herself forwards, twisting and scraping. She hit the river full length, impact and icy chill driving the breath from her body.

Desperately, gasping, she swam, fighting the current, the cold, the fear that whispered, "You'll never make it. He'll come after you. You'll drown under the bridge. What a fool, what a fool, what a fool!"

There was mud under her feet. She clawed her way onto the bank, pushed through tangled bushes, saw the Nag's Head rising on her right. She had made it! A few staggering steps more and she saw in the moonlight the stone stairs built into the side of the bridge.

Seconds later she crouched in the shadows on the landing at the top of the steps and looked out onto the bridge. A rush torch burned in an iron holder over the inn's sign and the door stood open. Several men stood there, arguing, then some went in while two of them, a tipsy woman between them, passed her crossing the bridge away from the town.

"Time to go home, Dolly," said one soothingly.

Selena could not have agreed more, but another rowdy group was approaching from the Abingdon side. The slovenly woman, growing pugnacious, stopped her companions half way across the span. Selena shivered and tried to stop her teeth chattering.

The Nag's Head seemed to be the most popular hostelry in Abingdon. Farm hands, unruly apprentices, stolid bargees, and loud-voiced drovers came and went, laughing and quarrelling. One or two dark-faced gypsies slipped by, the gold rings in their ears glinting. The moon sailed in a clear sky, lighting the bridge as brightly as any newfangled gas lamp.

Selena crouched miserably in the corner of the parapet. She was chilled to the bone, but she had rather die of cold than show herself in her torn shift to the boisterous patrons of the Nag's Head!

— 15 —

As THE MOON rose on Monday evening, Lord Iverbrook reached Milford Manor. He entered the drawing room with considerable trepidation, feeling very unsure of his welcome.

"Hugh, dear, I'm so glad you are come!" exclaimed Lady Whitton. "We are in quite a worry."

"Is Peter ill again?"

"No, it's Selena," Delia put in. "At least, she is not ill, but she and Cousin Aubrey are not yet come home."

His lordship frowned at the clock. "They went out together? Where did they go, and when?"

Mr. Hastings explained about the outing to Abingdon and the luncheon at the Crown and Thistle. "And now I come to think of it," he added, "the fellow was acting very odd."

"Yes, he kept looking round at the door, and he was stammering terribly," agreed Delia.

"We were just leaving the inn when we ran into Mrs. P. Yes, yes, I know, my dear fellow, and maybe you could have got rid of her, though I have my doubts, but being a gentleman I did not tell her to go jump in the Thames! At all events, we went on to the abbey ruins and Miss Delia and I got to talking and before we knew very well what we were about, we were half way to Oxford and the others nowhere in sight. There's no need to look at me like that," Hasty added defensively. "Literary discussion, you know, mad monks and such."

"So you turned back?" asked the viscount impatiently.

"Well of course we did. No sense in walking to Oxford, was there? It was nearly five by the time we reached the abbey again, and no sign of Miss Whitton or the others. When we got to the Crown, Mr. Russell's carriage was gone so naturally we assumed he had driven them home."

"So we came home," said Delia, "and Selena and Cousin Aubrey were not here and if the carriage had broken down we would have passed them on the way and Mama said she expected they had gone in to see the Russells. And maybe they did, but I cannot see why they would have stayed so long, for Jane is not Selena's particular friend and Lady Anne disapproves of Selena amazingly."

"We must send to Bracketts and see if she is there." Iverbrook strode to the bellpull and jerked on it.

"Do you think some harm has come to Selena?" asked Lady Whitton anxiously. "Surely not, with both Clive and Aubrey to look after her, not that she has ever needed looking after."

Delia was thoughtful. "Remember," she said slowly, "when Jem went with the invitation to Bracketts, what a long time he took? And it took Cousin Aubrey forever, just to go down to the stables to give him his orders. And when we went to the ball, they were talking together before we left, so that I thought we should never get going. It's a plot!"

Mr. Hastings and Lord Iverbrook stared at her.

"Delia, you must stop reading so many romances," protested her mother as Bannister came in.

"Send Tom to me," ordered the viscount, "and I think we had best see Jem as well." He turned to Lady Whitton.

"If you will," she said helplessly, "though I am sure you refine too much upon trifles."

His lordship paced up and down the room, looking grim. "You have not yet heard the full story of what happened to me at the ball," he said, "and this is not the moment for it, but I am inclined to believe that Amabel and Sir Aubrey are on better terms with each other than we know. They have at least a common motive, in preventing a marriage between me and Selena. How well they have succeeded in turning her against me I cannot tell; I fear there is something more sinister afoot tonight."

Lady Whitton and Mr. Hastings exchanged a glance of understanding. Delia gazed at the viscount in astonishment.

"You and Selena marry? But you are always quarrelling!"

Iverbrook flushed.

"No need to explain," said Mr. Hastings hurriedly. "What sort of mischief did you have in mind?"

Before the viscount could answer, there was a knock on the door; Tom Arbuckle and Jem entered.

Tom received orders to ride to Bracketts and left at once.

"You wanted to see me, my lady?" asked the groom.

"Lord Iverbrook wishes to ask you some questions, Jem. I am sure you have done nothing wrong."

"You went to Bracketts with a message, or a letter, yesterday," said Iverbrook. "Why did it take you so long?"

"There were t'other letter too, my lord. 'Tis a fair way to Cowley and back."

"To Cowley! Sir Aubrey sent you there?"

"He give me the letters, my lord. One to young Mr. Russell, to wait for an answer, and t'other to Mrs. Parcott, no answer expected. So I leaves the one at Bracketts and calls for an answer on me way home."

"Did not you think that strange?"

Jem looked puzzled. "What, my lord?"

"Never mind. What about Saturday evening? Sir Aubrey ordered you to fetch Mrs. Parcott on the way to Oxford?"

"Yes, my lord. He said he were afeared my lady and Miss Whitton might of forgot, what with the excitement of the dance and all. They did, too. Begging your pardon, my lady. I weren't too sure of the way, but the Bart, I mean Sir Aubrey, give me directions and I found the place all right and tight."

"And you did not guess that Lady Whitton might not know of the plan to pick up Mrs. Parcott?"

"No, my lord! I knows she's a friend o' theirn acos she keeps coming by. I ain't done aught to harm Miss Whitton?"

"I hope not, Jem. In any case, you are plainly not to blame. You may go now, but have my horses ready to put to the curricle at a moment's notice."

"Yes, my lord." The groom looked at his mistress. "My lady, I wou'n't do nowt to harm Miss Selena!"

"I know, Jem. I trust you absolutely. Now go and do as his lordship ordered." Lady Whitton turned to Iverbrook. "Hugh, I cannot believe that Aubrey acted with malice, any more than Jem did. His understanding is not superior. He surely meant only to give Amabel pleasure by inviting her to join us."

"Possibly, though I think it unlikely. You are too charitable, ma'am! How, pray, do you propose to exculpate Amabel?"

Her ladyship sighed. "Perhaps Lady Anne was right and I ought not to have welcomed Amabel. But how could I guess?"

"Guess what, Mama?" queried Delia.

Iverbrook had the grace to colour and ponder momentarily the unfairness that excluded his mistress, but not him, from polite society. Lady Whitton looked flustered. Mr. Hastings stepped into the breach.

"Never you mind, young lady," he said, conveniently forgetting that it was he who had revealed to her mother the relationship between the viscount and the Merry Widow. "Hugh, what do you mean to do now?"

"Nothing, I suppose, until we hear from the Russells." He resumed his pacing, with increased energy. "If that loose fish has harmed a hair of her head, I shall horsewhip him!"

"No, no, I say, my dear fellow, can't do that! Fellow's a gentleman. Have to call him out."

"Gentleman!" snorted his lordship. "If the Bart is a gentleman, then I am a dandy!"

Mr. Hastings took one look at his friend's ruffled hair, loosened neckcloth, and dusty boots, and conceded the point.

Lady Whitton, striving for calm, discovered that Hugh had not dined; she sent for refreshments. He was methodically disposing of a plate of cold beef and plum tart when young Mr. Russell burst into the room.

"My lord, your servant says Miss Whitton did not come home with Delia! I'd never have left had I guessed . . . had I not supposed . . . I beg your pardon, ma'am, but I hold myself to blame." He looked wretched.

"Oh fustian, Clive!" said Delia firmly. "Of course you supposed that Selena would go with us, and when we found you gone we supposed she had gone with you."

"I should have left a message at the Crown."

"It might have helped," said Lord Iverbrook, abandoning his meal. "The best thing you can do now is to tell us exactly what happened at the abbey."

Clive flushed to the roots of his hair and studied his boots. "Dee went off with Mr. Hastings," he said in a low voice, "and I was telling the others a bit about the place. Ghost stories and such. We went into the building where the monks lived and . . . and Mrs. Parcott wanted to see what it was like to be shut up in a cell. We went into one—all of us went in—that had an undamaged door. Most of them are rotted away, you know. And I closed the door and she was frightened—Mrs. Parcott, that is. It was sort of murky in there, with just a tiny hole in the wall for light. So I opened the door again and she rushed out. She was holding onto my sleeve and she pulled me with her. Miss Whitton and Sir Aubrey stayed in the cell, talking."

"Selena *never* talked to Cousin Aubrey," Delia said with conviction.

"Are you calling me a liar, Dee?" demanded Clive belligerently.

"I expect she was listening politely to one of his discourses," soothed Lady Whitton.

"Pretending to listen!" said Delia.

"Go on, Mr. Russell," said Lord Iverbrook. "This grows interesting."

"Anyway, they did not go with us. We went back along the corridor a little way and then Mrs. Parcott tripped. There was all sorts of debris on the floor. She hurt her ankle quite badly. Or so she said," he frowned, "for later she had no limp, now I come to think of it."

The viscount stood up, as if inaction was more than he could bear. Clive looked at him in alarm and he sat down again.

"Go on."

"She begged me to fetch my carriage and drive as close as I could. She was to meet the person who had brought her to Abingdon at the Crown, but could not walk so far. So I left her seated on a fallen beam and went to get the carriage. When I returned I helped her to the carriage, and then it seemed silly just to take her to the Crown, so I drove her home. She invited me in," Clive's face was scarlet again, his eyes on his feet, "for refreshments. When I left, it was nearly dark and it seemed pointless to go back to the abbey. I was sure everyone must have left. So I went home."

"Thank you," said his lordship, wondering just what form Amabel's gratitude had taken. He stood up again. "Unless anyone has other suggestions, I believe we can assume Selena is still at the abbey. I shall go and fetch her."

"I'll come with you!" offered Delia, Clive, and Mr. Hastings all at once.

"I think not." Iverbrook smiled at Lady Whitton. "I shall bring her home safe, ma'am, never fear."

"Dear Hugh, I'm sure you will," she said simply.

Jem was just as determined to go with the viscount.

"If the Bart's hurt Miss Selena, I'll help you give him a taste o' home-brewed!" he suggested.

"Thank you, Jem, but you may rest assured that if the baronet stands in need of a dusting, I shall administer it."

"His lordship peels to advantage," said Tom Arbuckle drily. "He won't need no help to darken the Bart's daylights."

"Handy with your fives, eh, my lord?" The groom looked over his tall, rangy form with a knowledgeable eye. "Good reach, I'd say."

"And good science, and all the will in the world. Spring 'em!"

Jem stood away from the horse's heads and his lordship took them out of the stableyard at a rattling pace. Not since the day he had found Peter had he driven down the drive in such haste, but then he had been in a fury, distracted. This time he was coldly collected, in control, aware of every moon-shadow that might force him to slacken his speed. The curricle swung into the lane and he let the greys have their heads. They had done one stage already today but they were once again the prime cattle he remembered. They flew towards Abingdon.

Selena knew that if she did not move soon, she would not be able to move at all. She trembled constantly and the numbness that had started in her toes was creeping up to her knees.

The torch over the Nag's Head sign had guttered out some time ago. A merry couple went into the tavern and closed the door behind them. There was no one on the bridge, only the moonlight to give her away.

She pulled herself painfully to her feet and staggered out onto the bridge. One hand on the parapet, she had taken several faltering steps when, with a ring of hooves on paving, a carriage appeared out of the darkness and started towards her.

It was moving fast. Perhaps the driver would not see her. She cowered against the wall, lost her balance, and fell full length in the roadway.

With an oath from the driver, the horses pulled up inches from her head. He jumped down and strode towards her. She tried to move, managed to rise to her knees, and faced him, holding her torn shift together with shaking hands.

"Selena!" Iverbrook dropped to his knees and hugged her to him. "My darling, I thought you were a ghost! Ye gods, you are cold enough to be one, and wet through!"

He picked her up, his strong arms holding her close. She tried to speak; numb lips and chattering teeth would not obey her.

"Hush, my love. You shall tell me later." He bent his head and kissed her, and she discovered her lips were not as numb as she had thought. He lifted her into the carriage and climbed up beside her. "First we must dry you, and I cannot take you to an inn for in your present condition the damage to your reputation would be beyond all repairing. You will have to take off your wet, uh, garment." He pulled a fur rug from under the seat and held it so as to shield her from anyone coming out of the tavern.

"Close your eyes," she whispered, and when he did, she struggled out of her shift. Reaching to take the rug from him, she touched his fingers and he opened his eyes. He caught a glimpse of her slim, pale body gleaming in the moonlight and quickly closed them again.

Eyes screwed shut, he helped her pull the rug around her. His hand brushed her naked breast. She shivered, not, this time, from cold.

The horses moved restlessly. Quickly Selena arranged the rug to cover her toes yet provide maximum decency. Already she felt much warmer.

"Ready," she said.

Iverbrook took one look at her bare shoulders and stripped off his many-caped driving coat. As he draped it about her, somehow their lips met and he held her for a long moment, until the jingling of the horses' bits reminded him of where they were. His left arm still around her, he picked up the reins in his right hand and urged the greys on.

He turned the curricle in the deserted marketplace, needing both hands for the job, and they drove back across the bridge in silence. How beautiful the Thames looked under the moon! A faint mist rose from its glimmering surface and a swan floated downstream in proud solitude.

Selena cleared her throat.

"How did your business go in London," she asked.

They were on the pike road, and the viscount could have spared an arm for his companion. Somehow, he felt, it would have been taking advantage of her dependence on him.

"Very well," he answered. "I had to sign some papers for my lawyer before ten o'clock this morning, in order to put a final end to that wretched lawsuit."

"Peter?"

"Yes."

"Oh." A pause. "Mama did not expect you back until tomorrow."

"I could not stay away, knowing that you thought . . . not knowing what you thought! Selena, what has your mother told you, or Hasty, about Saturday night?"

"Only that you are not, perhaps, the villain that you seemed, and that I must hear the tale from you."

"I seemed a villain to you?"

"What could I suppose when Cousin Aubrey announced that he had seen you going upstairs with Amabel!"

"He did not, I feel sure, explain that I was unconscious at the time."

"Unconscious! Oh Hugh!"

"Drugged. After what has happened today, I would wager half my fortune on it."

Ignored, the horses slowed to a walk as he told what he had learned of Amabel's and Aubrey's actions over the past few days. She reciprocated with the story of her escape from the abbey, which led to many expressions of admiration and the return of his arm to her waist. Selena leaned against him.

"I know that Aubrey wants to marry me," she said in puzzlement, "but why should Amabel wish to help him?"

Iverbrook was glad she could not see his flushed face. "If he marries you," he pointed out, "then I cannot. And she has been setting her cap at me for years."

Selena was silent and straightened a little in her seat, but did not remove his arm. Emboldened, he continued.

"You may remember that I once asked you to marry me?"

It was her turn to blush.

"I was not listening at the time," she confessed, "but afterwards, when I thought back, I knew you had."

"Your response did not precisely encourage me to try my luck again. However, fool that I am, I cannot help myself! Selena, there is nothing I

138

want more in this world than to have you for my wife. Will you marry me?"

She did not answer for a moment, then said with difficulty, "You are not asking me because of tonight? Because you feel you ought to?"

"No!" The explosive violence of his reply startled the horses into a trot. For a moment he was occupied with the reins, slowing them one-handed to a walking pace again. Selena had stopped shivering and he was in no hurry to return her to her family. "No," he said again, in calmer tones, "and I hope, indeed I know, that you have too much strength of mind to allow such considerations to influence your decision. I should be no better than Sir Aubrey were I to take advantage of you in such a way. No one need ever know in what condition I found you."

She giggled. "Except Bannister. You will never succeed in smuggling me past his watchful eye. And Polly will wonder what has become of my gown, not to mention my pelisse and my shoes and my hat and my gloves!"

"You did not leave your clothes with your cousin!"

"No, I threw them into the river. I thought they would compromise me as thoroughly as my presence."

"Clever girl! Now, with that problem out of the way, how about an answer?"

She turned and, promptly forgetting her state of undress, flung her arms about his neck. "Oh yes, Hugh, I will marry you. And I promise never to suspect you unjustly again!"

"No promises you can't keep!" he mumbled into her hair, returning her embrace with fervour. Then he came to his senses and wrapped her up again in rug and coat. "You will get cold again," he said severely.

"If I catch an inflammation of the lungs, will you nurse me?"

"Willingly, my love, but I suspect your mama might have something to say about that. Do you feel unwell?"

"Not in the least. I have never felt better. Hugh, do you know the story of Artemis and Actaeon?"

"Was he not the one who saw her swimming naked, and she was so angry she turned him into a stag? He was torn to pieces by his own hounds. You do not mean to turn me into a stag, I trust?"

"No." She turned and kissed his cheek. "It would be such a waste. Do you know about Endymion too?"

"That is not the sort of tale I should tell to a gently bred female!"

"That is what Papa always said. But now we are betrothed, could you not tell me?"

He looked down at her. Even by moonlight he read the mischief in her face, and she heard the laughter in his voice as he answered.

"Minx! Very well. I obey the moon goddess, but only because it will bring such a blush to your face as will stop you feeling the cold. To begin with, the situation was reversed. Endymion was sleeping naked on a mountain . . . "

"That makes me feel colder!"

"Come closer then, and don't interrupt."

"I can't get any closer."

"As I was saying, Endymion was asleep and Artemis—or shall I call her Selene?—saw him and fell in love with his beautiful form. She, uh, visited him in his sleep and he enjoyed the visit so much that he prayed to his father, Zeus (who, I'm sorry to say, was her father too), to give him eternal youth and eternal sleep so that he could go on dreaming. Selene—oh very well, Artemis—bore him fifty daughters, and for all we know still visits him regularly. Now, are you hot all over?"

"Warmer," she admitted. "What shocking morals the ancients had!"

The sound of the carriage crunching up the gravel drive brought the family to the doorstep and the entire staff of the Manor to the front hall.

"So much for smuggling you in unseen," grunted Lord Iverbrook, carrying Selena up the steps as Tom ran to lead the horses away.

"Never mind," she said blithely. "Mama, I am to marry Hugh!"

"How delightful, dearest," said Lady Whitton. "I knew he would bring you back safely. But where is Aubrey?"

The viscount looked at her blankly, and then a broad grin spread across his face.

"Do you know," he said, "I had quite forgot him. Poor Aubrey is going to have to spend the night all alone in a monk's cell at the haunted abbey!"

— 16 —

EARLY THE NEXT morning, Lord Iverbrook and Mr. Hastings set off for Abingdon in the barouche. Jem was driving, "it being my lady's carriage," and Tom kept him company on the box in case another pair of strong arms was needed to release Sir Aubrey from his prison.

Both Selena and Delia had expressed a desire to be present, only to have the suggestion grimly vetoed by the viscount.

"Hugh, you will not come to blows with him!" Lady Whitton said anxiously. "To be sure, he behaved very shabbily in trying to take advantage of Selena's situation, but there is no proof that he had a hand in planning it."

She had to be content with his assurance that he would take her point of view under consideration.

Clouds had blown in from the west overnight, and when they reached Abingdon Bridge a light rain was falling. Mr. Hastings turned up his collar and remarked that it was ill weather for rescuing rogues.

"Hush," said his lordship. "What's that noise?"

Across the water came a confused babble of voices. As Jem drew the horses to a standstill, Tom stood up precariously on the box and gazed at the far side of the river.

"There's a whole fleet of boats over there, m'lord," he said. "Over by that wall. We c'd likely see more a bit further on."

Jem drove on past the Nag's Head and stopped just before the end of the bridge. Lord Iverbrook and Mr. Hastings both rose to their feet and looked up-river.

Nine or ten small boats had gathered near the wall. Boys in skiffs and dinghies were laughing and jeering, while two men in a fishing dory shouted advice and encouragement, judging by the sound of their voices. The source of the excitement was a pale blob, high on the wall.

The viscount's eyes gleamed with unholy joy.

"Jem, can you row?" he demanded.

"Aye, my lord. I've lived by the river all me life."

"Find us a boat. Hasty, we are going for a short cruise."

Mr. Hastings looked down at his spotless fawn unmentionables, sighed, and agreed that if things were as they appeared to be, he would not miss the sight for the world.

They were not mistaken.

The crowd fell silent at their approach. "Why, Sir Aubrey, what a pleasure to see you here!" said Lord Iverbrook.

The baronet was not his usual striking self. His yellow hair hung in lank locks, dripping rainwater into the river below. The sleeves of his cerise coat were torn and begrimed. Beyond that they could not see, for only his head and arms protruded from the wall. He groaned and grimaced.

"Very bad *ton*," said Mr. Hastings disapprovingly. "Not at all the thing to make yourself a bobbing-block for the local citizens."

"Get me out of here!" Sir Aubrey croaked in desperation.

"Usn tried to reach him wi' the boathook," reported one of the men in the dory. "But he can't hardly move his arms and we was afeard to snag his coat case of hurting him."

"How long has he been here?" asked the viscount, trying with poor success to hide his grin. Apparently none of these bumpkins had thought to attempt a rescue from the gentleman's nether end.

"Dunno," answered one of the boys. "Usn come down at dawn to fish offn the island and there he were, like a cork in a bottle."

"Stuck tighter'n a penny in a miser's pocket," confirmed one of his mates.

"Hafta take the wall down," opined another, a witticism greeted with general laughter.

"Have none of you business elsewhere?" asked Lord Iverbrook. "I intend to go round into the abbey to see what can be done there to release this unfortunate. Should it prove necessary to eject him in this direction, will you remain here to haul him out?"

"Aye, sir," said the man, "us'll stay, for 'tis too late in the day to do any other sort o' fishing."

Jem turned their commandeered skiff and headed back to the jetty below the bridge.

" 'Tis my belief, my lord," he said, "as 'twill be a sight easier to push the Bart out nor it will to pull him in."

His lordship laughed. "Do you know, Jem, I'm inclined to agree with you!"

Tom had taken the carriage to the Crown and Thistle and he met them on the bridge. The four men sauntered into the abbey grounds, in no hurry to put an end to the baronet's captivity. They found the door of his cell without difficulty.

A long beam from the ruined roof, not thick but less decayed than most, was wedged across the corridor, from a point about a third of the way up the door to the angle of floor and wall on the opposite side.

"Very clever, m'lord," said Tom admiringly. "Could almost have happened by accident, like. If 'twas leaning 'gainst the wall here, wouldn't have took but a shove and a moment to put in its place."

"'Tain't too heavy, neither," Jem pointed out, freeing it with a jerk and laying it aside.

"But immovable from inside," said Iverbrook. "An effective piece of work indeed."

Tom swung the door open.

"Hinges oiled," he said, peering at them. "After you, m'lord."

The cell, its window blocked, was murky and it took the viscount's eyes several moments to adjust. He shivered in the damp, cold air and tried to imagine Selena trapped in here alone with her cousin, shouting for help as the light faded. No wonder the river had seemed an acceptable alternative! Sir Aubrey's plight no longer seemed a joke but an inadequate retribution.

He regained his sense of humour with his sight. The baronet dangled from the waist, most of his upper body stuck within the width of the wall. His nether garments had split open in his struggles. Less farsighted than Selena, he had kept on his boots as well as his coat, and their toes hung scant inches from the stone-paved floor.

Iverbrook waved Tom and Jem forward.

"Give it a try," he said, "but don't pull too hard or you might hurt him. Lady Whitton urged me not to inflict any damage."

A glance of complicity passed between the erstwhile rivals. They advanced on Sir Aubrey, grasped the heels of his boots, and with the utmost delicacy pulled them off.

"Tut!" said Mr. Hastings. "You ought always to wear gloves when removing a gentleman's boots."

"I fear that did not work," Iverbrook grinned. "I had best warn the Bart that he is going for a swim." He moved closer to the window and called, "Sir Aubrey! Our attempt to pull you back has failed. Hold your breath!"

Without further ado, the servants lifted his legs till his body was parallel to the floor and pushed with all their strength. Sir Aubrey, screeching, disappeared.

The splash was followed by a clamour of voices offering conflicting advice. Lord Iverbrook did not look out, but listened in silence for a few moments with the look on his face of a man who has just won a fortune at cards. Then he sighed and put his hand in his pocket.

"Thank you!" he said, handing Tom and Jem a guinea each. "A magnificent job! I suppose Lady Whitton expects us to take him back to the Manor with us. I only wish I had brought Selena after all!"

On her mother's orders, Selena breakfasted in bed. She ate heartily, having missed her dinner last night in all the excitement. Several muffins with marmalade, four thick rashers of bacon, and a whole pot of tea disappeared before she pushed the tray aside and rang the bell. She lay back, luxuriating in the warmth and comfort, and hoping Hugh would be back soon.

Polly came in, red-eyed, her usually merry face sombre. She removed the tray from the bed, set it by the door, and laid out Selena's best lilac silk morning gown.

"Shall I help you dress, miss?"

"No, thank you, Polly. I am sure you must be busy and I can manage. You do not look well. Is something amiss?"

"Oh, no, miss. Only . . . the other servants was saying as Sir Aubrey's a wicked man. Is he, miss?"

"Not half so wicked as he is foolish."

"Where is he, miss? He never come home last night."

"His lordship went to fetch him. No doubt they will return at any moment. I must get up."

144

"Yes, miss. I'm ever so glad you're going to marry his lordship."

"Thank you, Polly. So am I! Put out my walking shoes, if you please, and then you may go."

Selena dressed with a song in her heart. She spent more time than usual arranging her curly locks, then went up to the nursery.

"Did Uncle Hugh comed back, Aunt Sena?" asked Peter, looking up from the primer he was reading to Nurse. "I want to ride Leo today."

"Now you finish your lesson afore you start thinking on that pony, Master Peter," advised Mrs. Finnegan. "He knows his letters fine, Miss Selena, but he don't have much patience with the words. Oh dearie, it's happy I am to hear you'll soon be a married lady!"

Selena hugged the old woman, then noticed Peter looking at her in alarm. "That is what I have come to tell Peter about," she said. "If you don't mind, Finny, I think we had best talk alone."

Mrs. Finnegan picked up some knitting and retired to the next room. Selena sat down in a chair by the fire and pulled up a footstool beside her. Peter did not join her.

"You mustn't not marry Uncle Aubrey!" he said with anxious determination.

Selena smiled at him reassuringly. "I'm not going to, love. Should you mind if I married Uncle Hugh?"

Peter squeaked, jumped down from his seat at the table, and ran to throw himself into her arms.

"Really truly?" he asked. "Are you going to?"

"Yes."

"That's the bestest thing in the whole world! Aunts and uncles is s'posed to be married to each other. Timmy Russell says so." He was silent for a moment, hugging her, then said shyly, "Will I still belong to you?"

"Of course, darling. And to Uncle Hugh too."

"Will Uncle Hugh live here for ever and ever?"

"I don't know yet. He might want us to go and live with him in London, or at Iver. Should you mind that very much?"

His lips trembled. "What about Grandmama, and Auntie Dee?"

"They would come and visit us ever so often, and we would come and visit them here, too."

"That's not the same."

"No," she said gently, "it wouldn't be. I hope Uncle Hugh will choose to live here, for most of the year at least, but it is his decision."

"Aks him. Tell him it's *home.*"

"I will, Peterkin, only remember that it is not *his* home."

"It is now," said Peter.

Going in search of her mother, Selena ran into her sister on the stairs.

"You do look smart this morning," approved Delia. "Very different from last night." She giggled.

"I suppose you will never let me forget that fur rug," said Selena resignedly. "Not that I am in the least likely to forget it anyway."

"I am so glad you are going to marry Hugh. Shall I be allowed to call him Hugh when he is *my* brother-in-law, not just Phoebe's? I have not known how to address him this age."

" 'Your lordship' will be proper for a schoolroom miss of your tender years."

"I hope you are roasting me! Selena, shall you bring me out in the spring? It would be famous, so much better than going to Aunt Ringold as you and Phoebe did."

"So that is why you are glad I am to marry Hugh! I daresay we shall be in London for the Season, since he will be busy in the House of Lords. I shall see if I can persuade him to put up with my little sister for a few months, if Mama will entrust you to my care."

"Thank you! Do you mean to abandon the farm then? And go to live in Hugh's houses? I'm sure I cannot run it for you."

"I don't know, Dee. I haven't had time to work things out yet with Hugh. You are dressed for riding. Are you going out? I thought it was raining."

"Only a mizzle. Clive came to ask after you and I am going back with him, to see Jane and tell her all about it."

"Not all, I beg of you!"

"Jane won't tell, I promise."

"Not the world, but probably her mother. Lady Anne stands in no need of further ammunition against me."

"But it is such a romantic tale! Oh, very well, I will be discreet. I know you have no taste for romance."

"You'd be surprised!" said Selena with a smile.

She waved goodbye to her sister and went to the stillroom. Lady Whitton was busy with her aromatic potions.

"Just a moment, dear," she said. "I am preparing an infusion of catnip for poor Aubrey, to prevent a cold. You had best take some as well."

"Thank you, Mama, but I do not feel in the least old cattish this morning! Cousin Aubrey may have it all."

"I have made an elderleaf salve for bruises, but I do hope Hugh has not felt it necessary to chastise him."

"I am not so generous. I hope he has been exceedingly uncomfortable, and if Hugh wants to give him a leveller, he may do so with my full approval!"

"A leveller, dearest?"

"One of Peter's words, learned from Jem. Meaning, I collect, to knock someone down. It is just as well we shall soon have a gentleman in the family to teach him to speak like a gentleman. Mama, I am so happy!"

Lady Whitton hugged her daughter.

"I'm sure Hugh will make a delightful husband, my love, but we shall miss you," she said.

"I hope Hugh will want to live here at the Manor."

"Do you think he might? Delia and I could rent a small house nearby so that we would see you often."

"Nonsense, Mama! If we should stay here, the farthest you will remove is from your chamber to mine, and you shall take your dragon curtains with you."

"It never answers, Selena, having two mistresses in one household."

"Is not that how we have been living these four years? I do not recall that we have quarrelled yet!"

"Ah, but Hugh will not wish to live with his mama-in-law. He is a dear boy and I expect he would agree, but it will not do."

"I own I should not wish to live at Iver with the dowager viscountess. However, you and she are like cheese and chalk, and if Hugh should object, I'll not marry him, I vow!"

"Do not say such a thing, dearest! Of course you will marry him, and live happily where and with whom he chooses."

"I am not so conformable. I have no ambition to rule the roost but I do not mean to let him dictate to me. He will be wanting to run my farm, next!"

Selena retired to the library in a decidedly ruffled state of mind. Marriage to the viscount suddenly looked less like the blissful future she had envisioned, more like a source of endless complications and strife.

The way the corners of his eyes crinkled when he smiled; his gentle teasing and quick understanding of her own; his forgiveness of her temper, his admiration for her competence, his nascent idealism and determination to better the lot of his fellow man; were these enough to set in the balance against the disruption of her life, the loss of autonomy, perhaps the loss of all she had worked for for so many years?

She sat at her desk, gazing blankly down the long room, trying to work out what she wanted most.

Her mother and sister liked him. Peter adored him. That must weigh with her. Peter's future weighed heavily on Hugh's side. So did the memory of his arms around her, of the shivering thrill that swept through her at his touch, his mouth on hers . . .

The door opened and he came in. She looked at him, startled, unable to connect the reality with the dream.

"Come here," he said.

Like a sleepwalker she went to him and was enfolded in his arms.

"I've missed you," he muttered into her curls.

"Oh Hugh, twelve hours!"

"Thirteen hours and twenty-three minutes. I was afraid you might change your mind."

She had to prove to him that, rather to her own surprise, she had not, so it was some time before she was able to ask the question that had seemed all important.

"Hugh, where shall we live?"

"Here, I hope, at Milford Manor. It will be best for Peter, will it not? You do not want to set up in state at Iver Place, do you?" he asked apprehensively.

"Good heavens, no! I should not dare to try to displace your mama, *or* the pigs."

"Good."

"I shall be the Viscountess Iverbrook! Shall I have to be very . . . stately and proper and aristocratic?"

"Sometimes, perhaps. I am head of a large family of distant relatives, most of whom I have not seen for years, and once I have taken my seat in the House I suppose there will be occasions of state. I am as little practised as you! I know you will be equal to it, for when you are dressed up in all your finery, you have the bearing of a queen."

She blushed. "And when I am not dressed up?" she asked.

"You look like a farmer! Selena, I shall have to spend some time in London, in Parliament and working with Wilberforce. Will you come with me? If I find you a good bailiff who will follow your orders and manage the marketing and castrating of the bullocks? Will you come with me?"

Selena twisted in his arms until she could see his face. He looked so uncertain, half hopeful, half doubtful, that she had to kiss him.

"If you promise to take care of the harvest for me," she said teasingly, "then I promise to go to London with you. Hugh, Mama says that if we choose to live here, she and Delia will rent a house nearby and . . . "

"Never! You cannot mean to turn your mother out of her home!"

"Hush, love, it is her notion, not mine. If you protest as vehemently as I already have, I am sure we will change her mind."

"I most certainly shall protest! I shall tell her I am marrying you for your family and that she is an essential part of your dowry."

"And not my farm? You will not try to take over the farm?"

"Heaven forbid! The harvest is quite as much farming as I care to indulge in. Unless, of course, you mean to take up pig farming, in which case I shall most definitely interfere!"

"We do have a few pigs," she said thoughtfully. "I daresay you have not seen them. Come to think of it, there is room for a few more pens. We could even convert some of the cow byres, and keep the next few litters of piglets instead of selling them . . . "

"Selena! If I thought for a minute that you were not roasting me!"

"Roast pork is one of my favourite dishes, and one cannot live without bacon and ham and sausage and lard, and pigskin makes excellent leather, not to mention a dozen uses for the bristles."

"That," he said, "is why I am so rich, but believe me, my love, riches are not everything. For instance, I obtained your betrothal present as much by knowledge, influence, and charm as by handing over the ready."

"A betrothal present? Hugh, what is it? You have not had time to buy anything. We have only been betrothed for half a day."

"Roughly fourteen hours and forty-five minutes. I cannot be precise as to the minutes since it was dark and I could not see my watch."

"Odious wretch! What is it, Hugh?"

"A certain three fields, ideal for cattle pasture and most unsuitable for pigs."

"Not Lord Alphonse's water-meadows! You mean the water-meadows? Oh Hugh! But you cannot have purchased them this morning!"

"I had intended to give them to you anyway. You need not marry me to have them. I clinched the deal with Addlepate's man on Monday, since I was in town. Yesterday, that is."

"While I still thought you had run off to avoid having to explain your behaviour at the ball. That seems such a long time ago. I was so miserable when I thought you preferred Amabel to me. She is so beautiful."

"If you admire that type of beauty," he said indifferently. "*I* prefer tall, slender blonds with curly hair and eyes that change colour every time I look into them." Looking into them, he fell silent, then roused himself with an effort. "Selena, I must go to Iver to tell my mother of our engagement. She will be deeply offended if I inform her by letter and not in person."

"Of course, but not today."

"Also, there is a very old betrothal ring in the family—an heirloom—which I must fetch for you."

"But not today?"

"Not today, my darling. I obey your every whim."

"That is no whim," said Selena firmly. "It is past noon and much too late to leave."

Iverbrook laughed. "Always practical!" he said lovingly.

— 17 —

ON HIS RETURN from Abingdon, Sir Aubrey retired to his chamber to nurse bruised spirit, bruised ribs, and an incipient cold. For the last two Lady Whitton provided remedies; for the first she had no sympathy. The baronet had endangered her daughter, and only her innate kindness led her to allow him to stay.

The story of his plight lost nothing in the telling. Bannister went about his duties with a grin on his usually impassive face, and even Cook was seen to crack a smile. Delia returned from Bracketts in time to hear the gentlemen's version over luncheon, and was much inclined to take umbrage at her exclusion from the spectacle.

In the afternoon Selena and Hugh went walking along the river, leading Peter on Leo. Peter was blissful, and did not in the least mind being ignored for long periods. The rain had stopped and none of them noticed what a grey, chilly day it was.

They crossed Lord Alphonse Sebring's water-meadows, Selena busy with plans for drainage and mowing.

"I'll call them Addlepate's Acres," she said. "It will intrigue the country folk no end. They still argue over Farthing Field, which has been called that for generations. There's a record of it in a book of farm accounts three hundred years old."

"The Whittons have been here so long?"

"Since Richard II, and baronets since the Wars of the Roses, having cleverly chosen the winning side."

"Four hundred years, then. To think I once called you petty squires!"

"We have never claimed nor aimed at nobility. But it is a respectable family history, is it not? Peter will have it all now. Perhaps I ought to have married Cousin Aubrey after all."

"Just to preserve the name at Milford Manor? God forbid! Besides, you can always require that Peter change his name from Carrick to Whitton in order to inherit."

"I don't want to change my name," said the child firmly. "I like being Peter. You said you won't marry Uncle Aubrey, Aunt Sena. He's a bad man. Finny says he maked Polly cry."

"Does he snap at her? I have noticed that he is not good with the servants, and I'm afraid they do his bidding unwillingly. Is Mr. Hastings's valet still taking care of his clothes, Hugh?"

"As you say, unwillingly, though I think your cousin does not try to come the high and mighty with him. Dimbury is not easily impressed, and Hasty is of the opinion that Sir Aubrey stands in some awe of him. At least the hummingbird waistcoat has not been seen for some time, has it?"

Iverbrook debated whether to reveal to Selena his meeting with the baronet and the maid in the village. It seemed unwise to do so in Peter's hearing, and by the time they returned to the Manor, he had forgotten the subject.

At dinner he asked Lady Whitton for a love-potion.

"Selena is as changeable as the moon," he explained, eyes twinkling at her blush, "as I have cause to know! She may forget me while I am gone."

"I wish I could provide you with one," said Lady Whitton regretfully. "There must be magic involved for I have never read of a truly efficacious receipt. You need a real witch."

"Absence makes the heart grow fonder," pointed out Mr. Hastings.

"Out of sight, out of mind," Delia contradicted, "but you will not be gone for long."

"No. With luck just two days, at most three. I dare not leave her longer!"

"Do you think Lady Lavinia will wish to come and inspect me?" asked Selena uneasily. "I have only met her once, when Gil and Phoebe were married."

"Mama has not left Iver for years, even to go to London."

"When Phoebe was betrothed, she and I went to stay at Iver Place for a few days," said Lady Whitton. "I daresay you have forgotten, Hugh, but as head of the family and our host, you were present."

He laughed. "Have you a potion to restore the memory, ma'am? I suppose Selena must go with me soon to do the pretty, but there is no hurry. We'll let Mama recover from the news first."

Sir Aubrey had still not emerged from his chamber when, early the next morning, Lord Iverbrook set off for Iver Place.

"Keep an eye on him for me, Hasty," requested his lordship from his seat in his curricle. "And the other eye on Selena. I do not wish to hear when I come home that she has been abducted."

"Do you think he is plotting?" asked Delia eagerly.

"I don't trust him. Selena, you are not to leave the house with him on any pretext."

"As you wish, my lord." She curtseyed and dimpled at him, her curls shining in the pale October sunlight.

"I mean it! Let's be off, Tom, before she openly defies me."

He blew a kiss to Selena as the greys trotted sedately down the drive.

Selena walked down to the river. A few late roses bloomed among the Michaelmas daisies and autumn crocuses. The great oak was golden now, its leaves falling in slow spirals to float away downstream, following Hugh.

In a mood of gentle melancholy, Selena returned to the house. In a couple of hours John Peabody would be coming to see her. She had scarcely thought about farm business for several days and she must have clear instructions ready for the bailiff or nothing would be done right. At first it was difficult to concentrate on winter wheat and hedging and ditching, but as usual the details soon absorbed her. There were buildings in need of repair before the weather deteriorated, honey to be taken from the beehives, and Addlepate's Acres must be ploughed and sown to good grass.

By two o'clock she had seen John Peabody, brought her accounts up to date, and written some letters. She was sealing the last of these when there was a knock on the door and Mr. Hastings's round face appeared.

"My dear Miss Whitton, you have been closeted in the library long enough! I am in need of fresh air; will you ride with me?"

"Willingly. I expect Delia will go too."

"She is gone out for a drive with Mr. and Miss Russell."

"And you stayed behind?"

"I promised Hugh to keep an eye on you. I should not dare to leave the house without you!"

"This will never do. Have you been sitting in the hall, watching the library door for six hours lest I should escape you, like a cat at a mousehole?"

"Certainly not. Dimbury has not yet forgiven me for the depredations on my wardrobe caused by my boat ride the other day. If I were so lost to propriety as to crouch on the floor like a cat at a mousehole, I daresay he would leave me."

"Thus effectively destroying your reputation at a blow?" Selena laughed. "Have you eaten luncheon, sir?"

"Yes, I joined Lady Whitton. She will not make a love philtre for me, either."

"If I understand you aright, Mr. Hastings, I hope you will use no love philtre, nor any other persuasion until Delia has seen a little more of the world. And perhaps I ought to warn you that she is looking for—now how did she put it?—a man who *is* as romantic as he *looks.*"

Mr. Hastings grimaced. "I qualify in neither. And young Clive is the image of a hero in a novel."

"She has known him forever and he has quashed her flights of fancy time without number."

"I shall encourage them! But do not fear, I'll not press my suit yet awhile. Shall we go?"

"Unlike you, I have not eaten. Allow me a few minutes to change my dress and visit Cook, and I will be with you."

They rode into Abingdon, where Mr. Hastings had an errand to perform.

"Lady Whitton mentioned that she is running short of oil of sweet almonds," he explained. "If I may not court the daughter, I must needs court the mother. Besides, it is time I expressed my appreciation for her hospitality."

He was doomed to disappointment. It would have to be sent for, said the grocer, to Oxford or even to London.

"What else do you have?" asked Mr. Hastings. When the grocer shrugged and spread his arms expressively, he started wandering around, sniffing and poking in bags and barrels. "I've never been in a grocer's shop before," he confided to Selena. "Fascinating place. Just smell these spices. Does your mother grow these?"

"Most of them grow in the tropics, I believe."

"I'll get some. If she can't use 'em, Cook can have 'em. Incidentally, Miss Whitton, are you aware of that little romance?"

"Cook in love?" Selena was startled. "You must be mistaken. She has been with us since before I was born and never had an admirer to my knowledge."

"Cook and Hugh's Tom," confirmed Mr. Hastings. "I asked Dimbury and instead of denying it he went all prim and proper on me, really pokered up, so I'm ready to wager on it. Hi, boy! Let's have a pound of this, what is it, nutmeg, and one each of turmeric, cumin, cinnamon, cloves, coriander, cardamom—deuced if they don't all start with a C!"

"We usually sell them by the ounce, sir," said the grocer's boy, awed. "I'll have to ask Mr. Turney. They're ever so expensive."

"And they are used in very small quantities," Selena added as her companion looked alarmed. "They lose their flavour quickly."

"Very well, an ounce of each of them." Mr. Hastings recovered his poise. "Don't want to waste the stuff. Besides, we are riding and we don't want to carry a lot of parcels."

"We can deliver it, sir."

"No, I'll take it. Present for a lady. Just tie 'em up nicely, my dear fellow."

The package disappeared into the capacious pocket of his riding coat without producing a bulge large enough to spoil its line. They turned homewards across the fields.

"Past quarterday," explained Mr. Hastings sheepishly. "I'll have to go up to town to pick up my allowance when Hugh gets back. I'll be sorry to leave, dashed if I won't. Never thought the country could be so amusing."

"You'll always be welcome at Milford, Mr. Hastings, as Hugh's friend if not Delia's suitor. You have known Hugh forever, have you not?"

"Since Harrow."

"Was he a good student? He has a good memory for Greek myths."

"Only the scandalous ones, I'll be bound! Oh, beg your pardon, Miss Whitton. Shouldn't have said that."

Selena waved aside his apology. "Phoebe once described him to me as a 'wild and reckless blade.'"

"No, ma'am, did she? I say, that's going too far! An out-and-outer, up to every rig and row in town, but never going beyond the line, I do assure you. Always welcome everywhere, especially by the match-making mamas. Hugh's had more caps set at him than any man I know and never cared a fig for any of 'em. Dashed if I thought he'd take my advice."

"Your advice?"

"That's right. Wouldn't take it about a coat or a horse, but 'Marry her, my dear fellow,' I said, and here he is, betrothed."

"You advised him to marry me?"

"Don't know if you've noticed it, but he's a determined fellow, Hugh, once he's made up his mind about something. Says he's going to abolish slavery, he'll abolish slavery, all right and tight. Says he's going to be guardian to his heir, come hell or high water. 'Easy,' says I, 'marry her.' And here we are. He's within ame's ace of being guardian to his heir."

Mr. Hastings rattled on. He had lost his audience, and Orion was left to pick his own way along the muddy cart track. Selena rode in a daze, stupefied, unaware of her surroundings until they reached the Manor.

She parted from Mr. Hastings politely, and went upstairs with an unseeing look that left him feeling distinctly uneasy.

The emptiness within her expanded until it was hard to breathe. It hurt her throat. Dry-eyed, she mechanically took off her riding habit and hung it in the wardrobe.

Phrases passed through her memory.

"I mean to obtain custody, by hook or by crook."

"It will be best for Peter."

"I am marrying you for your family." She had thought he was joking when he said that.

How easily he had hoaxed her! How ready she had been to believe that he loved her! Confused and humiliated, she pressed her hands to her burning cheeks. It had all been a plot, a scheme thought up months ago to wheedle her into giving up control of Peter. Mr. Hastings had suggested "Marry her," and the noble Viscount Iverbrook had promptly set about laying siege.

How dare he!

Selena flung on the first gown that came to hand and ran down to the library. It was the work of a moment to pen a note to his lordship, declaring their engagement at an end. A few angry tears fell on the paper; she blotted them savagely, smearing the ink, then folded, sealed, and directed it.

If she put it on the table in the hall, to be taken to the post tomorrow, it might miss him. Jem must ride with it, leaving at once. But no, Jem was needed in the stables since that detestable man had taken Tom Arbuckle with him. It was typical of his unfeeling, inconsiderate ways.

Ten minutes later, Selena was on her way to the village, striding down the lane in a mannish way that would have shocked Lady Anne Russell. Behind her scurried Polly, a last minute concession to the proprieties, who looked none too pleased at being hustled out into the dusk.

Mr. Liddell, landlord of the Royal Oak, was "right flambusticated," as he later told his wife, when Miss Whitton marched into his inn at the busiest time of day. He left half a dozen farm hands calling for ale and hurried to greet her.

"Evening, miss!" he boomed. "What can I do for you today?"

"Good evening, Mr. Liddell. I want a letter delivered by morning to Iver Place. It's just this side of London. Can you send your ostler's boy? I'll pay you for his time and the horse, and there will be a tip for him if it arrives in time."

"Right you are, miss." Selena winced as the innkeeper raised his voice to a bellow. "Alf! ALF! Go fetch Ted here and step lively, mind! If you'll just step into the parlour, miss, you can give young Ted his instructions and he'll be off right away. Can I get you anything, miss?"

Selena declined. She and Polly went into the parlour, an oppressively overfurnished room hung with purple velvet, which was Mrs. Liddell's pride and joy and where the Royal Oak's rare visitors of Quality were invariably incarcerated.

In a few minutes the stableboy appeared, bashfully wiping his hands on his smock. Selena gave him directions to Iver Place, handed over the letter, and followed him out of the room.

As she paid the landlord, he asked anxiously, "The little master's not sick again?"

"No, he's very well, thank you."

"Ah!" said Mr. Liddell with a knowing look. As she left, she heard him telling his wife in an attempted whisper, "Our Ted's off to Iver Place, Maisie, with a love letter from Miss Whitton."

"Isn't that nice now?" came Maisie's answer, loud and clear.

With heightened colour and an aching heart, Selena hurried home.

— 18 —

THAT EVENING, SELENA'S forced gaiety alarmed everyone. Mr. Hastings, afraid that his unthinking words were to blame, was so alarmed that he confirmed his resolve to depart for London in search of his quarterly remittance.

"I owe Iverbrook fifty guineas," he pointed out, "so I'd best be gone before he returns. You can tell him he will be paid when next I see him."

"He will not mind!" cried Delia. "I am sure you need not fear that he will dun you. Won't you stay a little longer?"

"I'll see you next spring in town, shall I not, my dear Miss Delia? I expect to waltz with you at Almack's."

"You will always be welcome at Milford Manor, Mr. Hastings," said Lady Whitton.

The sparkle in Selena's eyes suggested to him that his welcome in that quarter had been withdrawn. "Thank you, my lady," he said. "I hope to visit you again. However, I really must leave tomorrow morning. Who knows but that my man of business will send the money back to my father? I have never before waited so long past quarterday to avail myself of it!"

Later that evening Lady Whitton, becomingly attired in a dove grey peignoir and frilly nightcap, tapped on Selena's chamber door, opened it, and peeped in.

"I think we had better have a little cose, my love," she suggested.

"Oh Mama, I am by far too sleepy to talk tonight," Selena answered, yawning hugely.

"In the morning then, dear. Goodnight and sweet dreams."

Lady Whitton retired to her chamber shaking her head, and Selena tossed and turned for hours before falling into a troubled sleep.

She woke late and went downstairs with dark rings shadowing her eyes. Her mother and sister had already breakfasted, Bannister informed her, and Mr. Hastings and Sir Aubrey had not yet descended.

"I wonder if Cousin Aubrey will put in an appearance today," she said uninterestedly. "I suppose Mama has told you that Mr. Hastings is leaving?"

"Yes, Miss Selena. And I wish it was the Bart instead, begging your pardon, miss. As do the other servants."

"I daresay we shall soon be back to normal, Bannister, just the three of us and Master Peter. I'll take a piece of toast and some tea, please."

She nibbled her toast without enthusiasm but drank three cups of tea, warming her hands on the forget-me-not painted china and sipping slowly, until she could procrastinate no longer.

"Is Mama in the stillroom?" she asked.

"Her ladyship was consulting with Cook, miss, but I expect she's finished by now. I'll send young Polly to find her."

Polly reported that my lady was now talking to Mrs. Tooting but would join Miss Selena in the drawing room shortly. Selena found Delia there, practising a funeral march on the pianoforte. She looked up as her sister entered and attacked immediately.

"Have you quarrelled with Mr. Hastings, Selena? He said nothing about leaving before you went to Abingdon with him."

"Of course not."

"You have such a quick temper, you must have said something that upset him."

"On the contrary. There's no need to be in the mopes, Dee, you will see him soon in London."

"I'm not moping. I'm sure I do not care if I never see him again. I expect he will visit you often when you are married, since he and Hugh are bosom-bows?"

"I'm not going to marry Lord Iverbrook after all."

"What? Selena, do you mean it? Then I shall have to go to Aunt Ringold. You are the meanest creature, I vow! I daresay Mr. Hastings will never call on Aunt Ringold." Delia flounced out of the room in a huff, nearly knocking over one of the housemaids, who had come to build up the fire.

Selena huddled in a chair, cold in spite of the blazing logs in the fireplace. The day outside was as bleak as her thoughts. What was she going to tell her mother? That she had gone off half-cocked again and ruined her own life forever? She should have given Hugh a hearing, however despicable he was.

Delia had said that she had a quick temper; it was not true. In general she was calm and collected, dealing with crises on the farm with unruffled composure. It was Hugh's fault she had been so impetuous recently. She hoped she would never see him again!

Lady Whitton came in, sat down beside her, and took one of her cold hands between her own.

"What is it, dearest?" she asked.

Selena wanted to cry, but no tears came.

"I'm not going to marry Hugh," she said, speaking with difficulty because of the lump in her throat. "I wrote him a letter. He'll never forgive me this time."

"What was it this time?"

"I can't tell you. Maybe it's not even true. Only I was so hurt and humiliated I did not stop to think and it's too late now. Mama, were you so confused and . . . and *birdwitted* when you were in love with Papa?"

"No, love, but our situations are very different. I was a mere girl, living with my parents, and had known your father forever. You are a strong-willed young woman, in charge of your own life, used to being looked up to. Had I considered, I should have predicted a stormy courtship."

"Well, it's too late now," repeated Selena miserably. "I am sorry, Mama, to have let my foolishness disturb you. I shall do very well, I promise, for I always expected to be an old maid."

"Nonsense, child." Lady Whitton had more to say, but suddenly Selena could not bear the thought of hearing her words of comfort and reassurance.

She jumped up. "I have work to do, Mama. Life goes on, you see!" With a bright smile, she hurried from the room and went to earth in the library, where she started the same business letter five times before giving up. She ripped her last effort in half and sat doodling on the pieces, wondering if Hugh had read his letter yet and if so, whether he was more angry, or relieved, or blue-devilled. It served him right!

Within the hour, the entire household knew that Miss Selena was not going to marry his lordship after all.

Mr. Hastings was so informed by Dimbury. He hurried his dressing, to the valet's distress, and raced downstairs to take his leave. His escape was foiled by Delia who, dressed in her prettiest winter walking dress of a cerulean blue the precise colour of her eyes, persuaded him that he had time for one final stroll by the river, in spite of the weather.

When the news reached Sir Aubrey, he also donned his finery with unusual alacrity. For the first time he noticed the absence of his hummingbird waistcoat, which he generally saved for special occasions. In its place he chose one with cherry and white stripes. He had had reservations about it since Dimbury pointed out its resemblance to a barber's pole, but it matched to perfection the cherry red of his coat. Besides, cherries were indubitably agricultural, so the colour must please his cousin, he thought. He gazed in the mirror, admiring the Waterfall, in which elaborate style Dimbury had taught him to tie his cravat. Still more he admired his guinea gold locks. Carefully arranging one careless curl at each temple, he descended to dazzle Selena.

Dazzled she was. She had as good as forgotten his existence when he minced into the library and raised his quizzing glass to study the inkstains on her fingers. In a guilty reflex she hid them under the desk.

"What can I do for you, Cousin?" she asked coldly.

"Fairest Selena, my beloved cousin, I am come to appeal to you one more time. Your eyes have been opened to the falseness of the high nobility, the unthinking arrogance of the aristocracy towards those but a step lower in the social scale. Allow me to console you. Do me the honour of accepting my hand in marriage. I shall protect you from the world and make your happiness my only care. Let us be wed, I beg you on bended knee!"

Sinking to the floor, he almost vanished behind the great oak desk.

"You have been practising," said Selena as he reappeared, somewhat discomposed. "That speech was a vast improvement over your previous efforts. Do take a seat and stop hovering!" she added.

With a sulky expression he sat down on the hard chair by the desk.

"Well, will you?" he demanded.

"Will I what?" she asked absently. To her own surprise she was considering the advantages of being married to her cousin. In spite of his gypsy mother he was of respectable birth. He was a fool, and a weak one; whatever his expectations she knew she could rule him with ease. His tastes might be expensive but the farm was doing better every year, she was well beforehand with the world, and she would hold the purse strings. He was good-looking (if she managed to break him of his passion for red), titled, and Milford Manor would remain in Whitton hands. As a married lady, it would be easier in many ways to do business, and however much one despised such conventions it would be more comfortable to be a wife than an old maid.

She looked at him, at his eager face, and avid eyes of Whitton blue. Above all, she knew his motives. He would never cast her into confusion, drive her to distraction with jealousy or fury, because she did not care. Nor would he laugh with her, tease her, thrill her with a touch, but Hugh was gone, whistled down the wind, to be shut out of her mind and heart forever.

"I'll think about it," she said.

He stared at her, mouth open in a witless gape.

"Of course, my own!" he gabbled. "Though naturally impatient for a decision which will decide my fate, I shall await your decision with what patience I can muster. My fate is in your hands, the decision is yours, only the impatience is mine! Or the patience," he added, confused. Seizing her hand he planted a kiss on her knuckles before she could withdraw it.

"Oh do go away, Aubrey!" said Selena.

Obediently he left, backing out of her presence as if she were royalty. Amused, exasperated, confirmed in her belief that the baronet would adapt with ease to life beneath the cat's paw, Selena sat contemplating matrimony for a few moments, then went to see Peter.

She climbed the stairs slowly, feeling tired. Peter rushed into her arms as she entered the nursery, and held her tight.

"Mrs. Tooting told Finny you're not going to marry Uncle Hugh!" he gasped, anguish in his voice. "Why because, Aunt Sena? Why because won't you?"

She picked him up and sat down, holding him on her lap. He looked up at her, blue eyes full of tears, lips trembling.

"I was mistaken, Peterkin. We shall not suit after all."

"You're not 'staken! Course you'll suit just right, like me and Leo. *Please* marry him, Aunt Sena?"

"I'm sorry, love."

"Promise you won't marry Uncle Aubrey, 'stead of Uncle Hugh."

"I can't promise. I don't know what I'm going to do. You ought to have a papa, especially when you are older."

"But not Uncle Aubrey!" The child sounded desperate. "He's a bad man. I wish my own mama and papa didn't die!"

Selena hugged him. "So do I, sweetheart."

Peter pulled away from her. "Is Mr. Hasty going home today?" he asked.

"Yes," she said, surprised. "I don't believe he has left yet. Do you want to say goodbye to him?"

"Mayhaps. I want to get down now."

She released him. He slipped to the floor and stood facing her, hands folded, face blotched with tears, expression resolute.

"Are you all right now?" she asked. "Remember, I have not yet made up my mind, and I'll think about what you have said. Don't worry about it, Peter. Everything will turn out all right."

She stooped to kiss him and went back to the library, wishing she believed her own words. She tried to consider dispassionately the pros and cons of marriage to Aubrey, an unprofitable exercise soon interrupted by the entrance of her mother.

"Bannister told me Aubrey came out looking smug as the cat that got the cream," she said. "What is he up to now?"

"Bannister has no business reporting to you! It is none of his concern."

"Now Selena, you know very well that all the servants have your best interests at heart."

"They are all excessively inquisitive. Aubrey is up to nothing new. He proposed to me again and I told him I would consider it."

"You didn't!"

"I did, and I am. The one thing that troubles me is that Peter does not like him, but he needs a father and he would soon grow accustomed."

"The thing that troubles *me*," said her mother, "is that *you* do not like him!"

"I care not a fig for that. It will make life easier, for I shall not feel obliged to take his wishes into account."

"Selena! Pray do not talk in that calculating way! It is not at all like you, and besides being highly unbecoming it . . . " There was a knock at the door. "Bother! Who is it?"

"It is I, my lady." Dimbury stepped into the room, bowing deferentially. He had one arm around Polly's shoulders, and after one look at the maid's tear-stained face, Lady Whitton sighed and resigned herself to the interruption.

"Yes, Dimbury? What is it?"

"I fear I may appear impertinent, my lady, but I must ask Miss Whitton whether she has accepted an offer of marriage from Sir Aubrey."

"Impertinent you are!" snapped Selena. "I must suppose that you are not run mad but have a good reason for it. Sir Aubrey has offered; I have not yet made up my mind."

With a wail, Polly turned and buried her face in the valet's shoulder.

"There now," he said, patting her hand. "I've a bit saved up after all these years and if my lady throws you out, as I don't doubt she's a right to do but I don't believe she will, well, you come to me and I'll see you all right. Understand? I never wanted a wife," he explained, turning back to the astounded ladies, "but I always did fancy a daughter. I'll be off now, my lady, if you'll excuse me, for there's a deal of packing still to be done. Mind you tell everything now, Polly, there's a good girl."

With another fatherly pat, he detached himself from the weeping maid and left.

Lady Whitton swept forward, put her arms around Polly, and led her to a chair.

"Sit down, my dear," she said gently. "What is the matter?"

"It's Sir Aubrey!" The words burst out, interspersed with racking sobs. "He tell me we'd get married and go to Jamaica and nobody wouldn't know or care I'm not a lady. He said we'd have a grand house and pretty clothes and go to parties and balls and all. He said he loved me, my lady, and now he's after Miss Selena again and me in the family way!"

"You are with child?" asked Lady Whitton in a faint voice. "Oh dear, my poor girl!" She sat down rather suddenly.

Selena pulled herself together and came round the desk. "Are you quite sure?" she asked searchingly, "and sure it was Sir Aubrey?"

"I'm no lightskirt, miss, there weren't no one else. He promised he'd marry me. I'm that sorry, miss, honest I am, to be such a trouble to her la'ship. Oh miss, what am I going to do?"

Selena sat down on a footstool and took one of Polly's twisting hands. "Do you still want to marry Sir Aubrey, after this?"

"I dunno, miss. He's ever so handsome, and there ain't no one else'll marry me now."

"We'll see what we can do, then. You can rest assured *I* shall not marry him! All the same, I doubt he'll come up to scratch."

Lady Whitton concurred. "You need not fear we'll abandon you, Polly," she comforted. "You will not need to take advantage of Dimbury's kind offer."

"Mr. Dimbury's been that good to me, my lady. He seen I was moped right off, and bin like a real father to me. You won't throw me out, my lady, and the baby? I'll work ever so hard to earn its keep."

"We'll decide what's to be done when we know what Sir Aubrey will do," said Selena. "Do you want to be present when we talk to him?"

"Oh no, miss. I never want to see him again, lessn he'll marry me. You'll tell me right off, miss?"

"Of course, Polly. You run along now, and tell Bannister I wish to see Sir Aubrey in here."

"Right, miss. Bless you, miss, and you too, my lady."

Polly jumped up, bobbed a curtsey, and scurried out.

"Poor child!" murmured Lady Whitton.

Grim-faced, Selena arranged a second chair behind the desk and invited her mother to join her.

"Like a court of law," she explained. "I hope it will make it more difficult for you to sympathise with the defendant."

"In this case I cannot sympathise, or rather, only with Polly. If he will not marry her, he must go. I will not have a . . . a *loose fish* in the house."

"Bravo, Mama! Stick to your guns, now, I hear him coming."

The baronet's eager anticipation faded to puzzlement as he entered the library and found himself face to face with a pair of stern ladies.

"Did you not send for me, Cousin?" he asked plaintively, looking about for a chair with a helpless expression on his handsome features. Selena had taken care to move all the chairs to an uncomfortable distance from the desk, forcing him to stand.

"I did, Cousin. Or more precisely, my mother did."

"Aunt?"

"We have just now spoken to Polly," said Lady Whitton with an austerity foreign to her nature. "She is in great distress, and her story has greatly distressed us, also."

"I didn't do it!" cried Sir Aubrey at once.

"Do what, Cousin?"

"Seduce the wench," he answered sulkily.

"Then how do you know that is what we are speaking of?"

"I suppose some other fellow has put a bun in her oven."

"Don't be vulgar, Aubrey," admonished Lady Whitton. "Polly has always been a good girl. You grossly deceived her with your promises of marriage."

"She cannot have supposed that I meant it! I, a baronet, to wed a serving maid! It is unthinkable. She pretended to believe me in order to have a ready excuse for indulging her animal passions."

"Aubrey!"

"I never realised how excessively vulgar you are," said Selena wonderingly. "I always knew you for a fool, but this is beyond anything."

"Selena, marry me! Nothing like this will ever happen again, I swear it. Give Polly her notice and we will forget she ever existed and live happily ever after."

Selena was too astonished to answer.

"Indeed you won't!" said her mother, standing up, her face pink with indignation. "You will marry Polly at once or you will leave this house for ever."

"Dear Aunt, you cannot have considered the scandal. Whether I marry the creature or you bar me from the Manor, people will talk. The family name will be dragged through the mud."

"I do not care *that* for scandalmongers," said Lady Whitton, snapping her fingers under his nose and making him jump. "Do you marry Polly or do I call the servants to throw you out?"

"I'll not wed a low-born slut." Sir Aubrey was petulant but determined. "You need not throw me out, I'll go. But you'll call me back when Selena realises she's on the shelf, I'll wager."

"Go!" chorused the ladies.

"I'm going, I'm going. I'll need some time to pack my things and order a carriage."

"You have an hour," said Lady Whitton inexorably as he backed out, this time as if he expected a knife in the back.

"If you are ever seen on my property after that," added Selena, "I shall have you taken up as a vagrant."

"You'll regret this!" muttered the baronet, and fled, not even pausing to close the door.

Pale and shaken, Lady Whitton sat down.

"I blame myself," she said. "By my age I ought to be a better judge of character. Poor Polly! I must go and tell her."

Bannister appeared in the open doorway, looking alarmed.

"My lady!" he exclaimed, "Sir Aubrey just came rushing out with a face like a thundercloud and told me to send to the Oak for a carriage. And here's the chaise from the Crown just come for Mr. Hastings and him and Miss Delia playing least in sight. And Polly, what's usually such a levelheaded lass, she's in hysterics and Mrs. Tooting's thrown another fit and Mr. Peabody's sent to say he has to see Miss Selena this afternoon urgent and what shall I do, my lady?"

"Coming!" answered Lady Whitton and her daughter in unison.

Polly was soothed, Mrs. Tooting put to bed with a draught of vervain, Jem sent to the Royal Oak for a carriage, and Mr. Hastings found. While Mr. Hastings distributed his loose change in vails for the servants and said his farewells to the Whittons, Dimbury packed his luggage into the smart yellow chaise from Abingdon. As they set off, none too soon for the impatient postilion, they met in the drive the shabby gig from the Royal Oak, the only vehicle for hire in Kings Milford. The postilion turned up his nose, but Ted, the ostler's boy, scarce returned from Iver, was too tired to do more than stick out his tongue in response.

"Young varmint," said Jem, sitting beside him, from the lofty height of three years advantage in age. "You won't never be a gentleman's groom if you don't behave proper."

Bannister instructed Ted to wait, and went off. Jem suggested that he tie up the horse and come round to the kitchen for a drop of something to warm him.

"'Tis a raw day," he said, and Ted, agreeing, followed him.

Bannister sent one of the housemaids to inform the baronet that his carriage had arrived.

"Ooh sir, do I 'ave to?" she wailed.

"You can't come to much trouble in half a minute, Doris, now can you?" he asked. "You come right back down straightaway. I've a nasty feeling, what with all the commotion, as all the servants is too busy to help the Bart with his bags."

Not only the staff but the family was invisible when the baronet descended the stairs. He rang the bell in the hallway several times, with as little result as his chamber bell had produced. Scowling, he managed to bring down all his luggage in four trips. As he stowed the last portmanteau in the rear of the gig, young Ted appeared, rubbing his hands.

"Ready to go, guv?" he asked, examining with interest Sir Aubrey's hot and flustered face. "Cold day, innit. 'S a rug inna back 'fyou wannit."

"Devil take the rug," growled the baronet as his driver swung up onto the box. "Let's get moving!"

Its breath steaming, the bony piebald horse hauled him away from the silent Manor.

The Whittons gathered in the dining room for luncheon.

"How cosy," said Lady Whitton brightly. "Just family again."

"I'm going to Bracketts this afternoon, Mama, if you do not need me," announced Delia, helping herself to a large slice of cold chicken and some bread and butter.

"I believe I shall go to John Peabody's, instead of waiting for him here," said Selena. "I need to get out of the house." She cut up an apple, took two bites, and pushed her plate away.

Their mother sighed. "It does seem quiet, does it not? I expect we shall soon become accustomed again. You may go, Delia, if you make sure to return by dark. And both of you dress warmly."

"Yes, Mama."

By the time Selena returned to the Manor it was raining, a cold, steady, drenching downpour. She changed out of her wet riding habit, putting on a round dress of Thibet cloth in a muddy green colour she despised. She had had it for years and generally wore it for inspecting the cow byres and pigpens, but it looked the way she felt at the moment: drab.

She went to see Peter, suddenly realising that she had not told him of Sir Aubrey's dismissal. How right he had been! Uncle Aubrey was a bad man and she and Hugh would suit perfectly. What did she care if he was going to marry her for Peter's sake? That would have been part of her motive too, after all, quite apart from the fact that she loved him desperately. Only it was too late now.

She opened the nursery door. Mrs. Finnegan, snoozing in her rocking chair, blinked owlishly at her. There was no sign of her nephew.

"Where is Peter, Nurse?"

"He went down to his granny a few minutes ago, dearie. Oh my, but it's nearly dark! I must of dropped off. Forty winks just don't seem to be enough at my age."

"When did he go, Finny? What time?"

"Right after his lunch, it was. He says he sees a carridge in the drive and he's got to say good-bye to Mr. Hasty. That's what he calls Mr. Hastings."

"But that was hours ago! He was not with us when Mr. Hastings left. What did he do after I talked to him this morning?"

"He were ever so quiet for a while, then he goes to his treasures," she pointed at the carved and painted wooden chest in the corner, "and sorts out his favourites. He says he wants to play Dick Whittington and the cat and will I tie his stuff up in a bundle, which I does. Then Doris come up with lunch, saying all's at sixes and sevens below, so when Peter's ate, not that he did eat much, being downright fidgetty, and he says he's going to see his granny I says not on your life while they're all in a fuss. Then a whiles later I catches him a-trying to sneak out with his bundle. He says kind of desperate like as he's got to see Grandmama now, so I lets him go, first taking the bundle off of him, for Mrs. Tooting don't like toys all over below stairs, as well you know, Miss Selena, having tried that trick on your own account a dunnamany years agone."

"He's run away!" said Selena. "He asked me if Mr. Hastings was leaving today. I wonder if he thought he would take him to Iverbrook? But he cannot have hidden in the chaise—Mr. Hastings would surely have found him by now and brought him back."

"Likely he got in the wrong carriage by mistake. There were his Uncle Aubrey's carriage too, weren't there?"

Selena paled. "That's right. And I have no idea where he was going. That was hours ago!" She picked up her skirts and ran out of the room.

Half way down the stairs she met Bannister, somewhat out of breath, coming to find her.

"Miss Selena!" he panted. "There's a boy from the Crown brought a letter. He says as how 'tis urgent and he won't give it into any hands but yourn."

"Where is he?"

"In the kitchen, miss, and dripping all over Cook's nice clean floor."

Selena was nearly at the bottom of the stairs before he finished his sentence. She hurried to the kitchen and found the lad steaming in front of the fire. Assured that she was Miss Whitton, he handed her a soggy paper.

She unfolded it with care. The ink had run but the writing was still plainly legible. She read it, and put out a hand to the table to steady herself, her face white.

"How did you come by this?"

"A man brung it, and paid to have it delivered tonight, miss. Dunno who he were. Di'n't think to ask, miss."

"No, of course not. What, Cook? No, I'm all right. I must see my mother at once."

"My lady's in the drawing room," said the butler, who had just caught up with her. "Miss Delia too."

"Thank you, Bannister. Tell Jem to come to me there, if you please." She walked slowly this time. There was no need to hurry. As she entered the drawing room she heard Delia.

"Honestly I'm not wet, Mama. Clive brought me home in the carriage. I'll change later."

"Yes, don't go yet, Dee," said Selena, her voice sounding strange in her own ears. "You'll have to know sooner or later."

They turned to her.

"Know what?" Delia asked.

"Selena, what is it? You look ill. Come and sit down, dearest."

She sank into a chair and unfolded the grubby letter again. "This is from Cousin Aubrey. He has Peter. If I don't marry him, he'll sell him to the gypsies for his fare to Jamaica and we'll never see him again."

"We must rescue him! Call all the farmhands together and we'll go after him!"

"We don't know where he is, Dee. You know how the gypsies move about."

"Someone must know. The boy from the Royal Oak! Send Jem to ask him."

Selena and her mother looked at each other with dawning hope.

"Good idea! Jem should be here in a minute."

"If he has not told you where he is, how does he expect you to contact him?" asked Lady Whitton.

"I am to be at the Crown and Thistle at seven o'clock." Jem came in and she waved at him to wait. "Someone will meet me there and take me to him."

"Then the men can follow you and rescue you as well as Peter," said Delia.

"No. If anyone goes with me, even a maid, I will not be contacted and Peter will disappear."

The groom gasped, and Selena turned to him.

"Jem, go down to the village and ask the ostler's boy at the Oak where he took Sir Aubrey this afternoon. Try not to arouse curiosity, but be as quick as you can."

"Right, miss." Wasting no more time on words, he left.

The half hour before his return passed with agonising slowness. Outside, gloomy dusk merged into blackest of black nights, and rain still fell in sheets. Polly came in to draw the curtains and light more candles. She looked at the three sombre figures and burst into tears.

"It's all my fault!" she moaned, and ran out. Lady Whitton could not summon the energy to go after her.

"I know Aubrey's mama was a gypsy," said Selena, "but I never saw him talking to them."

"We never saw him with Polly either," pointed out her mother sadly.

"Where else could he have gone?" asked Delia. They fell silent again.

At last Jem came in, bootless, coatless, his damp hair sticking up in spikes where it had been roughly dried.

"Ted ain't come home yet, my lady," he reported. "Mr. Liddell says he were that wore out after being out all night on an errand, he prolly fell asleep somewheres. He don't look for him till morning."

Chickens come home to roost, thought Selena. If she had not written that letter, if Ted had not taken it to Iver . . . "I shall have to marry Aubrey," she said, her voice leaden.

"I'll go wi' you to Abingdon, Miss Selena," the groom said. "They'll never see me ifn I take care they don't. Wi' the two of us, we'll save Master Peter right enough."

"No," said Selena flatly. "We cannot risk it. I shall go alone. Have Orion saddled for me by half past six, if you please."

"Yes, miss." Jem looked mutinous but did not persist. He padded out in his stockinged feet, muttering ominously.

At half past six, he brought Orion to the side door. Selena was waiting with her mother and sister.

"You will never find your way to Abingdon!" exclaimed Lady Whitton. "It is pitch dark."

"That is one thing you need not worry about. Orion could find his way there blindfolded. Do not cry, Mama! Only this afternoon I was wondering whether to marry Cousin Aubrey, and now I find my mind made up for me. Dee, take care of Mama."

She kissed them both, Jem helped her mount, and she rode off into the night.

= 19 =

BEING IN NO hurry to confront his mother, Lord Iverbrook drove south at a leisurely pace, stopping en route for luncheon. He did not arrive at Iver Place until late afternoon, and even then did not hasten to Lady Lavinia's side.

As Tom Arbuckle drove the curricle round to the stables, he mounted the brick steps and rang the bell, as usual feeling like a visitor to his own house.

A liveried footman he did not recognise opened the door. "Yes, sir?" he enquired.

"I'm Lord Iverbrook, dammit!" exclaimed the viscount. "Where the devil is that old hoaxer Prynn?"

"Beg pardon, my lord. I'll find him at once, my lord. Shall I take your lordship's coat, my lord?" stammered the servant.

"Is my stepfather at home? Mr. Ffinch-Smythe, clothhead!" he added as the footman gaped. "Lady Lavinia is my mother, Mr. Ffinch-Smythe is my stepfather, and *this is my house!*"

The butler sailed out from the nether regions to investigate the commotion.

"What is it, Frederick?" he asked. "Oh, my lord! Your lordship was not expected." His demeanour was frosty.

"This," pointed out Iverbrook again, his voice equally cold, "is my house. I hope I may come and go as I please?"

"Naturally, my lord. I shall at once inform her ladyship of your lordship's arrival."

"Don't. I wish to speak to Mr. Ffinch-Smythe first."

"Certainly, my lord. I believe Mr. Ffinch-Smythe is, ah, down at the farm."

"In that case, Frederick, I shall keep my coat. Prynn, in future when you hire new staff during my absence, I suggest you take them up to the long gallery to study my portrait, *before* I arrive home unexpectedly."

"Yes, my lord. An excellent idea, my lord. Might I make so bold, my lord, as to enquire whether your lordship intends to make a long stay at the Place?"

"Two nights at most. And for God's sake stop 'lording' me!"

"Yes, my . . . sir."

In a high dudgeon, the viscount strode down to the pigpens. The exercise cooled his temper, and the last of it was banished by his stepfather's usual greeting.

"What-ho, Iverbrook! Come and look at Primrose."

The black and white sow looked much the same as the last time he had seen her, though if possible even fatter.

"She's put on weight?" he offered dubiously.

"Ha! Right on the mark. She'd just had a litter when you were here in July, takes it out of the poor old girl, you know. Nearly time to breed her again now."

"Is it that long since I was at Iver? The devil! I daresay my mother has been enacting you a Cheltenham tragedy on the subject of Prodigal Sons."

"Fine litter it was, too. Growing fast, not too plump. Must confess Lady Lavinia has mentioned Turkish treatment once or twice."

"Turkish . . . ? Oh, you mean she has complained of my absence. For a moment I thought you had plans for importing pigs from Turkey!"

"No, no. Don't know if they breed 'em. Mohammedans, you know. Naples, it was, we talked of, but I spoke to Lord Liverpool and he says it won't do. At least until Boney's beaten. Wouldn't worry about your mama, if I was you. She'll come round, what?"

"Under normal circumstances, yes. However, I have news for her that I fear won't be welcome."

"Want us to move out? 'Fraid that's one thing won't wash. I've asked her a hundred times if I've asked her once to live at Ffinch House. My house, after all. Fond of it, what? She won't budge."

"I know. It's not that. I'm getting married."

Mr. Ffinch-Smythe looked puzzled and scratched his wig. "Funny.

Thought you was talking of bringing your nevvie here, not a bride. Must have misheard. Getting leg-shackled, are you? Who's the lady?"

"Miss Whitton. My nephew's aunt."

"Ah, I see." The old gentleman's brow cleared momentarily. "Good thought that. But you'll be wanting to live here and it don't do to have two females in the same house, my boy, take my word. Have to come up with a way to persuade her to remove to Ffinch House, what?"

"I believe it would kill her, sir. Fortunately my betrothed owns her own property and we plan to reside there. You know I never could abide the Place, and all the pomp and circumstance that go with it."

His stepfather brightened. "Excellent notion! Had me worried for a minute. Shouldn't be too hard to bring her round then. Better wait till morning though. Always at her best just after breakfast. Fine woman, your mother, but touchy. Like Primrose here. Downright temperamental at times, ain't you, Primrose?"

Since the sun was setting behind the hill, Mr. Ffinch-Smythe consented to accompany his stepson back to the house. It looked more attractive than usual, with golden evening light softening the harsh brick and lamps shining in the windows. They entered by a side door, thus avoiding Prynn.

"Better change right away," suggested Mr. Ffinch-Smythe. "Lady Lavinia likes to dine early in winter. Knee-breeches, mind! Bring your man with you?"

"Yes, thank you, sir. You don't think I should visit Mama first?"

"No, no. See her at dinner. Won't be able to rake you over the coals with the servants present, what?"

"That's a point."

"Just takes a little savvy-fair, my boy. French for know-how. Women need managing."

Thinking of his temperamental beloved, Lord Iverbrook laughed. "I wish you had said that four months ago! It would have saved me a great deal of time and anguish and I should not now be quaking in my shoes at the prospect of meeting my neglected mother!"

"Wearing boots," pointed out his stepfather. "Muddy ones too."

Tom Arbuckle had ascertained the precise hour of dinner, thus enabling his master to descend from his chilly chamber to the chillier gallery a mere five minutes before the gong. Lady Lavinia, fragile as porcelain in her floating pearl grey drapery, had only time for the indispensable tenderly maternal greeting before her husband offered his arm to lead her into the dining room. Her dutiful son, following with the frigidly disapproving Miss Sneed, noted that she walked with firm steps, not making use of the support.

The viscount took his place at the head of the table. His mother, at the other end, was a good twenty feet distant, his view of her obscured by a large silver epergne embossed with excessively ugly Chinese mandarins. The servants would not be the only barrier between him and a scolding, he realised. Apart from distance and obstacles, Lady Lavinia had always been most particular about the propriety of conversing only with those seated directly to one's left and right.

It was a long meal, enlivened only by Mr. Ffinch-Smythe's discourse on pig breeding. Lord Iverbrook had plenty of leisure to compare the high-vaulted room, its dark panelling hung with the more distinguished of his ancestors, to the cosy dining room at Milford Manor. Having grown used to perfectly cooked plain roasts and stews and pies, he nibbled distastefully at the elaborate creations of his mother's expensive cook, as often as not singed or curdled or half raw. My lady ate like a bird and was not interested in food. Her husband consumed ravenously anything that was put before him, talking round mouthfuls of grey fricassee or blackened pastry with equal ease. Her son watched the last course removed with a hollow in his stomach and, when she and her companion withdrew, drank a glass too much of the excellent port his father had put down before his birth.

The extra glass stood him in good stead. Lady Lavinia apparently did not consider the drawing room an appropriate place to comb her son's hair with a joint stool. Nonetheless it was a painful evening, from Miss Sneed's wooden performance of a Handel suite upon the spinet, to a game of whist for penny points during which my lady called for her smelling salts every time she was trumped. Iverbrook only survived it by remembering and anticipating other evenings. In his mind, Delia sang ballads and thumped out merry gigs. Peter sat on his knee while Lady Whitton's kindly voice read a fairytale. He caught Selena's eye, and almost rose to his feet to go and sit beside her before he realised it was all in his imagination.

He wished he'd had two glasses of wine too many, and wondered at his stepfather's continual good humour.

At eight thirty, to the second, Prynn brought in the tea tray. At nine, Lady Lavinia rose and held out her hand to her son. He jumped up and kissed it.

"You will come and see me first thing tomorrow morning, Hugh," she commanded.

"Yes, Mama. Goodnight."

"Lady Lavinia rises at ten," said Miss Sneed severely, and supported her ladyship's tottering steps from the room.

"Brandy?" offered Mr. Ffinch-Smythe.

"I think not, thank you, sir. I shall need all my wits about me in the morning."

"I believe I'll take a glass. Come to think of it, it's your brandy, my boy. You don't mind?"

"Of course not."

"I generally retire at ten. The pigs rise early, what? No need for you to do so though. Make yourself at home." He laughed at his little joke.

The viscount looked around the drawing room and wondered what he was supposed to occupy himself with for the rest of the evening. "I think I'll go to bed too," he sighed. "I have grown accustomed to country hours at Milford."

Iverbrook woke early next morning and went downstairs. It was a wet, blustery day, made no warmer by Prynn's sour greeting. The butler's manner did not thaw as he served his lordship's solitary breakfast. He waited until Iverbrook had abandoned a half-full cup of lukewarm coffee and pushed back his chair before he announced ponderously:

"I believe, my lord, that an urgent letter for your lordship was delivered late last night." He ruminated. "Or possibly early this morning, my lord. Would your lordship wish to see it now?"

Iverbrook looked at him in exasperation. "Yes," he said shortly.

"I shall ring for Frederick, my lord, to fetch it from the hall table for your lordship."

"Don't bother. I shall fetch it for myself." He strode out, ignoring the butler's smug face.

He recognised the writing at once, though it was less neat than usual.

Selena, he thought. The darling! She must have written it only a few hours after he left the Manor. Smiling in anticipation, he went to the library to enjoy it in comfort.

The smile faded as he read the salutation.

"My lord,

"Pray do not trouble yourself to return with the betrothal ring. It will not be needed after all. I daresay I should be flattered that you finally decided marriage to me was preferable to a lawsuit. I find I am not. As no doubt you will be pleased to hear, Mr. Hastings is delighted that you have at last taken his advice. S. Whitton."

"The devil!" he said aloud. "Next time I see you, Hasty, I'll wring your wretched neck, or better, pull out your tongue with red-hot pincers. Selena, my love, for an intelligent woman you are the veriest featherhead! Now what do I do next?"

A clock striking ten reinforced his dilemma. Prynn's lethargic service had left him no time to think. How could he tell Lady Lavinia of his betrothal when his poor, deluded sweetheart had just cried off? On the other hand, if he waited until he had persuaded her of her error, he would have to come right back to Iver Place, starve through another dinner, doze through another endless evening, and suffer through another painful interview.

Put that way, the choice was easy.

He made his way to his mother's boudoir. As he expected, she had risen from her bed only to collapse immediately upon her chaise longue, guarded by Miss Sneed. Not for the first time, he wondered if she was really the frail invalid she appeared; unfortunately, he could think of no way to test the matter that would not lead to disaster if it was true.

The elegant, diaphanous gown was the colour of woodsmoke this time, a fashionable shade described in *Ackerman's* as *soupir d'automne.*

"Charming, Mama!" said Iverbrook hopefully. "How well that dress becomes you."

"But I am very unwell, Hugh," she sighed. "If your poor, sainted papa can see how you neglect me, he must be turning in his grave. Four months with never a word."

"Three and a half."

"Don't contradict me, Hugh! I am sure a few days are neither here nor there. What have you been doing all this weary time that is more important than comforting a sick mother?"

Seeing an opening for his main purpose, Hugh began to explain that he had been getting to know his nephew.

"A child, a mere child, can be of no interest to a gentleman of your years. Or indeed of any age. I regret to say that I do not believe you, my son." Agnes Sneed was heard to snort in agreement. "You have returned to your libertine ways, the shocking conduct you dare not describe to your loving mama. How well I know the lies, the evasions! My vinaigrette, Agnes!"

Hugh backed away from the acrid vapours and tried not to listen as his character was torn to shreds. It was very unjust, he felt, since he had turned over a new leaf. At last, despairing of an end to the peroration, he interrupted.

"I have news for you, Mama, which I hope will please you. I mean to settle down and live respectably. I am engaged to be married."

Silenced at last, Lady Lavinia gaped at him. Before Miss Sneed could take up cudgels on her behalf, Hugh continued.

"You need not fear that I mean to ask you to remove from the Place. Miss Whitton has her own house and we shall live there and in London."

"Miss Whitton! I feel a Spasm coming on, Agnes. Who is Miss Whitton?" demanded Lady Lavinia in a failing voice.

"Well really, Mama! She is Gil's sister-in-law. You remember your son Gilbert and his wife?"

"There's no call to be sarcastic," said Miss Sneed sharply.

"Of course I remember Phoebe Whitton. A nobody! Unexceptionable for a younger son, perhaps, even if he was a Carrick of Iver, but you are a viscount, Hugh. It is your duty to the family to make a grand match and I'm sure I do not see any reason why you should not. You were born hosed and shod and have not yet managed to bring an abbey to a grange, thanks to my dear Mr. Ffinch-Smythe. Your lineage is impeccable and your looks passable, and though your character is unstable I do not by any means despair of an eligible connection."

"I have formed a connection, Mama. I am not informing you of my intentions but of a *fait accompli*. Miss Whitton and I are betrothed." Iverbrook crossed his fingers behind his back. "And I want to bring her to see you soon, because I do not care for long engagements." Not with a volatile lady like my Selena, he added silently.

"You have sent a notice to the *Gazette?*"

"Not yet."

"Then Miss Whitton must be persuaded to see that it will not do." Lady Lavinia regained sufficient strength to sit up straight and push away Miss Sneed's anxious hands. "No one need know you have cried off. I have the very girl in mind for you: Lady Mary Hodgkiss. Superior breeding, prettily behaved, and thirty thousand pounds if she has a penny."

Iverbrook ignored Lady Mary's claims; he laughed.

"You might as well resign yourself to it, Mama," he said, "for Lennox Hastings knows all about it and his tongue has a greater circulation than the *Gazette!*"

His mother wilted. "Mr. Hastings!" she said with loathing. "As well tell the world. You may write to Miss Whitton and tell her that I will receive her next week."

"Thank you, Mama. I shall go in person to inform her of the honour. I mean to leave at once."

"But Hugh, you only arrived yesterday. Agnes, the smelling salts! Four months with never a word and then you stay only one night. Your poor, sainted papa must be turning in his grave."

Realising that the interview had returned to its starting point, the viscount dropped a kiss on Lady Lavinia's hand and slipped out of the room under cover of the fuming sal volatile.

= 20 =

IT RAINED FROM Iver to Beaconsfield. It rained from Beaconsfield to High Wycombe, and from High Wycombe to Watlington it rained some more. Between Watlington and Kings Milford darkness fell, but it didn't stop raining. Watery needles glinted in the light of the carriage lamps, hissed when they hit them, turned the road beneath the horses' hooves to a quagmire.

Inside the Iverbrook travelling carriage, with its crested doors, his lordship was almost as wet as Tom Arbuckle on the box outside. The roof leaked. For years Lady Lavinia had refused to leave home if there was a cloud in the sky, though in any case she never ventured more than five miles from Iver Place, and no one had thought to investigate whether the aged vehicle was still as waterproof as it was impressive.

His lordship cursed as a drip ran down the back of his neck, and wondered if any woman was worth it. At least Selena could hardly turn him out on a night like this.

They drove past the Royal Oak and turned up the lane towards the Manor. Dry clothes, thought Iverbrook hopefully, and a hot meal. Then he would explain matters to his beloved; he would be patient, kind, and firm, forgiving her flights of fancy, her unreasonable reproaches. He would take her in his arms and she would forget that Hasty had ever spoken.

The carriage crunched to a halt at the front door. Iverbrook sprang down and dashed up the steps. The door opened as he reached it.

"My lord!" exclaimed Bannister in surprise. "I thought . . . My lord, thank heaven you've come!"

Lady Whitton hurried into the hall, Delia close behind her.

"Hugh, thank heaven you've come!"

"Peter has been abducted by gypsies and Selena has gone after him," announced Delia. "Alone!"

"Alone? Gypsies? What on earth are you talking about?" Iverbrook handed his soggy hat and coat to the butler and took Lady Whitton's arm. "You are worn to a shadow, ma'am. Come and sit down while Delia explains what is going on."

He led them back into the drawing room.

"It's really Cousin Aubrey," Delia said. "She has to marry him to get Peter back, so she had to go alone or they wouldn't have met her to take her there. Gypsies sell little boys to chimney sweeps, you know."

"Take her where? Where is Hasty?" demanded his lordship, utterly confused and hoping for a rational explanation.

"He went up to London because he owes you some money. That was before it all happened. Mama made Cousin Aubrey leave because of Polly only she won't tell me about that and then Peter was missing again and a letter came for Selena and he is in league with the gypsies. . . . "

"A letter? Where is it?"

"Selena left it on the table there," said Lady Whitton. "Yes, there it is."

Iverbrook picked up the still damp paper and studied it. He looked up grimly.

"Sir Aubrey says he will sell Peter to the gypsies," he stated, "but I do not believe he is with them now. I recognise the hand. This was written by Amabel Parcott!"

"You think they are at Cowley?" asked Delia eagerly. "That is famous! We can carry out my plan after all, Mama."

"What is your plan, Dee?" asked the viscount.

"Call out the farmhands and go take Peter back. And Selena too, now."

"It would take too long, I fear. If she leaves the Crown at seven . . . it is near that now. By the time we had gathered everyone together, in the darkness and this weather, she must have been in his hands for several hours. No, I shall go alone as she did."

"That you won't, m'lord," said Tom Arbuckle, dripping in the doorway. "It seems young Jem's missing and it's my belief he went after Miss Selena. I'll be coming with you, m'lord, and if you've got your duelling pops, I've got me horse pistols."

The viscount nodded in approval. "Right you are, Tom. Now don't you worry, ma'am. Tell Cook to keep our dinner hot and we'll be back with them in time to eat it. Look after your mother, Delia." He followed his servant into the hall.

Bannister was on his knees unpacking a bag. "Here's a dry coat, my lord," he said.

"Good man. Tom, go saddle a pair of horses quickly. We'll ride."

"I c'n take the carridge round to the stable, my lord," volunteered Polly, brushing his hat. "Me and Doris'll rub the horses down good. I'll just get me cloak on."

"Here's a mug o' mulled ale, my lord, to put some warmth into you," offered Cook. "There be one for you in the kitchen, Tom, and dinner'll be waiting when you come back wi' Miss Selena and Master Peter."

It was still pitch dark outside, and though the downpour had slackened rain still fell. Tom held a lantern aloft but the going was slow.

"We must come up with her before she reaches the house," fretted Iverbrook. "Who knows what that devil has planned for her arrival."

"Miss Whitton won't be travelling no faster nor us, m'lord," Tom pointed out.

"But she is ahead of us. We must go faster." He urged his unwilling horse to a canter.

As they reached the post road, the rain stopped. A rising wind chilled the riders but it scattered the clouds and a half moon shone intermittently. At a gallop they raced past the turning to Abingdon and flew on towards Oxford.

There was a mile still to go before Cowley when they saw a gig before them in the road. The driver looked nervously over his shoulder, and saw them bearing down upon him out of the night. He whipped up his nag. The single figure huddled in the back did not stir.

"It must be her!" cried Iverbrook, and drew one of his pistols.

Tom waved his weapon in reply and they thundered on, parting on each side of the gig to pull up before it, swinging their mounts around. Guns levelled at the driver's head, they shouted together, "Stand and deliver!"

Whinnying in fright, the nag reared between the shafts. The light carriage tilted and driver and passenger slid gracefully into the mud.

Before the amateur highwaymen could dash to the rescue, another voice was heard. From the shadow of the hedge it came, young, scared, but resolute.

"Hold still an' drop them pops! I got you all covered!"

"Jem!" Selena sat up. "It's all right, it's Lord Iverbrook. Oh Hugh, I'm so glad to see you but what are we going to do now? He won't take me to the gypsy camp now!" She burst into tears.

Dismounting, the viscount strode to her side and knelt in the road. He gathered her wet, muddy form to his heart. "Don't cry, love," he murmured. "Don't cry. Peter is not with the gypsies, he's at Amabel's house. We'll be there in a few minutes, with or without the rogue's help."

Jem emerged from the shadows, leading Pippin. Tom, with the other two horses, met him by the recumbent driver.

"Well done, young feller," he said. "What are we a-going to do with this 'un?" He nudged the man with his toe.

Jem cocked his pistol suggestively.

"I ain't done nothing," gabbled Amabel's groom. "Mrs. Parcott said to fetch the lady from the Crown an' that's all I done. Honest!"

"That there's the Royal Oak's gig," said Jem. "Where's young Ted?"

"Still sleeping, fer all I know. Dead tired, he were. I ain't done nothing to him."

"Ahem! My lord!" Tom reluctantly interrupted Iverbrook. "What would you wish done with this 'un?"

Iverbrook looked up. "He'd best drive the gig. We'll need it to get home."

"I won't go in it!" declared Selena.

"Of course not, love. You ride with me." He helped her to rise.

"We must hurry. Poor Peterkin must be frightened half to death."

"Selena, if we hurry you will not suppose that I followed you only for Peter's sake?" There was a laugh in his voice.

"No, oh no, Hugh!"

He kissed her hot cheek and mounted. Tom threw her up before him and they set off. With his arms encircling her, her head on his chest, she asked, "Did you get my letter, Hugh?"

"Yes, love. I decided to ignore it."

"Oh." Pause. "Good. It did not make you angry?"

"Not in the least. I have decided to make allowances for your megrims in future."

She sat up straight. "You are odiously condescending!" she said.

"You must learn to make allowances for me too. If you love me as much as I love you, you will not find it difficult."

"I shall try," she said, relaxing against him again. "I do love you, Hugh. If I didn't, I shouldn't be so . . ."

"Skittish?"

"Yes, only that sounds like a high-bred horse."

With Jem leading, they turned off the high road at Cowley and soon rode between ornate stone gateposts, up the short drive to the Gants' baroque mansion. The moon shone full on the facade, illuminating every scroll and curlicue with pitiless brilliance.

"Good God!" said Iverbrook. "A piece of Florence set down in the middle of the English countryside." He turned as the gig pulled up behind them. "You there! What were you to do when you arrived?"

"Just show the lady in, my lord. Most of the servants is off for the night."

"Very well. Go harness a fresh horse and wake the lad from the Royal Oak to drive us back."

"But my lord . . ."

"Do you wish to make the acquaintance of the local magistrate?" asked his lordship politely.

"No, my lord! I ain't done nothing, my lord. I'm going, I'm going!"

Iverbrook helped Selena to slide to the ground, and swung down after her.

"Jem, go and keep an eye on that rascal. Tom, come in with us, but I want no interference unless it proves necessary to defend Miss Whitton and Master Peter. Understood?"

"Yes, m'lord," said Tom grimly as they trod up the steps.

"Hugh, you are not going to challenge Aubrey to a duel?" Selena hung on his sleeve, stopping him.

"As Hasty pointed out, whatever his manners and morals he is a gentleman. I cannot decently horsewhip him."

"So you will offer to let him try and kill you! I shall never understand men's idiotish notions of honour. And if instead you kill him, you will have to flee the country. Either way, I am a widow before I am a wife. Hugh, you must not!"

"Indeed I must. I could never hold up my head again, else. I am generally accounted a good shot; I'll engage not to kill your cousin."

Tom intervened. "Mr. Dimbury did mention as Sir Aubrey don't have no firearm to his name. He can't ride nor drive. Maybe he can't shoot neither."

"You see, Selena, I am quite safe."

She was unconvinced, but followed him into the house. The marble-floored entrance hall, crowded with a bewildering display of statuary in varying degrees of disrepair, had several doors leading off it. Only one was open, the room beyond it well lighted.

"Wait here, Tom," said the viscount.

Selena ran forward, Iverbrook close behind her.

"Peter!" she cried. "Thank heaven! Are you all right?"

He was sitting cross-legged on the table in an otherwise empty dining room. The table was set with a lavish cold collation. His chin liberally smeared with whipped cream, he was attacking the apple pie in his lap with a large fork.

"This is a good pie," he said, manoeuvring a chunk towards his mouth. "You want some, Aunt Sena?"

"No, thank you, pet. You *are* a mess." Relieved as she was to find him unharmed, Selena hesitated to embrace the sticky brat.

"So are you," pointed out her nephew. "So's Uncle Hugh, only he's not as bad as you."

Selena looked down at herself. The horrid green dress she was still wearing was no longer green but an indescribable brownish black. "Oh dear," she said, "you're right. I am more likely to make you dirty than the other way about."

"Might I enquire as to the present whereabouts of the villain?" Hugh was leaning against the wall, lips twitching at the picture presented by his hovering beloved and the matter-of-fact victim.

"Yes, where's Uncle Aubrey?"

"Being sick," said Peter with considerable satisfaction. Abandoning his pie, he swung his legs over the side of the table and explained. "I putted some black mustardseed in his wine and he drinked it and he went sort of green and putted a napkin on his mouth. And then he runned out and Mrs. Parrot runned after him and I 'spect she's holding his head like Grandmama does when I be sick."

"I expect so," agreed Selena faintly. "Wherever did you come by the black mustardseed?"

"I keep some in my pocket, case I eat some bad berries again by mistake. I gived it to Uncle Aubrey 'cos I knowed you'd come and get me soon."

"You're a most ingenious young man!" said his Uncle Hugh. "Tell me, how did Uncle Aubrey manage to make off with you in the first place?"

"Aunt Sena said she may marry Uncle Aubrey so I wanted to go with Mr. Hasty to find you, only it wasn't not Mr. Hasty's carriage it was Uncle Aubrey's. I hided under the rug."

Iverbrook looked at Selena in dismay. "You actually considered marrying the man?" he asked incredulously.

She coloured. "I don't believe I'd really have done it, but after I wrote that letter I was in such despair, anything seemed better than that emptiness."

"Poor darling!" In two strides he was at her side, holding her close.

"You'll get all muddier, Uncle Hugh," warned Peter.

He released her and looked down at his clothes. "I don't think that is possible," he said. "Well, I daresay I had best go and confront the wicked baronet." He put his finger to Selena's lips, stilling her protest. "You stay here with Peter, my love. You might try what a wet napkin will do for his appearance, though you and I are beyond repair. Do not leave this room until I return, or Tom comes for you."

"Hugh!"

He took her face between his hands and kissed her very gently, then turned and left the room, his tall, lean figure moving with jaunty insouciance. Cold with fear, Selena watched him go.

"Do you want some bread and butter?" asked Peter.

Declining, she dipped a napkin in the water jug and set about scrubbing his face and hands. He submitted patiently. Whenever it was safe to open his mouth, he told her about his adventures with Uncle Aubrey. She did not hear a word.

She was listening for a shot.

It took the viscount several minutes to run Sir Aubrey to earth. The baronet was reclining on a wooden bench in a well-scrubbed scullery, strategically close to the sink. The ghastly hue of his countenance was intensified by the pinkish orange of his coat.

Beside him, a rose velvet angel of mercy, Mrs. Parcott knelt on the stone-flagged floor, wiping his face with a lace handkerchief. She heard Iverbrook's footsteps and jumped up.

"Hugh!"

"Correct, Amabel."

"What are you doing here? Aubrey said you were at Iver."

"I was. I have come to settle accounts with Aubrey." He drew his duelling pistols from his pocket and offered one to the baronet, who groaned and turned away.

"You desire a more formal arrangement?" queried his lordship. "Seconds, a meeting at dawn, perhaps a doctor in attendance?"

"How can you be so insensitive!" stormed Amabel. "Aubrey is extremely unwell and cannot possibly answer your challenge now."

Grinning, Iverbrook returned the guns to his pocket.

"Clever lad, my nephew," he commented. "His Grandmama is a witch, you know. It's a mistake to abduct a witch's grandson."

"The little brat did this?" Sir Aubrey sat up abruptly. "He has poisoned me!" His face turned a still more interesting shade of green and he subsided, clutching his stomach.

"I hope you will punish him severely," said Mrs. Parcott, billowing to her knees again and patting the baronet's hand soothingly.

Iverbrook looked at her in amazement. "I consider his behaviour an exemplary instance of self-defense. I suppose you think that instead of shooting Sir Aubrey I ought to pay his fare back to Jamaica?"

"There is no need for that," she said stiffly. "If he chooses to go, I shall pay his fare."

"Oh, but he most definitely chooses to go! He has already discovered how unhealthy the English climate can be. If he should stay, he might find it fatal. What is more, Bel, I'd join him if I were you. No telling but that you might find the Indies healthier too."

She shot him a look of dislike, but before she could speak Sir Aubrey groaned again, struggled to his feet and leaned over the sink.

Lord Iverbrook beat a quick retreat.

When he entered the dining room, Selena was standing in front of a long mirror framed with gilt cherubs, attacking her own face with a damp cloth. Their eyes met in the reflection.

"Are you hurt?" she whispered.

"Not in the least."

"Did you . . . did you kill him?"

"I'm afraid not. He was by far too ill to be shot. He will shortly return to the Indies, and I have a feeling that Mrs. Parrot will accompany him. In fact, I should not be surprised if they made a match of it. Sir Aubrey wants money, Mrs. Parrot wants a title, they are perfectly suited."

Selena giggled. "I like to hear you call her Mrs. Parrot," she confessed, turning at last.

"You'll like it even better when I call you Lady Iverbrook." He held out his hands and she ran into his arms.

Swinging his legs, Peter watched with tolerant interest. Some minutes passed before Hugh became aware of his scrutiny.

"Your aunt and I are going to be married after all," he announced, slightly flushed, over Selena's shoulder.

"That's all right," said Peter benignly. "I told Aunt Sena already, aunts and uncles is s'posed to be married to each other!"